John P. K

Annals of Quodlibet

John P. Kennedy

Annals of Quodlibet

1st Edition | ISBN: 978-3-75233-160-8

Place of Publication: Frankfurt am Main, Germany

Year of Publication: 2020

Outlook Verlag GmbH, Germany.

Reproduction of the original.

ANNALS OF QUODLIBET.

EDITED BY

THE AUTHOR OF "SWALLOW BARN," ETC. ETC.

INTRODUCTION.

FRIENDLY READER:—

Of a truth, we are a great people!—and most happy am I, Solomon Secondthoughts, Schoolmaster of the Borough of Quodlibet, that it hath fallen to my lot, even in my small way, to make known to you how in our Borough that greatness hath grown toward its perfect maturity—feeling persuaded that Quodlibet therein is but an abstract or miniature portrait of this nation. Happy am I, although sorely oppressed with an inward perception of my defective craft in this most worthy task, that I have been thought by our Central Committee a fit expounder of that history wherein is *enchrysalized* (if I may be allowed to draw a word, *parce detortum*, from the Greek mint) the most veritable essence of that recently discovered Democratic theory, for distinction called the Quodlibetarian, which is destined to supplant all other principles in our government, and to render us the most formidable and the most imposing people upon the terraqueous globe.

How it came to pass that this duty has been committed to my hands, you shall learn.

In the days of the late Judge Flam, now thirty years gone by, and long before Quodlibet was, that very considerate and astute gentleman honored me, a poor and youthful scholar, with a promotion to the office of private tutor in his family, then residing at their ancient seat in this neighborhood. It was my especial duty, in this station, to prepare Master Middleton, the eldest born, for college; which in three years of assiduous labor was achieved, much to my content, and, I need not scruple to affirm, no less to my honor, seeing how notably my pupil has since figured in high places among the salt of the nation. Far be it from me to take an undue share of desert for this consummation; it would be disingenuous not to say that my pupil's liberal endowments at the hand of Nature herself rendered my task easy of success.

By the aid of my early patron the Judge, whose memory will long be embalmed in the unction of my gratitude, I became, after Master Middleton was passed from under my care, the head of our district school, which at first was established in that lowly log building under the big chestnut upon the Rumblebottom, about fifty rods south of Christy M'Curdy's mill—which tenement is yet to be seen, although in a melancholy state of desolation, the roof thereof having been blown away in the famous hurricane of August, 1836, just two years and ten months after the Removal of the Deposits. This unfortunate event—I mean the blowing off of the roof—it was the mercy of

Providence to delay for the term of one year and a fraction of a month after I had removed into the new academy which my former pupil, and now, in lineal succession to his lamented parent the Judge, my second patron, the Hon. Middleton Flam, had procured to be erected for my better accommodation in the Borough of Quodlibet. Had my removal been delayed, or the hurricane have risen thirteen months sooner than it did, who shall tell what mourning it might not have spread through our country side—who shall venture to say that Quodlibet might not have been to-day without a chronicler?

This long inhabiting of mine in these parts has afforded me all desirable opportunities to note the growth of the region, and especially to mark out the beginnings, the progression, and the sudden magnifying of our Borough; and being a man—I speak it not vaingloriously—of an inquiring turn, and strongly gifted, as our people of Quodlibet are pleased to allow, with the perfection of setting down my thoughts in writing; and having that essential requisite of the historian, an ardent and unquenchable love of my subject, it has ever been my custom to put into my tablets whatsoever I have deemed noteworthy in the events and opinions of my day, accompanied by such reflections thereon as my subject might be found to invite. Some of these memorabilia, with discourses pertinent to the same, have I from time to time, distrustfully and with the proper timidity of authorship, ventured to contribute to our newspaper, and thereby has my secret vanity been regaled by seeing myself in print. By what token I have not yet ascertained, but these lucubrations of mine were not long ago discovered to our "Grand Central Committee of Unflinching New-Light Quodlibetarian Democrats," who have been charged with the arduous duty of maintaining the integrity of the party in the present alarming crisis, and of promoting, by all means in their power, the indefeasible, unquestionable, and perpetual right of succession to the Presidential Chair, claimed by and asserted for the candidate of the great, unterrified New Democratic school of patriotic defenders of the spoils. This Central Committee now hold their sessions weekly in Quodlibet—and having discovered my hand in the lucubrations to which I have alluded above, they have been pleased to express a favorable opinion thereon; and, as a sequence thereto, it has occurred to them to fancy that my poor labors being duly given to the compiling of such a history as my tablets might afford of the rise and progress of the New Democratic principle in Quodlibet, the same would greatly redound to the advantage of the cause in the present great struggle. Acting upon this suggestion, the Grand Central Committee have honored me with a request to throw into such shape as I might deem best these scattered records of opinion and chronicles of fact, whereof I was supposed to have a rich magazine.

Readily and cheerfully have I acceded to this request; and with the more relish, as I shall thus be furnished with an authentic occasion to present to the world the many valuable thoughts and eloquent utterings of my late distinguished pupil, and now beneficent patron, the Hon. Middleton Flam, long a representative of this Borough and the adjacent district in the Congress of the United States.

I pretend to no greater merit in this execution of my task than what an impartial spirit of investigation, a long acquaintance with persons of every degree connected with this history, an apt judgment in discriminating between opinions, a most faithful and abundant memory, a careful store of documentary evidence, an unalterable devotion to the great principles of Quodlibetarian Democracy, and, for the expounding of all, a lucid and felicitous style, may allow me to claim as the chronicler of this Borough.

The better to assure you, my friendly reader, that, in temper and condition, I may demand somewhat of the confidence due to the character of a dispassionate commentator on the times, I would have you understand that I am now on the shady side of sixty, unmarried, and in possession of an easy revenue of four hundred dollars per annum, which is voted to me by our commissioners, for instructing in their rudiments thirty-seven children of both sexes; that I have a plate at the table of my patron, the Hon. Middleton Flam, my former pupil, every Sunday at dinner; and that he, being aware for some time past of my purpose to treasure up his remarkable sayings, has, with a generous freedom, often repeated to me many opinions which otherwise would have been irretrievably lost. Moreover, since I am now brought before the public under circumstances in which reserve on my part would be no better than affectation, I would also advertise my indulgent reader of the fact that I belong to the Quodlibetarian New-Light Club, whereof I some time officiated as Secretary, and which club generally meets on Saturday night at Ferret's; that the members of the same, noting my staidness of deportment and the careful deliberation with which I guard myself in the utterance of any discourse, do frequent honor to the temperance of my judgment by making me the arbiter of such casual controversies as arise therein, touching the true import and application of the principles of our New-Light Democracy; and— if I run no risk of being charged with offering a trivial evidence of the reputation I have earned in the club—I would also mention, that some of our light wags have gone so far—facetiously and with a commendable good nature, knowing that I would not take it ill, as more peevish men might, in their jocular pleasantry—as to call me, in allusion to my natural sedateness, SOBER SECONDTHOUGHTS:—the rogues!

And now, amiable and considerate reader, you have "ab imo pectore" my honest avouch for what I propose to lay before you, and a plain confession of my weaknesses. I come with a clean breast to the confessional. We shall have a frugal banquet of it, but the fruits, I make bold to promise, shall be wholesome and of the best. Now turn we to it in good earnest. If this little chronicle—for my book shall not be overgrown and apoplectic, but rather, as you shall find it, "garrulous and thin"—do not bring you to a profound sense of the value of this Amaranth of Republicanism, the New-Light Quodlibetarian Democracy, then say it to my teeth, there is no virtue in SOBER SECONDTHOUGHTS. Go thy ways—"The wise man's eyes are in his head, but the fool walketh in darkness."

S. S., SCHOOLMASTER.

QUODLIBET.

CHAPTER I.

ANTIQUITIES OF QUODLIBET—MICHAEL GRANT'S TANYARD DESTROYED BY THE CANAL—CONSEQUENCES OF THIS EVENT—TWO DISTINGUISHED INDIVIDUALS TAKE UP THEIR RESIDENCE IN THE BOROUGH—ESTABLISHMENT OF THE PATRIOTIC COPPERPLATE BANK— CIRCUMSTANCES WHICH LED TO AND FOLLOWED THAT MEASURE— MICHAEL GRANT'S OBJECTIONS TO IT.

It was at the close of the year 1833, or rather, I should say, at the opening of the following spring, that our Borough of Quodlibet took that sudden leap to greatness which has, of late, caused it to be so much talked about. Our folks are accustomed to set this down to the Removal of the Deposits. Indeed, until that famous event, Quodlibet was, as one might say in common parlance, a place not worth talking about—it might hardly be remarked upon the maps. But since that date, verily, like Jeshurun, it has waxed fat. It has thus come to pass that "The Removal" is a great epoch in our annals—our Hegira—the A. U. C. of all Quodlibetarians.

Michael Grant, a long time ago—that is to say, full twenty years—had a tanyard on Rumblebottom Creek, occupying the very ground which is now covered by the canal basin. Even as far back as that day he had laid up, out of the earnings of his trade, a snug sum of money, which sufficed to purchase the farm where he now lives at the foot of the Hogback. Quodlibet, or that which now is Quodlibet, was then as nothing. Michael's dwelling house and tanyard, Abel Brawn's blacksmith-shop, Christy M'Curdy's mill, and my school-house, made up the sum-total of the settlement. It is now ten years, or hard on to it, since the commissioners came this way and put the cap-sheaf on Michael's worldly fortune by ruining his tanyard and breaking up his business, whereof the damage was so taken to heart by the jury that, in their rage against internal improvements, they brought in a verdict which doubled Mr. Grant's estate in ready money, besides leaving him two acres of town lots bordering on the basin, and which, they say, are worth more to-day than the whole tanyard with its appurtenances ever was worth in its best time. This verdict wrought a strange appetite in our county, among the landholders, to be ruined in the same way; and I truly believe it was a chief cause of the unpopularity of internal improvements in this neighborhood, that the commissioners were only able to destroy the farms on the lowlands—which fact, it was said, brought down the price of the uplands on the whole line of the canal, besides creating a great deal of ill humor among all who were out of the way of being damaged.

With the money which this verdict brought him, Mr. Grant improved a part of his two acres—which he was persuaded to cut up into town lots—by building the brick tavern, and the store that stands next door to it. These were the first buildings of any note in Quodlibet, and are generally supposed to have given rise to the incorporation of the Borough by the Legislature. Jesse Ferret took a lease of the tavern as soon as it was finished, and set up the sign of "The Hero"—meaning thereby General Jackson—which, by-the-by, was the first piece of historical painting that the celebrated Quipes ever attempted. The store was rented by Frederick Barndollar for his son Jacob, who was just then going to marry Ferret's daughter Susan, and open in the Iron and Flour Forwarding and Commission line, in company with Anthony Hardbottle, his own brother-in-law.

This was the state of things in Quodlibet five years before "The Removal," from which period, up to the date of the Removal, although Barndollar & Hardbottle did a tolerable business, and Ferret had a fair run of custom, there were not above a dozen new tenements built in the Borough. But a bright destiny was yet in reserve for Quodlibet; and as I propose to unfold some incidents of its history belonging to these later times, I cannot pretermit the opportunity now afforded me to glance, though in a perfunctory and hasty fashion, at some striking events which seemed to presignify and illustrate its marvelously sudden growth.

I think it was in the very month of the Removal of the Deposits, that Theodore Fog broke up at Tumbledown, on the other side of the Hogback, and came over to Quodlibet to practice law. And it was looked upon as a very notable thing, that, in the course of the following winter, Nicodemus Handy should have also quitted Tumbledown and brought his sign, as a lottery agent, to Quodlibet, and set up that business in our Borough. There was a wonderful intimacy struck up between him and Fog, and a good many visits were made by Nicodemus during the fall, before he came over to settle. Our people marveled at this matter, and were not a little puzzled to make out the meaning of it, knowing that Nicodemus Handy was a shrewd man, and not likely, without some good reason for it, to strike up a friendship with a person so little given to business as Theodore Fog, against whom I desire to say nothing, holding his abilities in great respect, but meaning only to infer that as Theodore is considered high-flown in his speech, and rather too fond of living about Ferret's bar-room, it was thought strange that Nicodemus, who is plain spoken, and of the Temperance principle, should have taken up with him. It was not long after Mr. Handy had seated himself in Quodlibet, and placed his sign at the door of a small weather-boarded office, ten feet by twelve, and within a stone-throw of Fog's, before the public were favored with an insight into the cause of this intimacy between these two friends. This was disclosed in a plan for establishing The Patriotic Copperplate Bank of Quodlibet, the particulars whereof were made known at a meeting held in the dining-room of "The Hero" one evening in March, when Theodore Fog made a flowery speech on the subject to ten persons, counting Ferret and Nim Porter the bar-keeper. The capital of the bank was proposed to be half a million, and the stock one hundred dollars a share, of which one dollar was to be paid in, and the remainder to be secured by promissory notes, payable on demand, if convenient.

This excellent scheme found many supporters; and, accordingly, when the time came for action, the whole amount was subscribed by Handy and Fog and ten of their particular friends, who had an eye to being directors and officers of the bank—to whom might also be added about thirty boatmen, who, together with the boys of my academy, lent their names to Mr. Handy.

Through the liberality of Fog, the necessary cash was supplied out of three hundred dollars, the remains of a trust fund in his hands belonging to a family of orphans in the neighborhood of Tumbledown, who had not yet had occasion to know from their attorney, the said Theodore Fog himself, of their success in a cause relating to this fund which had been gained some months before. As Nicodemus managed the subscriptions, which indeed he did with wonderful skill, these three hundred dollars went a great way in making up the payments on considerably more than the majority of the stock: and this being adjusted, he undertook a visit to the Legislature, where, through the disinterested exertions of some staunch Democratic friends, he procured a most unexceptionable charter for the bank, full of all sorts of provisions, conditions, and clauses necessary to enable it to accommodate the public with as much paper money as the said public could possibly desire.

In consideration of these great services, Nicodemus Handy elected himself Cashier; and, at the same time, had well-nigh fallen into a quarrel with Fog, who had set his heart upon being President—which, in view of the fact that that gentleman's habits were somewhat irregular after twelve o'clock in the day, Nicodemus would by no means consent to. This dissension, however, was seemingly healed, by bringing in as President my worshipful pupil, the Hon. Middleton Flam, now our member of Congress, and by making Theodore one of the directors, besides giving him the law business of the bank. It was always thought, notwithstanding Fog pretended to be satisfied at the time with this arrangement, that it rankled in his bosom, and bred a jealousy between him and his associates in the bank, and helped to drive him to drinking faster than he would naturally have done, if his feelings had not been aggravated by this act of supposed ingratitude.

I should not omit to mention that Nicodemus Handy was a man of exact and scrupulous circumspection, and noted for the deliberation with which he weighed the consequences of his actions, or, as the common saying is, "looked before he leapt"—a remarkable proof of which kind of wisdom he afforded at this time. Having been compelled by circumstances to live beyond the avails of his lottery business, and thereby to bring himself under some impracticable liabilities, he made it a point of conscience, before he could permit himself to be clothed with the dignity of a cashier, or even to place a share of stock in his own name on the books, to swear out in open court, and to surrender, for the benefit of his numerous and patient creditors, his whole stock of worldly goods—consisting, according to the inventory thereof on record, which I have seen, of a cylindrical sheet-iron stove, two chairs, a desk and a sign-board, this latter being, as I remember, of the shape of a screen, on each leaf of which "NICODEMUS HANDY" was printed, together with the scheme of a lottery, set forth in large red and blue letters. He barely retained what the law allowed him, being his mere wearing apparel; to wit, a bran new suit of black superfine Saxony, one dozen of the best cambric linen shirts, as many lawn pocket handkerchiefs, white kid gloves, and such other trivial but gentlemanlike appurtenances as denoted that extreme neatness of dress in which Mr. Handy has ever taken a just pride, and which has been so often remarked by his friends as one of the strong points in his character. These articles, it was said, he had procured not more with a provident eye to that state of destitution into which the generous surrender of his property was about to plunge him, than with a decent regard to the respectability of appearance which the public, he conceived, had a right to exact from the Cashier of the Patriotic Copperplate Bank of Quodlibet. All right-minded persons will naturally commend this prudence, and applaud Mr. Handy's sense of the dignity proper to so important and elevated a station—a station which Theodore Fog, in his speech at "The Hero," so appropriately eulogized as one "of financial, fiscal, and monetary responsibility."

There was one circumstance connected with the history of the establishment of the bank that excited great observation among our folks: that was the dislike Michael Grant took up against it from its very beginning. It was an indiscriminate, unmitigable, dogged dislike to the whole concern, which, by degrees, brought him into a bad opinion of our Borough, and I verily believe was the cause why, from that time forward, he kept himself so much at his farm near the Hogback, and grew to be, as if it were out of mere opposition, so unhappily, and indeed I may say, so perversely stubborn in those iniquitous Whig sentiments which he was in the habit of uttering. I have heard him say that he thought as badly as a man could think, of the grounds for starting the bank, and still worse of the men who started it,—which, certainly, was a very rash expression, considering that our congressman, the Hon. Middleton Flam, was President and one of the first patrons of the institution, and that such a man as Nicodemus Handy was Cashier; to say nothing of Theodore Fog, whose habits, we are willing to confess, might, in the estimation of some men, give some little color to my worthy friend's vituperation.

Now, there was no man in Quodlibet whom Handy and Fog so much desired, or strove so hard, to bring into the bank scheme as Mr. Grant. They made every sort of effort and used all kinds of arguments to entice him. Nicodemus Handy on one occasion, I think it was in April, put the matter to him in such strong points of view, that I have often marveled since how the good gentleman stood it. He argued, with amazing cogency, that General Jackson had removed the deposits for the express purpose of destroying the Bank of the United States, and giving the State banks a fair field: that the Old Hero was an enthusiastic friend to State rights, and especially to State banks, which it was the desire of his heart to see increased and multiplied all over the country; that he was actually, as it were, making pets out of these banks, and was determined to feed them up with the public moneys and give them such a credit in the land as would forever shut out all hope to the friends of a National Bank to succeed with their purpose: and, finally, that although Clay and the Whigs were endeavoring to resist the General in his determination to establish new banks in the States, that resistance was already considered hopeless. It was with a visible air of triumph that Mr. Handy, in confirmation of this opinion, read from the Globe of the 21st of December previous these words:—

"The intelligent people of the West know how to maintain their rights and independence, and to repel oppression. Although foiled in the beginning, every Western State is about to establish a State bank institution. They are resolved to avail themselves of their own State credit, as well as of the National credit, to maintain a currency independent of foreign control. Mr. Clay's presses in Kentucky begin now to feel how vain are all their efforts to resist the determination of the people of the West. Ohio, Indiana, Illinois, Missouri, and Kentucky are resolved to take care of themselves, and no longer depend on the kind guardianship of Biddle, Clay & Co."

Having laid this fact before Mr. Grant, by way of clinching the argument Mr. Handy pulled out of his pocket a letter which he had just received from the Secretary of the Treasury. It contained a communication of the deepest import to the future fortunes of our Borough; which communication, as I have been favored by Mr. Handy with a copy, I feel happy to transcribe here for the edification of my reader. It is a circular, and came to our cashier printed on gilt-edged letter-paper, having the title of the bank, the date, and some other items filled up in writing.

"TREASURY DEPARTMENT, *April* 1, 1834.

"SIR:—The Patriotic Copperplate Bank of Quodlibet has been selected by this Department as the depository of the public money collected in Quodlibet and its vicinity; and the Marshal will hand you the form of a contract proposed to be executed, with a copy of his instructions from this Department. In selecting your institution as one of the fiscal agents of the government, I not only rely on its solidity and established character, as affording a sufficient guarantee for the safety of the public money intrusted to its keeping, but I confide also in its disposition to adopt the most liberal course which circumstances will admit toward other moneyed institutions generally, and particularly those in your vicinity. The deposits of the public money will enable you to afford increased facilities to commerce, and to extend your accommodations to individuals; and as the duties which are payable to the government arise from the business and enterprise of the merchants engaged in foreign trade, it is but reasonable that they should be preferred in the additional accommodations which the public deposits will enable your institution to give, whenever it can be done without injustice to the claims of other classes of the community.

"I am, etc.,   R. B. TANEY,

"*Secretary of the Treasury.*

"*To the President of the Patriotic Copperplate Bank of Quodlibet.*"

"There, sir," said Mr. Handy, after he had read this paper to Mr. Grant—"read that over again and tell me if there is any Quodlibetarian that ought not to rejoice in this great event, and lend his endeavors, with both heart and soul, to promote and sustain an institution so favored by the government. The Secretary, you perceive, has confidence in the 'solidity and established character' of our bank—how can you refuse *your* confidence after that? Sir, the Secretary is an honor to the Democracy of Quodlibet:—what does he say? Does he tell us to keep the public moneys locked up only for the selfish purposes of the government? Oh no: far from it; 'the deposits' says he, 'will enable you to afford increased facilities to commerce, and to extend your accommodations to individuals.' Mark that! there's a President and Secretary for you! True friends, Mr. Grant—true friends to the people. How careful are they of our great mercantile and trading classes! Sir, the government cannot do too much for such people as we are—that's the true Democratic motto— we *expect* a great deal—but they outrun our expectations. No more low prices for grain, Mr. Grant—no more scarcity of money:—accommodation is the word—better currency is the word—high prices, good wages and plenty of work is the word now-a-days. We shall have a city here before you can cleverly turn yourself round. Depend upon it, sir, we are destined to become a great, glorious, and immortal people."

"Sir," said Theodore Fog, interposing at this moment, with a look that wore a compound expression of thoughtful sternness and poetical frenzy—"when the historic muse shall hereafter contemplate the humble origin of Quodlibet ——"

"Fog," interrupted Nicodemus, somewhat petulantly—and I feel sorry to be obliged to record this inconsiderate language—"Blame the historic muse!— we are now on business."

"As a director, sir," replied Fog, with a subdued air, but with a dignified gravity, "I have a *right* to speak. I meant to say, sir, in plain phrase, that Quodlibet must inevitably, from this day forth, under the proud auspices of democratic principles—obedient to that native impulse which the profound statesmanship of this people-sustaining and people-sustained administration has imparted to it, soar aloft to place herself upon the proud pinnacle of commercial prosperity, wealth, and power. I have no doubt, Mr. Grant, your tavern lot will increase to three times its present value. You *ought* to take stock;—let me tell you, sir, as a citizen of Quodlibet, you ought. As to the cash, that's a bagatelle. Handy and I can let you have any number of shares on your own terms. Flam will do anything we say to let you in. By-the-by, he got us the deposits. Flam's a man of influence—but whether on the whole he will make us the best President we could have procured, is perhaps somewhat apocryphal."

"You cannot fail to see," said Mr. Handy, "that we must all make our fortunes, if the government is only true to its word; and who can doubt it will be true? We start comparatively with nothing, I may say, speaking of myself—absolutely with nothing. We shall make a large issue of paper, predicated upon the deposits; we shall accommodate everybody, as the Secretary desires—of course, not forgetting our friends, and more particularly ourselves:—we shall pay, in this way, our stock purchases. You may run up a square of warehouses on the Basin; I will join you as a partner in the transaction, give you the plan of operations, furnish architectural models, supply the funds, et cetera, et cetera. We will sell out the buildings at a hundred per cent. advance before they are finished; Fog here will be the purchaser. We have then only to advertise in the papers this extraordinary rise of property in Quodlibet—procure a map to be made of our new city; get it lithographed, and immediately sell the lots on the Exchange of New York at a most unprecedented valuation. My dear sir, I have just bought a hundred acres of land adjoining the Borough, with an eye to this very speculation. You shall have an interest of one-half in this operation at a reasonable valuation—I shall want but a small profit, say two hundred per cent.—a mere trifle—in consideration of my labors in laying it off into streets, lanes, and alleys;—and if there is any convenience in it to you—although I know you are a moneyed man—you have only to make a proposal for a slice of accommodation—just drop a note now and then into the discount box. You understand. The Secretary will be delighted, my dear sir, to hear of our giving an accommodation to you. But there's one thing, Mr. Grant, I must not forget to remark—the Secretary, in fact, makes it a sort of *sine qua non*—you must come out a genuine—declare yourself a Whole Hog—and go for Flam in the fall elections. The Secretary expects, you know," and as he said this he laid his finger significantly upon his nose, "that the accommodation principle—is to be measurably—extended—in proportion to the—Democracy—of the applicants. You understand?—a word to the wise—that's all. It couldn't be expected, you perceive, that we, holding the deposits, should be quite as favorable to the Whigs, who rather charge us with experimenting on the currency—you know—and who, in fact, don't scruple to say that our banking system will be a failure—it couldn't be expected we should be as bountiful to them as to those who go with us in building up this concatenation—tweedle dum and tweedle dee, you know, betwixt you and me;—but it's made a point of—and has its effect on ulterior expectations—you understand. The long and the short is, without being mealy-mouthed, we must prefer the old Hero's friends;—but, after all, that's a small matter:—be a Democrat, and go for Flam!"

"Flam and the immutable principles of civil liberty!" said Fog, with great animation. "Middleton Flam, the embodiment and personification of those deep and profound truths, based upon the eternal distinctions of the greatest good to the greatest number! Diffusive wealth, combined capital, increased facilities to commerce, and accommodation to individuals—there is the *multum in parvo* of General Jackson's Democratic creed!—there is the glorious consummation of the war with the great money power, which, like Juggernaut, was crushing down the liberties of our Republic!"

Michael Grant was a patient listener, and a man of few words. He stood all the time that Fog and Handy were plying him with this discourse, with his thumbs in his waistcoat pockets, looking down, with a grum cogitation, at his own image in the water of the basin, on the margin of which the parties had met, and every now and then rocking on his heels and flapping the soles of his feet sharply on the ground, denoting, by this movement, to those who knew his habit, that he was growing more and more positive in his opinion. Once or twice he was observed to raise his head, and with one eye half shut, seemed as if studying the heavens. At length he broke out with an answer which, from the vehemence of his tone, caused Handy and Fog to prick up their ears, and gaze upon each other with a look of incredulous surprise.

"Your bank, gentlemen," said he, "is a humbug. Your speculation in lots, your accommodations and the fortunes you are going to make, are humbugs. Flam and the immutable principles of civil liberty are humbugs, and the greatest humbug of all is your Democracy."

With these very rash and inconsiderate words, Mr. Grant turned on his heel and walked away, leaving Handy and Fog looking significantly at each other. From that time Mr. Grant was generally considered an enemy to our bank, and, as far as I can learn, never had any dealings with it.

Mr. Handy set up a dry laugh as soon as Mr. Grant was out of sight, and laughed on for some moments. At last he said, somewhat mysteriously, and with a great deal of deliberation—

"Fog, it's my opinion that the old tanner has cut his eye teeth—what do you think of him?"

"He labors," replied Fog, "under a sinistrous and defective obliquity of comprehension; and from all I can make out of this colloquy, I rather incline to the opinion that he is not *very* willing to embark largely in our stock." And saying this, Fog folded his arms and looked steadfastly in Mr. Handy's face.

"Nor, as I should judge," said Handy in a kind of whisper, "is he likely to join me in my speculation in town lots. Fog, don't forget, you will indorse my note for the purchase-money of that hundred acres—I shall discount it to-morrow —I like to pay cash—that was always my principle."

"Undoubtedly—consider me a sure card in that line," replied Fog:—"it is understood, of course, that you reciprocate the favor on my purchase of the meadow?"

"Without question—assuredly, Fog—one good turn deserves another."

"Then, let's go up and take a drink," said Fog, imitating the tone of a tragedy-player—"we'll call it twelve, although my dial points but half way from eleven."

"You know I never drink," quoth Handy.

"Then come and look on me while I that act perform," said Theodore.

"Agreed," said Nicodemus. And thereupon these trusty friends went straight to Nim Porter's bar.

CHAPTER II.

GREAT USEFULNESS OF THE BANK—SURPRISING GROWTH OF QUODLIBET
—SOME ACCOUNT OF THE HON. MIDDLETON FLAM—ORIGIN OF HIS
DEMOCRACY—HIS LOGICAL ARGUMENT IN FAVOR OF THE POCKETING
OF THE BILL TO REPEAL THE SPECIE CIRCULAR—THE DEMOCRATIC
PRINCIPLE AS DEVELOPED IN THE REPRESENTATIVE SYSTEM.

In the course of the first year after The Removal, or as I should say, in the year One—speaking after our manner in Quodlibet—the bank made itself very agreeable to everybody. Mr. Flam came home from Congress after the end of the long session, and found everything prospering beyond his most sanguine expectations. Nicodemus Handy had put a new weather-boarded room to the back of his office for the use of the Directors, and the banking business was transacted in the front apartment where Nicodemus used to sell lottery tickets. There was one thing that strangers visiting Quodlibet were accustomed to remark upon in a jocular vein, regarding the bank—and that was the sign which was placed, as it were parapet-wise, along the eaves of the roof, and being of greater longitude than the front of the building, projected considerably at either end. Quipes has been held responsible for this, but I know that he could not help it, on account of the length of the name, which, nevertheless, it is due to him to say he endeavored, very much to my discontent, to shorten, both by orthographical device and by abbreviation, having painted it thus—

THE PATRIOTI^C COPERPLAT^E BANK OF QUODLI^{bet};

notwithstanding which, it overran the dimensions of the tenement to which it was attached. I say strangers sometimes facetiously alluded to this discrepancy, by observing that the bank was like the old Hero himself, too great for the frame that contained it. And, truly, the bank did a great business! Mr. Handy, who is acknowledged to be a man of taste, procured one of the handsomest plates, it is supposed, that Murray, Draper & Fairman ever executed, and with about six bales of pinkish silk paper, and a very superior cylinder press, created an amount of capital which soon put to rest old Mr. Grant's grumbling about the want of solidity in the bank, and fully justified the Secretary's declaration of his confidence in its "established character as affording a sufficient guarantee for the safety of the public money intrusted to its keeping."

As a proof how admirably matters were conducted by Mr. Handy, the Directors soon found no other reason to attend at the Board than now and then to hold a chat upon politics and smoke a cigar; and the President, the Hon. Middleton Flam, having his October election on hand, was so thoroughly convinced of Nicodemus's ability, that I do not believe he went into the bank more than half a dozen times during the whole season.

It was in the course of this year, and pretty soon after the bank got the deposits, that Mr. Handy began his row of four story brick warehouses on the Basin, which now goes by the name of Nicodemus Row. He also laid the foundation of his mansion on the hill, fronting upon Handy Place; and which edifice he subsequently finished, so much to the adornment of our Borough, with a Grecian portico in front, and an Italian veranda looking toward the garden. As his improvements advanced in this and the next year, he successively reared a Temple of Minerva on the top of the ice-house, a statue of Apollo in the center of the carriage-circle, a sun-dial on a marble pillar where the garden walks intersect, and a gilded dragon weather-cock on the cupola of the stables. The new banking house was commenced early in the summer, and has been finished of very beautiful granite, being in its front, if I am rightly informed by Mr. Handy, an exact miniature copy of the Tomb of Osymandias: it is situated on Flam Street, the first after you leave the Basin, going northward. All the Directors, except Fog, followed the footsteps of their illustrious predecessor, Mr. Handy, and went to work to build themselves villas on the elevated ground back of the Borough, now known by the name of Copperplate Ridge,—which villas were duly completed in all manner of Greek, Roman, and Tuscan fashions. These being likewise imitated, in turn, by many friends of the bank who migrated hither from all parts and cast their lines in our Borough, Quodlibet hath thereby, very suddenly, grown to be, in a figurative sense, a pattern card of the daintiest structures of the four quarters of the world. Perhaps I may be too fast in making so broad an assertion— cupio non putari mendacem—I am not quite sure that, as yet, we have any well ascertained specimen of the Asiatic: but if Nicodemus Handy's pagoda, which he talked of building on the knoll in the center of his training course, had not been interrupted by an untoward event, of which it may become my duty to speak hereafter, I should, in that case, have made no difficulty in reiterating, with a clear conscience and without reservation, the remark which distrustfully and with claim of allowance I have ventured above.

My valuable patron not being resident actually within the Borough, and being, as I have said, very busy in the matter of his election during the greater part of the first year of the bank, had not much opportunity to devote himself to its concerns. But the Directors, partly aware of their own knowledge, how valuable was his influence with the Secretary, and partly persuaded thereof by the Cashier, established, with a liberality which Mr. Handy remarked at the time was exceedingly gentlemanlike, his salary as President at three thousand dollars a year—which sum, Mr. Flam himself has, more than once in my hearing, averred upon his honor, he did not consider one cent too much. And

18

indeed, I feel myself bound to express my concurrence in this opinion, when I reflect upon the weight of his character, the antiquity of his family, the preponderance of his strong Democratic sentiments, and the expenses to which, as President, he was exposed in looking after the interests of the bank —more especially in the journeys to Washington, whereof I have heard him speak, for the purpose of explaining matters to the Secretary.

Connected with this matter of salary, and as having a natural propinquity to the subject, I may here cursorily, for I design to be more particular on this point hereafter, claim the privilege to enter a little into the family matters of my patron. And on this head, I would observe that the household of Mr. Flam is large. Of a truth, as some philosopher has remarked, mouths are not fed, nor bodies clad, without considerable of the wherewithal! There is Mrs. Flam, the venerated consort of our representative—a lady most honorably conducive to the multiplication of the strength and glory of this land; there is, likewise, Mr. Flam's sister Janet—truly an honor to her sex for instructive discourse and exemplary life; and there is Master Middleton, Junior, with his four sisters and three brothers, who may be all ranged into the semblance of a step-ladder. Great is Mr. Flam's parental tenderness toward this happy progeny— the reduplication and retriplication, if I may so express it, of himself and their respectable mamma. Yielding to the solicitude inspired by this tenderness, almost the first thing which our representative did, after the establishment of the bank—the means having thereby come the better to his hand—was to send Master Middleton, Junior, who was very urgent in his entreaties to that point, to Europe, that the young gentleman, by two or three years travel, might witness the distresses and oppressions of monarchical government, and become confirmed in his democratic sentiments. A refinement of sensibility in Mr. Flam, which I might almost denominate fastidious, has also operated with him to require the education of his daughters to be conducted under his own roof. He would never hear, for one moment, any persuasion to trust them, even at their earliest age, in the public school—considerately fearful lest they might form intimacies unbecoming the station to which he destined them in after-life. They have consequently been placed under the special tuition of a most estimable lady, Mademoiselle Jonquille, a resident governess, who is enjoined to speak to them nothing but French. This lady, among other things, teaches them music, and is aided in the arduous duties allotted to her by a drawing-master of acknowledged ability in water-colors, and a very superior professor of dancing, who instructs them in the elegant accomplishment of waltzing and galloping, which, Mr. Flam says, is now-a-days held to be indispensable in the first Democratic circles at Washington, where it has always been his design to introduce the young ladies into high life.

It will not be out of place here to mention that the worthy subject of this desultory memoir, my patron and former pupil, inherited a large fortune from his father, the late Judge Flam, who was especially honored by old John Adams, or, as the better phrase is, the elder Adams, with an appointment to the bench on the night of the third of March, Anno Domini 1801; and I have often heard Mr. Middleton say that his father had, up to the day of his lamented departure from this world, which melancholy event happened in the year of our Lord 1825, the greatest respect for General Jackson; which liking for the Old Hero descended to his son, along with the family estate, and serves satisfactorily to account for my former pupil's ardent attachment to Democratic principles, as in the sequel I shall make appear.

I do not desire to conceal the fact that Judge Flam, and even Mr. Middleton himself, for some years after he came to man's estate, were both reputed to belong to what was generally, at that time, denominated and known by the appellation of the Old Federal party, and what, in common parlance, has been sometimes scoffingly termed The Black Cockade; and that the Judge, who was always noted for being very stiff in his opinions, maintained his connection nominally with that party until the day of his death. I mention this not in derogation of Mr. Middleton our representative, but rather in the way of commendation, because I am by this fact the more strongly confirmed in my admiration of the greatness of his character—seeing that his conversion to Democracy is the pure result of reflection and conviction, which is more laudable, in my humble thinking, than to be "a born veteran Democrat," as I once heard a great man boast himself.

Now this conversion being a notable matter, I can by no means pretermit a veritable account of it, which happens to be fully within my power to disclose, I being, as I may say, a witness to the whole course of it.

Everybody remembers that most signal of all the literary productions of General Jackson's various and illustrious pen, his letter to Mr. Monroe, dated the 12th of November, Anno Domini 1816. It came—in the language of my venerated friend, Judge Flam—like the sound of a trumpet upon the ears of all of the Old Federalists. "Now is the time," says General Jackson, in that immortal letter, which I transcribed, as soon as I saw it in print, into my book of memorable things, and which I now quote *verbatim et literatim*:—

> "Now is the time to exterminate that monster called Party Spirit. By selecting characters most conspicuous for their probity, virtue, capacity, and firmness, without any regard to party, you will go far to, if not entirely, eradicate those feelings which, on former occasions, threw so many obstacles in the way, and perhaps have the pleasure and honor of uniting a people heretofore politically divided. The Chief Magistrate of a great and powerful nation

should never indulge in party feelings. His conduct should be liberal and disinterested, always bearing in mind that he acts for the whole, and not a part of the community."

This letter of the last of the Romans was published in the National Intelligencer, and I happened to be with Judge Flam when it first met his eye. He was sipping his tea. The venerable Judge read it twice; took up the cup, and, in a musing, thoughtful mood, burnt his mouth with the hot liquid so badly that he was obliged to call for cold water.—Just at that moment, Middleton, his son, came into the parlor: he had been out shooting partridges.

"My dear Middleton, read that," said the Judge.

Middleton sat down and read it; and then looked intently at his father, waiting to hear what he would say.

"Middleton, my son," said he in a very deliberate and emphatic manner, "There's our man. General Jackson has been called a Hero—he's a Sage, a wise man, a very wise man. *We* have been kept in the mire too long: these Jeffersons and Madisons, and Nicholases and Randolphs, and all that Virginia Junto (I think that was the very word he used) have trodden us in the dust. They, with all the Democracy at their back, have lorded it over us for sixteen years. We owe them an old grudge. *But our time is coming*, (this expression he repeated twice.) Remember, my son, if ever you get into a majority, stick to it. Bring up your children to it. You have a long account to settle:—*I shall bequeath to you the Vengeance of the Federal party*. We must rally at once upon Andrew Jackson. He will bring *us* what it is fashionable to call 'the people.'—We shall bring *him* the talent, the intelligence, and the patriotism of the land. In such an alliance how can it be otherwise but that we shall have all the power?—and then, if we fail to play our cards with skill, we shall deserve to lose the game. Let Jackson be our candidate for the next Presidency, and let our gathering word be, in the sentiment of this memorable letter, 'The Union of the People and the extermination of the Monster of Party.' Do not slumber, my son, but give your energies to this great enterprise."

Mr. Middleton took this advice of his venerable father greatly to heart. "Up with Jackson, and down with Party!" said he, after a long rumination; "good, excellent—nothing can be better!" And several times that night, before he went to bed, he audibly uttered the same words, as he walked backward and forward across the room.

From this time Judge Flam wrote many letters to his friends, disclosing the views he had expressed to Middleton; and by degrees the matter ripened and ripened, until things were so contrived as to bring about what Judge Flam used to smile and say, was "a spontaneous, unpremeditated burst of popular feeling," in the nomination of the General. And the Judge used to laugh outright, when the papers took strong ground in the General's favor, as the candidate who was brought out "without intrigue or party management." The Old Hero and Sage, we all know, was cheated out of his first election; which circumstance greatly embittered his early friends, who, from that time—Mr. Middleton among the rest—took a very decided stand for Reform, Retrenchment, Economy, and the Rights of the People.

The Judge did not live to witness this second effort which resulted so gloriously for the Democratic cause; but his son stuck close to the Old Hero, and was among his most ardent supporters to the last. When the General succeeded, his first care was to show his gratitude to that disinterested band of patriots who so freely surrendered their old principles and abandoned their old comrades in his behalf. *He* brought *them* into office, just to show that he was determined to carry out the doctrine of his letter; and *they* were loudest in their praise of *him* for the sake of the *old grudge*, of which Judge Flam spoke to his son, and to indemnify their long suffering in the cause of the country, in the course of which they had, for so many years, been strangers to power. So between these two persuasions, it is not to be wondered at that they should have become the principal friends and most confidential advisers of the General.

Having thus got upon an elevation, from whence they could look backward upon their past errors, and forward to their future hopes, a new light dawned upon every man of them; and thereupon they straightway became sick and sorry for having so long sinned against Democracy, and grew ashamed of that black cockade which George Washington wore in the Revolution; made open renunciation of their former pretended attachment to his principles; canonized Mr. Jefferson as a saint, whom they had formerly reviled as the chief of sinners; purged out their old Federal blood; took deep alterative draughts of detergent medicine; and, finally, like true patriots, came forth regenerated, thorough-bred whole-hog Democrats, sworn to follow the new Democratic principle through all its meanderings, traverses, dodgings, and duckings to the end. Indeed, Mr. Middleton Flam, our honorable representative, has more than once, in some of his later speeches before the people, contended, that although his father was attached to George Washington's school of politics, which, as he remarked, naturally arose out of the prejudices created by the revolutionary war—in which the old Judge had served as a soldier—yet, that he, Middleton, never was truly an admirer of that gentleman's theory of government or system of measures—but, on the contrary, held them in marked disesteem, and from his earliest youth had a strong inclination toward that freedom from restraint, which, in man and boy, is the best test of the new Democratic principle. In proof of this tendency of his youthful opinions, he mentioned, with most admirable effect, an exploit, in which, when not more than twelve years of age, he gallantly stood up at the head of a party of his school-fellows to bar out the tutor and take a holiday, on the ground of the indefeasible rights of man, with a view to attend a great political meeting of the friends of Jefferson, just previous to the second election of that Apostle of Democracy.

Be that as it may, our distinguished member of Congress is now, by force of reflection and conviction, as pure, unadulterated, and, as our people jocularly denote it, as patent a dyed-in-the-wool Democrat as Theodore Fog himself, whose attachment to popular principles, habits, and manners, and whose unalterable adhesion to the new Democratic theory, are written in every line of his face and in every movement of his body:—and so, Mr. Flam avers, is every one of his black-cockade friends who have got an office. "Thus it is,"— if I may be allowed to quote a beautiful sentiment from one of Fog's speeches —"thus it is, that by degrees, the errors of old opinions are washed out by the all-pervading ablution of the Democratic principle following in the footsteps of the march of intellect; and so true is it, that the body politic, like quicksilver, regurgitates and repudiates the feculence of Federalism."

Nicodemus Handy has an attachment for Mr. Flam, which is truly fraternal. It goes so far as to prevent him from ever contradicting Mr. Middleton in any fact, or gainsaying him in any opinion—although I did think at one time, when Nicodemus was thought to be rich, that he was a little bold in his sentiments on two or three matters wherein our member differed from him. One I remember in particular; it was when the Old Hero pocketed the Specie Circular Bill. Mr. Handy thought, for a little while, that the circular was too hard upon the banks and the trading people, and he seemed to insinuate that the General was rather cornered by Congress, when they ordered its repeal by two-thirds of both Houses; and that, consequently, as a good Democrat, he ought to have submitted to the will of the people in that matter, and allowed them to have the law after it was passed. Mr. Flam was diametrically opposed to him, and proved, I thought conclusively, that, according to the sound Quodlibetarian Democratic principle, the General was altogether right in putting the act of Congress aside and not allowing them to overset his plans by another vote of two-thirds. "For," he inquired with great force of argument, adopting the Socratic form, "what is Congress? The representatives of the people, by districts and by States. For whom can any one man in that body speak? For his own district, or for his own State—no more. Now, what is the President? Sir," said he, in that solemn and impressive tone in which he addresses the House at Washington, "the President himself has answered that question in his immortal Protest against the Senate—he is '*the direct representative of the American people*,' and, as he took occasion once to say in his Message, '*It will be for those in whose behalf we all act, to decide whether the Executive Department of the Government, in the steps which it has taken on this subject, has been found in the line of its duty.*' The President, sir, is the representative of the *whole* people—not of a district, not of a State, but of the *whole* nation. Why should these representatives of *the parts* undertake to dictate to the representative of *the whole*? It is for the people to decide whether, in putting that bill in his pocket, he was in the line of his duty. Sir, there is the broad buttress upon which the Democratic principle reposes, and will repose forever. Jackson has determined, as representative of the people, that the Specie Circular shall not be repealed, and every true Democrat will of course say that he is right. I am surprised that you, Handy, should give any countenance to the factious doctrine set up by the Whigs, that Congress has a right to array itself against the clearly expressed will of the people, when uttered through the paramount representative of the whole nation."

Mr. Handy was evidently confounded by this unanswerable argument, and, of course, did not attempt to answer. I confess, for my own part, I listened with admiration and amazement at the dialectic skill with which so abstruse a subject was so briefly yet so clearly elucidated, and I inwardly ejaculated, in the language of the afflicted man of Uz, "How forcible are right words!"

My late pupil's reflections were drawn to this question of the Specie Circular with more intensity of regard, from a very natural train of circumstances, which had great influence in inducing an elaborate study of the subject. Mr. Handy has often said that Mr. Flam was the very best customer our bank had from the beginning. Acting, as he always did, upon the principle that our first care is due to those who are nearest to us, or, according to the adage, that charity begins at home, the President of the bank refused to borrow from any other institution, but determined exclusively to patronize his own. This principle he carried to the romantic extent of borrowing four times as much as anybody else; and as he always contended for it as the most approved theorem in banking, that the wider and the more remote the circulation of the paper of a bank, the better for its profit, he employed these funds in the purchase of a large quantity of the Chickasaw Reserve lands. By these means Mr. Flam became the proprietor of a vast number of acres in that Southwest country; and as the Specie Circular was a most laudable contrivance to stop overtrading and speculating in the public lands, it occurred to our worthy representative that the less the public lands were sold, the more his would come into the market at good prices; and so, with a view to the benefit of Quodlibet, where he expected to invest the profits, he became a strong advocate of the Circular. This set him to studying the question of the pocketing of the bill for its repeal, whereof I have spoken above, and enabled him to convince himself how deeply that matter was connected with the development of the Democratic principle in the manner put forth in his argument to Mr. Handy.

Thus does it come to pass that, step by step, as our government rolls on, its fundamental features are successively disclosed in the practical operations of that sublime system which so securely intrenches the good of the people in the doctrines of genuine Quodlibetarian Democracy, as now of late, for the first time, fully understood and practiced.

Ever after that notable discourse, Mr. Handy showed himself, both in private and at our public meetings, the stern, uncompromising champion of the Specie Circular and of the broad representative character of the President. The other questions upon which I have found him to differ occasionally with Mr. Flam, shared pretty nearly the same fate as this. The Cashier ultimately fell into entire harmony of sentiment in all matters with the President; though, as I have insinuated before, in the flood-tide of Mr. Handy's fortune, when he began to be accounted a man of wealth, he was, in accordance with a principle of human nature founded upon the corrupting and debasing influence of riches, much more difficult to bring into perfect conformity of opinion with Mr. Flam, than in the ebb. Yet, I would here remark that, almost in the same degree that Mr. Handy yielded his assent to the doctrines of the Hon. Middleton Flam, did the rank and file of our sturdy and independent Democracy yield to Mr. Handy; the whole party being kept in a harmonious agreement and accord by what Fog terms "the electric diffusion of the Democratic principle through the whole circle of hand-in-hand, unflinching, unwavering, uncorruptible, and power-frowning-down yeomanry of the most virtuous and enlightened nation upon the terrestrial globe."

CHAPTER III.

FURTHER DISCOURSE RELATING TO THE HON. MIDDLETON FLAM—
CORRECTION IN THE ORTHOGRAPHY OF HIS FAMILY SEAT—HIS
RESPECT FOR THE PEOPLE—VERY ORIGINAL VIEWS ENTERTAINED BY
HIM ON THIS SUBJECT—HIS LIBERALITY IN MONEY MATTERS—
AVERSION TO THE LAW REGARDING INTEREST—DEMOCRATIC VIEW OF
THAT QUESTION—HIS ENCOURAGEMENT OF INDUSTRY AND THE
WORKING PEOPLE—INGENIOUS AND PROFOUND ILLUSTRATION OF THE
GREAT DEMOCRATIC PRINCIPLE.

Holding, as I do, our Democratic leader, the Hon. Middleton Flam, in the most deservedly profound respect, and knowing him to be, if I may be allowed the expression, a bright exemplar of Democracy, and containing in himself, metaphorically speaking, the epitome of all sound opinions, I am fully authorized by the common usage regarding public characters to bring him and his affairs conspicuously into the view of the world, not for censure, neither for praise, although no man is better entitled to the latter, but for instruction. Such is the destiny of distinguished men, that their lives are common property for the teaching of their generation. Duly acknowledging the weight of this maxim, I shall venture in the present chapter to give my reader a still closer insight into the private concerns of our representative; for which task I feel myself somewhat specially qualified, through the bountiful hospitality of that excellent gentleman, who has not only welcomed me to his board often on week days, and always on Sundays, but who has even flattered me, more than once, by the remark that he would not take umbrage at such impartial development of his life and opinions as he knew I, better than any other of his friends, (truly herein his kindness has overrated my worthiness,) had it in my power to make.

The old family seat of the Flams is about two miles from Quodlibet. It is upon the Bickerbray road; and, taking in all the grounds belonging to the domicile, the tract is somewhere about eight hundred acres; by far the greater portion of which is a flat range of woodland and field, watered by Grasshopper Run, which falls into the Rumblebottom. The tract used to be called, in Judge Flam's time, "The Poplar Flats," and the house, at that day, went by the name of "Quality Hall:" but ever since Mr. Middleton has had it, which, as may be gathered from what I have imparted in the last chapter, has been from the time that the old Black Cockades began to think of turning Democrats; ever since that day the spelling has been gradually changing, and the house now goes by the settled name of "Equality Hall," and the tract is always written by our people "The Popular Flats." Mr. Middleton greatly approves of this change, for two reasons which he has had occasion to take into his serious reflections

—First; "Because," he says, "in the Quodlibetarian Democratic system, as now understood, words are things." "Not only things, sir," said he, in a discourse one day, at his own table, "but important and valuable things. I have observed," he continued, "in our country, especially among the unflinching, uncompromising Democrats, that a name is always half the battle. For instance, sir, we wish to destroy the bank; we have only to call it a Monster: we desire to put down an opposition ticket, and keep the offices among ourselves; all that we have to do is to set up a cry of Aristocracy. If we want to stop a canal, we clamor against Consolidation: if we wish it to go on, it is only to change the word—Develop the Resources. When it was thought worth our while to frighten Calhoun with the notion that we were going to hang him, we hurraed for the Proclamation; and after that, when we wanted to gain over his best friends to our side—State-Rights was the word. Depend upon it, gentlemen, with the true Quodlibetarian Democracy, names are things: that is the grand secret of the 'New-Light system.'"

Mr. Flam's second reason for approving the change in the spelling of Poplar Flats and Quality Hall, did not depend upon such a philosophical subtlety as the first; it was simply because he had very nigh lost his first election to Congress from inattention to this material point of orthography. Quality Hall, some of the Democrats of our region were unreasonable and headstrong enough to say, was not so Democratic a name as their candidate ought to have for his place of residence; and if it had not been that our representative discovered this in time to convince them that it was an old-fashioned way of spelling Equality Hall, I believe, in my conscience, he would have made out very badly: but luckily for this district, and I may say, for the nation, this error in spelling was corrected in time to set all straight; and Mr. Flam, from that day, not only put the E before the Q, but, in token of that incident, and by way of a remembrancer, always spoke of Equality Hall as built upon Popular Flats, which sounded very well in the ears of the New Lights, and no doubt went a great way to keep him in Congress ever after. Therefore I repeat, after my patron and friend, words *are* things;—and, democratically speaking, in the sense of a New Light, I might even say *better* than things.

Equality Hall is a building which looks larger than it is, from the circumstance that it was originally a one-storied, irregular cottage of brick, but in the Judge's time a second story was put to it; and, almost immediately after Mr. Middleton came to be the owner, he enlarged the eastern gable by widening it to nearly forty feet, and building it up considerably above the roof, and then adding to it a grand Grecian Temple porch with niches for statues, and with fluted Doric columns of wood, which thus constituted what Mr. Middleton calls his façade and principal front to the building. The effect of this piece of magnificence was to screen the old-cottage from view, and to impress the beholder with the idea of a grand building peeping out upon the Bickerbray road between the foliage of two weeping willows, which the old Judge put there before Mr. Jefferson's election.

I have heard some fastidious, not to say malevolent critics, find fault with this new addition to the building, upon the score that it had too much pretense about it; and that one was always disappointed upon finding all this grandeur of outside to be but a mere piece of theatrical show, without having anything to correspond to it within. Mr. Flam has heard the same objection, but he has always treated it with the contempt it deserved. "It *was* intended for show," he observed one day addressing the people from the hustings, when he had occasion to notice a remark of one of these caviling gentlemen, who had said something about having walked behind the portico to find the house—and I shall never forget how his eye kindled and his form dilated as he spoke —"Show, sir! Of course, it was put there for show. What else could it be put for? What is any portico put up for? It faces toward the road, sir—it was designed to face toward the road. When I built that portico, I wished the people, sir, to see it; the best I have shall always be shown to the people. I trust, sir, that my respect for the people shall never so far abate, as to induce me to neglect *them*. My house, sir, intrinsically is that of an humble citizen; there are a dozen equal to it in this county; but that part of it which is intended to gratify the people is unsurpassed here or anywhere else. I have laid out, sir, a small fortune on that portico to gratify the people: all that I have comes from them—all that I ever expect to be, I hope to derive from them: who has so good a right as they to require me to put my best foot foremost, when they are the spectators? On the same principle, sir, when I appear in public, I dress in the most expensive attire, I drive the best horses, and procure the finest coach. My turnout is altogether elaborate, studiously particular—simply because I hold the people in too much esteem, to shab them off with anything of a secondary quality, while Providence has blessed me with the means of providing them the best. That, sir, is what I call a keystone principle in the arch of Democratic government: that is the sentiment, and that alone, which is to give perpetuity to this——"

"Fair fabric of freedom," said Theodore Fog, who was among the auditory, and perceived that Mr. Flam hesitated for a word to convey his idea.

"Thank you, my friend," courteously replied Mr. Flam, "I am indebted to you for the word—fair fabric of freedom."

Coming back from this digression, which I have the rather indulged because of the eloquence, as well as the just Democratic sentiment it breathes, I proceed with my sketch of the homestead of our distinguished leader of the politics of Quodlibet.

If I were asked what constituted the most striking feature in the arrangements of this very admirable establishment, I should say it was the judicious admixture of a laudable economy, with the greatest possible effect in the way of outward exhibition. For instance, the grounds were embellished with sundry structures, apparently at great cost, and producing a most satisfactory impression on the eye, but which, when examined, would be found to be, for the most part, painted imitations of a very cheap kind. Thus there was to be seen from the portico, peering above a thicket on the Grasshopper Run, an old castle with ivy-crowned battlements, greatly enriching the view; at the end of the long walk in the garden, a magnificent obelisk rose forty feet above a bed of asparagus; the entrance to the stable-yard was through the Gothic archway of an old chapel, exceeding pleasant to behold; and the ice pond was guarded by a palisade composed of muskets, lances, swords, shields, and cannon, flanked at each end by a pile of drums and colors. All these several embellishments a nice observation would determine to be executed in oil painting, upon wooden screens sawed into the requisite figures. But even this expense would, perhaps, have been avoided, had it not been that Quipes, our artist, owed Mr. Flam twenty-five dollars on account of a debt which Mr. Flam had to pay for him, to get him out of jail, for the sake of his vote, when we first elected our public-spirited representative to Congress. Owing to this circumstance, connected with the fact that Sam Hardesty, the joiner, became insolvent on his contract for building the big portico, whereby Mr. Flam was obliged to advance money to him in order to get it finished, our member conceived that it would be a good plan to work these debts out of his two friends, by setting them about the decorations I have described. Besides, he reasoned with himself that it was always well to give employment to the working people about him, with a view to encourage industry and afford a practical illustration of the benignant influence of the great Democratic principle upon society—a consideration which Mr. Flam on no occasion ever permitted himself to lose sight of. By this judicious management he accomplished a fourfold purpose: namely, the beautifying of Popular Flats; the execution of these rich specimens of art, at less than half their value; the employment of two very meritorious fragments of the people; and, above all, a most satisfactory development of the excellence and usefulness of the great New-Light Democratic principle.

Mr. Flam never was what you might call a moneyed man. For although his farms were very productive, and he had a considerable income from stock in the United States Bank; and although the expenses of his family were very far short of what the world might, from the show he made, suppose them to be; yet he was in the habit of parting with his money as fast as it came to hand. There were a great number of deserving but needy persons who were often at the Popular Flats, and who did not hesitate to borrow all the funds Mr. Flam could spare, (if he had a fault it was the generosity of his lendings,) and in this way to keep him, as he has often told me himself, very bare. To make sure against loss he had the prudence never to lend without bond and mortgage, with a power of attorney to confess judgment; and as he ever avowed what he called his most irrevocable opinion, that the interest law was exceedingly oppressive upon the industry of the country, he invariably made his own bargain on that point—sagaciously remarking, as I once heard him to Nicholas Hardup, the cattle dealer, who was under execution upon a judgment, and came to borrow the amount from Mr. Flam, "Money, sir, is a commodity like wheat or cattle; its value is regulated by the relations of supply and demand. Society will never prosper till that principle is universally recognized. *We* go for it, Mr. Hardup, as cardinal in the Democratic creed. Labor, to be free, requires that the money contract also should be free. Why should the poor man pay six per cent. when money is worth but five? Why should he be prevented paying seven, eight, or nine, even, if he finds it his interest to give it—or cannot do without it? No, sir, Equal Rights, Liberty of Conscience, and Unrestricted Freedom of Contract—there is the buttress of Democratic government!"

It often happened, as such things will happen, that Mr. Flam became the loser by his generosity; and as it was a maxim with him to inculcate the most rigid punctuality in all engagements, he has never felt himself at liberty to relax what he regarded this salutary rule; so that, on many occasions, he has been compelled to submit to the unpleasant and expensive operation of closing his accounts on the bond and mortgage, by taking possession of the mortgaged property; and in this way, as he sometimes feelingly complains to his friends, he has become encumbered with more land than he knows what to do with. He has, however, gradually got through a great deal of this trouble by renting out his farms; a course which he intends to persevere in until his children are able to take the management of them.

Mr. Handy has several times endeavored to persuade him to make his improvements rather more permanent, and to take down these embellishments I have been describing; rather rashly as I thought, calling them, to Mr. Flam's face, pasteboard scenery, gingerbread nonsense, and twopenny gimcracks: and he insinuated that if our worthy representative would lay out some of his "accommodation" in a more solid manner upon Popular Flats, it would tell hereafter to his advantage. But Mr. Flam turns a deaf ear to all Nicodemus's preaching. He says that the accommodation is better laid out in the Chickasaw Reserve, where he means to realize a large fortune; and as to what Mr. Handy is pleased to call *gimcracks* and *gingerbread*, that, in fact, is the only kind of decoration in which a man, who respects the simplicity and purity of

Democratic government, ought to indulge his taste. "If," said he, "my old castle, my obelisk, or my Gothic gateway were built of stone instead of white pine, a fair inference might be made against me of a lurking wish to restore the exploded aristocratic system of primogeniture and entails. It would be said I was building for my son and his eldest born. Thank God, no such treasonable design can be inferred from this *gimcrack* and *gingerbread*, as you wittily term it. When I go, sir, my estate is to be cut up as our Democratic republican laws ordain; and my gimcrack and gingerbread can be plowed in as easily as the dockweed. Strange as it may sound to the ears of some, gimcrack and gingerbread are the elements of our new Democratic theory. Sir, our government should glory in it:—it does glory in it. There is no reproach in the fact that we neither build, legislate, think, nor determine for the next generation. We attend to *ourselves*—that is genuine New-Light Democracy. We oppose Vested Rights, we oppose Chartered Privileges, we oppose Pledges to bind future Legislatures, we oppose Tariffs, Internal Improvements, Colleges, and Universities, on the broad Democratic ground that we have nothing to do with Posterity. Posterity will be as free as we are. Let it take care of itself. I glory, sir, in saying New-Light Democracy riots in gimcrack and gingerbread."

This eloquent outburst of sentiment effectually silenced Mr. Handy, and brought him thoroughly into Mr. Flam's opinion. I rejoice that my intimacy with this able statesman should have afforded me this opportunity to show the brilliancy with which his mind sparkles in the demonstration of political truth, and the wonderful power with which it converts apparently trivial thoughts into golden illustrations of the Democratic theory as lately discovered and practiced.

CHAPTER IV.

THE SECOND ERA—POPULATION OF QUODLIBET—INCREASE UNPARALLELED IN ANCIENT CITIES; EQUALED ONLY BY MILWAUKEE, ETC.—SUCCESS OF THE BANK—ATTACK UPON IT IN CONGRESS—THE HON. MIDDLETON FLAM'S TRIUMPHANT VINDICATION—SKETCH OF HIS CELEBRATED SPEECH BEFORE THE NEW LIGHTS—INIMITABLE IRONY ON THE DIVORCE OF GOVERNMENT AND BANK—MERITED COMPLIMENT TO THE HEAD OF THE SECRETARY OF THE TREASURY—THAT DISTINGUISHED GENTLEMAN'S OPINIONS.

It is no part of my design in the compilation of this little history to preserve the form of a regular, chronological narrative of the course of events in Quodlibet; for although the material for such a continuous recital abounds in the memoranda which I have preserved, yet it seems better to suit the purpose of the respectable committee who have invoked me to this labor, that I should rather make excerpts from the mass of my papers, in such wise as to bring before my reader the condition of the Borough at several epochs, with an occasional reference to such incidents as may serve to explain the opinions of our people and illustrate the course of that beautiful system of politics which the world—I mean that world of which our Borough is the center—has consented to honor with the epithet of Quodlibetarian; and in which designation, in my poor judgment, is comprehended the essence of the true theory by which this nation has advanced to its present unparalleled state of prosperity and grandeur.

Following this suggestion, I propose now to lead my reader to that epoch in the annals of the Borough which dates in the fourth year after the Removal, or, in the vernacular computation, the year of 1836-7. The population of Quodlibet had now reached to the astonishing amount of fifteen hundred and eighty odd souls—the increase being altogether without an example in the history of civilization, excepting, perhaps, in that of Milwaukee, Navarino, and some other of those seemingly incredible and fabulous creations of art which are said to have sprung up under the beneficent auspices of the Quodlibetarian theory, as the same has been practiced in this government for some few years past. Quodlibet, I repeat, had reached in population upwards of fifteen hundred and eighty inhabitants, as was ascertained by a diligent enumeration made under the direction of our New-Light Club, with a view to the election of a constable held this year in the Borough;—and when we reflect that at the date of the Removal, the whole settlement fell short of two hundred persons all told, it will be perceived that in three years our increase has exceeded seven hundred per cent.! Verily, neither London, Athens, nor Palmyra, Karnac, Luxor, nor even Milwaukee itself, I doubt, has ever manifested so prolific an augmentation.

Nicodemus Handy's row of stores on the Basin was the first improvement, as I have already informed my reader; then Copperplate Ridge was studded with buildings; at the same time Flam Street was enriched with the bank and seven brick buildings; then came the Female Lyceum, with the Town Hall in the second story of the same building, Peter Ounce's Boatmen's Hotel on the other side of the Basin, the Hay Scales, Zachary Younghusband's (the tinplate worker) shop, and Dr. Thomas G. Winkleman's Druggist Store and Soda Water Pavilion. These, as well as I can recollect, were the principal establishments erected in Quodlibet in the three years I have referred to. There were a number of private houses built in this period, and a whole settlement of free negroes made below the Basin, on the line of the canal. I ought to mention, too, that Nicodemus Handy this year dug out the foundations, and, I believe, built the cellar walls, of a second row of stores and of a new hotel designed on a very large scale, with extensive baths to be attached to it. These buildings, it pains me to say, in advance, never got higher than the first story, as I shall be obliged to relate hereafter.

The bank did a sweeping business all this time; and nothing can be conceived more beautiful than the theory upon which it was conducted. It has run out of my memory how many new bales of pink silk paper were turned off by it, but the amount would scarcely be believed if I were to set it down; and the accommodation principle was carried out to an extent that must have been truly gratifying to the Secretary. Still, even this most exemplary institution did not escape the malevolence of the Whigs. That ever-complaining party, as the Hon. Middleton Flam assured us by letter, were making a great ado in Congress about all the banks, but particularly about ours—alleging, in their usual factious manner, that the government would lose money by us, as well as by the others.

Deeming this charge as one of peculiar atrocity, we at once determined to take it up in our New-Light Club, and stamp upon it the most conclusive refutation. We accordingly fixed an evening for the discussion, during Christmas week, when we knew that our member would be at home to visit his family; and he was of course invited to attend and give his views upon this very interesting question. The meeting was in the Town Hall up stairs above the Female Lyceum. All Quodlibet was present. I shall be long thankful to Providence for the dignified station which it fell to my lot to fill on that memorable occasion. By a most unexpected but most felicitous chance, I was honored that night with a call to the chair; the worthy Mr. Snuffers, our President, not being able to attend, in consequence of the interesting condition of Mrs. Snuffers. As the subject of discussion was one of thrilling interest, the most intense anxiety prevailed to hear the speech of our eloquent representative. He came fully prepared, bringing with him a load of documents. Our Vice, Mr. Doubleday, who is a solid thinking, shrewd person, of that maturity of judgment which it is impossible to impose upon, and himself, by-the-by, a first-rate debater, told me, after we broke up, that Mr. Flam's discourse that evening on the banking system at large and on the *safety* of the banks in particular, was one of the closest pieces of reasoning he had ever listened to in his life. I regret that I have preserved so imperfect an outline of this speech, but such as it is I offer it to my reader.

The orator commenced very appropriately by remarking how impossible it was, in the nature of things, to satisfy the Whigs on any point. He said there were three parties in Congress: First, the Whigs—who still croaked about a National Bank—and his description of their croaking was to the last degree humorous; it produced peals of laughter. Second, the thorough-going Quodlibetarian Whole Hogs, who were steadfast and immovable for the State Banks; and a third party, small in numbers, "attenuated"—as he remarked with irresistibly comic effect—"and gaunt; feeble, shrill, and like crickets who might scarcely be seen in daytime;" and who, when the bill to Regulate the Deposits was up, presented what, in his opinion, was the most alarming, if it had not been the most ridiculous scheme, in relation to the public money, that had ever been hatched in the hotbed of faction. These men, he said called themselves Conservatives: "And what think you, Mr. President," he asked, "was *their* project? It was, sir, to separate the Government from the Banks." Here Mr. Flam was interrupted by a loud laugh. "A Mr. Gordon," he said, "was at the head of this little troop. He proposed a bill, two sessions ago, to place the revenue and public moneys in the hands of Receivers—the moneys were to be paid to these Receivers in GOLD and SILVER! and no bank was to be intrusted with a dollar!! And this," exclaimed Mr. Flam, with a tone of inimitable irony, "was to be done for the SAFETY of the public Treasure! Your money not safe in the hands of the banks, but *perfectly secure* in the keeping of these honest Receivers, who were to be furnished with vaults and iron chests to lock it up in!!! O rare Conservatives!—O wise Conservatives! —O honest Conservatives!"

We all thought the ceiling of the Town Hall would have toppled down on our heads from the laughter occasioned by this sally. In this admirable strain he continued for some minutes. At length, taking himself up, and falling into a tone of grave expostulation, he pulled out a copy of The Globe from his pocket, and proceeded—

"Admirably, sir, has this paper which I hold in my hand descanted on this most wicked project. These well-timed remarks, I beg leave to read. Hear the incomparable Blair. *'Had such a suggestion,'* says he, *'come from General Jackson, it would have been rung through the Old Dominion as conclusive proof of all the aspirations which may have been charged to the Hero of New Orleans. See here, they would say, he wishes to put the public money directly into the palms of his friends and partisans, instead of keeping it on deposit in banks, whence it cannot be drawn, for other than public purposes, without certain detection. In such a case, we should feel that the people had just cause for alarm, and ought to give their most watchful attention to such an effort to enlarge Executive power, and put in its hands the means of corruption.'* Most admirably again," continued Mr. Flam, "has this same incomparable Blair said, *'The scheme is disorganizing and revolutionary, subversive of the fundamental principles of our government, and of its practice from 1780 down to this day.'* Will you, freemen of Quodlibet, gentlemen of The New Light," exclaimed Mr. Flam, "if faction should go so far as to put this odious, disorganizing, and revolutionary yoke upon the country, will you, freemen of Quodlibet, submit to it?"

"No!" shouted the ready response of sixty-four voices.

"Gentlemen, listen to the words of the Old Hero," continued Mr. Flam, with a gratulatory smile playing on his face, presenting at the same time a printed document which he carefully unfolded—"listen to that 'old man eloquent' whose mouth is never opened but to breathe the precepts of wisdom and patriotism:—I read you from his last message. In remarking upon this absurd project, the President, in this able paper, holds the following language: *'To retain the Public Revenue in the Treasury unemployed in any way, is impracticable. It is considered against the genius of our free institutions to lock up in vaults the treasure of the nation. Such a treasure would doubtless be employed at some time, as it has in other countries, when opportunity tempted ambition.'* Now are you willing, men of Quodlibet," again ejaculated our eloquent representative, as he slapped the document upon the table, "are you willing, or can you consent to tolerate a proposition which is against the genius——"

"No!" thundered forth sixty-four New Lights again, before our orator had finished the sentence.

"Order, order, freemen of Quodlibet," I called out, as it was my duty to do, at this interruption. "Hear our distinguished representative to an end, before you respond."

There was a decorous silence.

"A proposition," continued Mr. Flam, "which is against the genius of our free institutions, and which would be a lure to tempt ambition to its most unholy purposes?"

The club looked at me for a sign, and I, quickly giving a nod of my head, a loud "No" ran over the whole room, like a *feu de joie* fired off at a militia training.

"Now, gentlemen," said Mr. Flam, "one word as to the *safety* of these deposits. Whigs—oh that some of you were present, to mark how a plain tale shall put you down! I have here the Secretary's own report," he added, as he selected one from the bundle of documents which lay before him. "There is no need for many words here—here is Mr. Secretary himself, than whom a more pellucid, diaphanous, transparent Secretary of the Treasury—a mind of rock-crystal, a head of sunbeams, a soul, sir, of pure fountain water, that gurgles and gurgles, perpetually welling forth its unadulterated intelligence in a purling stream, of which it may be said, in the beautiful language of the poet of antiquity

'Rusticus expectat dum defluat amnis, at ille
Labitur et labetur in omne volubilis ævum'"——

Here I gave a nod, by way of signal to the club, to applaud this splendid outbreak of Ciceronian eloquence; whereat the New Lights vociferated "Bravo—three times three!" and made the house ring with their approbation —"I say, sir, I have the Secretary himself here present."

Several of the members, not being accustomed to this parliamentary language, took the orator literally, and rose to welcome the distinguished person referred to; but a word from me explained matters, and brought the club again to order.

"The Secretary, gentlemen New Lights," said Mr. Flam, adroitly availing himself of the occasion to throw off a coruscation of wit—"the Secretary lives *in his reports*—profound, statesmanlike, recondite and deep, his report is in my hand—*it is himself!* I will read you what he says upon this matter of the safety of the banks."

Here Mr. Flam read as follows, from a report dated December 12, 1834:——

36

"It is gratifying to reflect, however, that the credit given by the government, whether to bank paper or bank agents, has been accompanied by SMALLER LOSSES in the experience under the system of State banks in this country, at their worst periods, and under their severest calamities, than any other kind of credit the government has ever given in relation to its pecuniary transactions." "Again," he continued, turning to another page, "it is a singular fact, in praise of this description of public debtors— the selected banks—that there is not now due, on deposit, in the whole of them, which have ever stopped payment, from the establishment of the constitution to the present moment, a sum much beyond what is now due to the United States from one mercantile firm, that stopped payment in 1825 or 1826, and of whom ample security was required, and supposed to be taken under the responsibility of an oath. If we include the whole present dues to the government from discredited banks at all times, and of all kinds, whether as depositories or not, and embrace even counterfeit bills, and every other species of unavailable funds in the treasury, they will not exceed what is due from two such firms. Of almost one hundred banks, not depositories, which, during all our wars and commercial embarrassments, have heretofore failed, in any part of the Union, in debt to the government, on their bills or otherwise, it will be seen by the above table (to which Mr. Flam referred as annexed to the report) that the whole of them, except seventeen, have adjusted everything which they owed, and that the balance due from them, without interest, is less than $32,000."

"There, gentlemen New Lights of Quodlibet," said Mr. Flam, when he had finished reading these extracts, "what can be added beyond this certificate from the Secretary, of the value of our State banks? Even the lips of Whiggism are sealed before it; and nothing is left but the confession that, in all their senseless clamor against our favorite and long-tried State bank system, the course of its enemies has been but the ebullition of disappointed ambition and peevish discontent. Are you willing, I ask, to see this glorious system prostrated to the earth?"

"No!" was again the general cry.

"Are you content to see your cherished banks stripped of the confidence of the government?"

"No—never, never!" shouted the New Lights to a man.

"Then, gentlemen Quodlibetarians, radii of the New Lights, you have justified all my hopes. Your applause rewards all my toils—your support and confidence enlist all my gratitude. With emotions of heart-felt satisfaction, I bid you each good night!"

With these words, this remarkable man gathered up his documents, and, with a countenance full of smiles, retired from the midst of this circle of his devoted—yes, I may say, his idolizing friends.

CHAPTER V.

EXCITEMENT PRODUCED BY THE THOROUGH BLUE WHOLE TEAM— MEETING OF THE NEW LIGHT—JESSE FERRET'S AMBIDEXTERITY— INTRODUCTION OF ELIPHALET FOX TO THE CLUB—HIS EXPOSITION OF PRINCIPLES—ESTABLISHMENT OF THE QUODLIBET WHOLE HOG.

Soon after the time referred to in the last chapter—that is, when we were favored by Mr. Flam with his views on the banking system—there was a question of the most profound interest in agitation, both in the New-Light Club and out of it; that question was the establishment of a newspaper. The Quodlibetarian Democracy were, I am sorry to inform my reader, most sorely and wantonly assailed, indeed I may say insulted, by an hebdomadal sheet which, through the aid, or, more properly speaking, *the abuse* of the post-office (for surely it was not the original design of that institution to afford the means of corrupting the people by the dissemination of such moral poisons) was distributed among sundry of our citizens, and even put upon the files of one of our public houses. I do not scruple to name the house—that of Jesse Ferret—Jesse being at this time a little amphibious in his politics, or, in Mr. Fog's expressive language, *rather fishy*. The paper to which I allude was published at Thorough Blue Court-House, a perfect hotbed of contumacious opposition, situate about fifty miles due west from Quodlibet. It was called "The Thorough Blue Whole Team," and was edited by Augustus Postlethwaite Tompkinson, an inchoate lawyer, who had set up for a poet, and whose sentiments were of the most dangerous Whig complexion. This paper was constantly filled with extracts of the ravings of Whig members of Congress against our admirable system of banking, and had gone to such an extreme of rashness, as to denominate that splendid measure of the purest and wisest statesman of the age—my reader perceives I mean Mr. Benton—for the introduction of the gold currency, a humbug! But this was not all; the unprincipled editor of that reckless journal had actually so far forgotten all the decencies of civilized society, had become so callous to the cause of virtue and truth, as to launch his puny thunderbolts at the fair fame of the Hon. Middleton Flam. He was ridiculed as a pretender! he was nicknamed a charlatan!! and the unbridled license of this unsparing defamer did not stop short of denouncing him as a Federalist!!! All Quodlibet—that is, all who possessed the soul of Quodlibetarians—raised up their hands at the political impiety of this libel. A spontaneous burst of feeling indicated the deep sentiment which called for immediate action on the subject. For a full week, the New Light was in a state of paroxysm. The club met every night. Nicodemus Handy was there; Fog was there; Nim Porter was there; Snuffers and Doubleday, Doctor Winkleman and Zachary Younghusband, recently appointed postmaster of the Borough, were there. Every thorough-bred Quod, even down to Flan. Sucker, was there. Jesse Ferret, I have already said, was fishy. I regret to say it, but it is true. Jesse, bending to the suppleness of the times, and forgetting a patriot's duty, which is first and foremost above all things to stick to his party, pleaded his public calling to excuse his vacillation, and even went so far as to say that "a publican should have no politics." Oh shame, where is thy blush! Not so with Nim Porter;—his soul towered above the bar-room; he would bet all he was worth on the side of his party. Everybody in Quodlibet knows how free Nim always was with his bets.

The decisive meeting of the club took place in the dining-room of Ferret's tavern. Nicodemus Handy did not often attend the meetings of the club: we looked to him rather for head work, for he was not the best of public speakers; but on the night of this assemblage he made it a point to be present. Mr. Handy is rather a short, fat man; his head is partially bald, his face is smooth and fair, his dress was always remarked for being of the best material, put on in the neatest manner—in short, Mr. Handy is a first-rate gentleman. I am particular in noting these matters, because THE WHOLE TEAM was in the habit of bragging that "all the decency" was on his side. Now I would challenge Thorough Blue Court-House, and the settlement ten miles around it—the whole region is Whig—to produce one man among them to compare either with the Hon. Middleton Flam or Nicodemus Handy. And I would take this occasion further to remark, in refutation of THE WHOLE TEAM's calumny touching "all the decency," that the true Quodlibetarian Democrats have as great a respect for appearance, and as profound a spirit of assentation and regard toward a man of wealth, as the people of any country upon earth: if anything, our tip-top Quods carry rather a higher head than the richest Whigs in these parts, and any dispassionate man who will examine into the matter will say so.

Snuffers was in the chair. The members of the club did not sit down: they were too much agitated to sit down. As soon as I, in my character of Secretary, read the minutes of the preceding meeting, Mr. Handy rose, and after some very appropriate remarks delivered in a modest fashion, (in which he assured the club that he was unaccustomed to public speaking and moreover oppressed by the intensity of his feelings in regard to the recent attack on his friend, the Hon. Middleton Flam, and in a slight degree agitated in the presence of this most respectable assemblage of Quods,) came at once to the point. "Who," he asked, "was Augustus Postlethwaite Tompkinson? His name told you who he was—an aristocrat, a poet, a sentimentalizer, *a dealer in fiction*! What was his calling? A pander, a pimp, a professional reviler of great and good men. What was his paper? That sink of infamy—THE WHOLE TEAM—twenty-four by eighteen, with a poet's corner, and an outside stuffed with a few beggarly advertisements. Would gentlemen submit to be led by the nose by a thing like that, twenty-four by eighteen?"

"Never," cried out Flanigan Sucker, who stood in the doorway, just behind Nim Porter—"will we, Nim?"

"Silence," said Mr. Snuffers.

"If gentlemen have my feelings of indignation on this subject," continued Mr. Handy, "they will concur with me in establishing a paper of our own."

"Go it, Nicodemus!" shouted Flan. Sucker, very indecorously putting in his word a second time.

Thereupon arose some confusion in the club, and Flan., being found upon examination to be muddled with liquor, was requested to retire; and not being very prompt to obey this invitation, he was turned out.

Mr. Handy then proceeded. "Gentlemen," said he, "a paper we must have, and I feel happy in the opportunity to introduce to your acquaintance a good friend of our cause, who is here present to-night, and who, under the auspices of this club, is willing to undertake the responsible duty of supplying this so much desiderated object. I beg leave to present to you Mr. Eliphalet Fox, a gentleman long connected with the press in a neighboring State, and who is prepared to submit to you his scheme."

Upon this a stranger, who had been seated in a back part of the room, wrapped up in a green camlet cloak with plaid lining, which I may add had apparently seen much service, stepped forward, and, disrobing himself of this outer garment, stood full before the President. He was a thin, faded little fellow, whose clothes seemed to be somewhat too large for him. His eye was gray and rather dull, his physiognomy melancholy, his cheek sunken, his complexion freckled, his coat blue, the buttons dingy, his hair sandy, and like untwisted rope. The first glance at the person of this new-comer gave every man of the club the assurance that here was an editor indeed. A whisper of approbation ran through the crowd, and from that moment, as Mr. Doubleday afterward said to me, we felt assured that we had the man we wanted.

"Mr. President," said he, in a feeble and sickly voice, "my name *is* Fox. I am in want of employment. Sir," he added, gritting his teeth and taking an attitude, "if the rancor of my soul, accumulated by maltreatment, set on edge by disappointment, indurated by time, entitle me to claim your confidence, then, sir, my claim stands number one. If a thorough knowledge, sir, of the characteristic traits of Federalism, long acquaintance with its designs, persecution, sir, from its votaries, a deep experience of its black ingratitude; if days of toil spent in its service, nights of feverish anxiety protracted in ruminating over its purposes; if promises violated, hopes blasted, labors unrewarded, may be deemed a stimulus to hatred—then, sir, am I richly endowed with the qualifications to expose the enemies of Quodlibetarian Democracy. I am a child, sir, of sorrow: the milk of my nature has been curdled by neglect. Mine is a history of talents underrated, sensibilities derided, patriotism spurned, affluence, nay competence, withheld. The world has turned me aside. I have no resting place on the bosom of my mother. Society, like a demon, pursues me. Writs in the hands of the sheriff, judgments on the docket, *fi. fas.* and *ca. sas.* track my footsteps. No limitation runs in my favor: the *scire facias*, ever ready, revives the inhuman judgment, and my second shirt—my first is in rags—is stripped from my body to glut the avarice of my relentless pursuers. Thank God, I have at last found a friend in that distinguished man who has been so ruthlessly, so recently assailed, by that fledgling of the aristocracy, Augustus Postlethwaite Tompkinson. Yes, sir, in the Hon. Middleton Flam I have found a friend. He has given me letters to this benevolent gentleman, Mr. Handy; he has recommended my establishment here; he promises to co-operate with this respectable club in giving me a foothold among you. With her Flams and her Handys, Quodlibet is destined to an enviable influence in this great Republic." (Here he was interrupted by loud cheers.) "My scheme is, Mr. President, with the aid of this club, and that of the benefactors I have named, forthwith to start THE QUODLIBET WHOLE HOG. It shall take a decided and uncompromising stand against THE THOROUGH BLUE WHOLE TEAM, (here he was again arrested by cheers;) pledged to contradict every word uttered by that vile print, (cheers;) to traduce and bring down its editor by the most systematic disparagement, (cheers;) to disprove all Whig assertions; unfailingly to take the opposite side on all questions; industriously to lower the standing of the members of the Whig party, (immense cheers;) through thick and thin, good report and evil report, for better and for worse, to defend and sustain the administration of the new President, who is about to take his seat, that incomparable Democrat of the genuine Quodlibetarian stamp, Martin Van Buren, (at this point the cheering continued for some moments, with such violence that the speaker had to suspend his remarks;) and finally, sir, to commend, exalt, and illustrate the character and pretensions of our unrivaled friend Mr. Flam, (immense cheering,) giving utterance to his sentiments, preponderance to his opinions, authority to his advice on all proper and suitable occasions, (loud cheering for a long time.) In short, sir, The Whole Hog shall be what its name imports, a faithful mirror of the Democracy of Quodlibet. Its publication shall be weekly; its size, twenty-six by twenty, having the advantage over the Whole Team by full two inches each way. There, sir, is an outline of my sentiments and proposed paper." Mr. Fox concluded this address in the midst of a congratulatory uproar, altogether unprecedented in the club.

Seizing upon the enthusiasm of the moment, and being rather fearful that Fog would attempt to make a speech, which that gentleman's condition would have rendered extremely improper at this hour, Mr. Handy immediately offered a resolution for the establishment of the Whole Hog, and its adoption as the organ of the party, on the principles proposed by Mr. Fox. This was carried by acclamation; and the members without further discussion adjourned to the bar-room, where Nim Porter offered a bet—and not finding any one to take him up, continued to offer it during the evening—of fifty dollars to twenty-five, or one hundred to fifty, that Eliphalet Fox would run Augustus Postlethwaite Tompkinson's Whole Team out of Quodlibet in six months from that day:—that there would not be but two copies of the Whole Team taken in the Borough, and that one of them would be Michael Grant's out at the Hogback:—"for," said Nim, with an oath, which I will not repeat —"I can see it in that Liphlet Fox's eye; if he isn't a gouger when his bile's fresh, there aint nothing in Lavender on Physiology, or Fowler on the Shape of Heads."

CHAPTER VI.

Eliphalet Fox's paper, "The Whole Hog," made its first appearance on the day of the inauguration of President Van Buren. Bright were the omens that heralded its birth. The lustrous orb of Jackson had just set in an ocean of splendor. Happy old man! Felix qui potuit rerum cognoscere causas! In the glowing language of his own immortal valedictory, he left "this great people prosperous and happy." That star of the second magnitude, Martin Van Buren, first among the sidera minora, had just risen. In the nearly equally immortal salutatory of this Sidus Minor, he spake the words, "we present an aggregate of human prosperity surely not elsewhere to be found." Fortunate omens, incomparable auspices! Under these cheering signs "The Whole Hog" appeared upon the stage.

Never was paper more faithful to the Quodlibetarian theory. Never was editor more richly endowed to sustain that theory than Eliphalet Fox. My reader will doubtless expect that I should impart such gleanings of the editor's life as my diligent researches have enabled me to collect. This reasonable expectation shall be indulged.

Eliphalet Fox was one of those men whose career furnishes so remarkable a commentary upon the beneficent character of our great Democratic Quodlibetarian principle. His ancestors, two generations back, were Federal and rich: in the last generation they were Federal and poor—a transition strikingly natural and eminently illustrative of our free institutions. Eliphalet was born in the town of Gabwrangle, in the adjoining State. His education was circumscribed to the circle of reading, writing, and arithmetic, which Eliphalet himself sometimes jocosely describes as algebraically denoted by the signs of the three Rs; to wit, Reading, Righting, and Rithmetic—a joke (mehercule) both ingenious and new!

His parents being, as I may say, inops pecuniæ, bound Eliphalet to a trade; but handicraft was abhorrent to his genius. His temper was sour and peevish; and though seemingly meek, even to a degree of asininity, in his demeanor, yet it was early discovered that, upon occasion, he could very deftly and nimbly, as the poet says, "unpack his heart with words and fall to swearing like a very drab." This art was too valuable in Eliphalet's time to go long without a patron; and, accordingly, after he had worked four most reluctant years in a printing-office, to which his respectable parents, thwarting the current of his genius, had devoted him, he was discovered and taken by the hand by Mr. Theophilus Flam, brother of the late Judge, and leader of the Federal party of

Gabwrangle. It was just before the war; and the party being hard set upon by its enemies, had, like a cat surrounded by curs, thrown itself upon its back, and essayed to defend itself, most cattishly, with claw and tooth. And sharply, as we well know, did they fight. Eliphalet, in this strife, played the part of a claw, showing most admirable spring nails, though ordinarily hid, and therefore but little suspected in his velvet paw. His position in this battle was that of conductor of "The Gabwrangle Grimalkin," a cross-grained, querulous, tart and vinegarish little folio, which hoisted the banner of Theophilus Flam, and swore in his words. Eliphalet Fox, in consequence of the trusty position which was thus confided to him, and still more by reason of a certain rabid but laudable hatred of all who bore the name of Democrat, in those days, (and here I would have my reader mark that a Democrat of 1812 was a very different thing from a Democrat of this our day, especially from a true Quodlibetarian Democrat,) rose to be a person of great consideration in Gabwrangle. The party of Theophilus Flam, like our illustrious chief of the new Democracy, Mr. Van Buren, made sturdy opposition to Madison and his unrighteous war, and finally enjoyed the satisfaction of a complete triumph over all their political adversaries in Gabwrangle, by an utter route of the spurious Democrats who opposed them: a point of good fortune which did not fall to the lot of our illustrious chief at Kinderhook; since history records the disastrous fact that he, so far from conquering, was obliged to give in, and was even unhappily compelled, by the force of adverse winds, to go over to the majority, (an event very distressing to his feelings,) when he found that that majority was so obstinate as to refuse to come on his side: he was, if I may so say, as it were, a prisoner-of-war, and acted under a vis major. But at Gabwrangle—thanks to the persevering tongue and pen of Eliphalet Fox!—it was all the other way; and "The Grimalkin," to the last, enjoyed a most enviable renown as the bitterest reviler of Mr. Madison and his doings.

Habit grows into an instinct, and as times change our habits are the last to follow the fashion. It is only by referring to this deep-seated principle of human nature, that I am able to account for the extraordinary vituperation which Eliphalet Fox, at a later day, poured upon the head of the Old Hero when he was brought out for President. The Grimalkin, like all poison-concocting animals, grew more venomous as it grew older; and were it not that Eliphalet has repented of this folly, and amply atoned for its commission, I should blush to record the almost savage ferocity, the altogether unpardonable acerbity, and, above all, the thoroughly unquodlibetarian freedom with which he assailed the purest man that in the tide of time—as another pure man has remarked—ever appeared upon this terraqueous globe. But the truth is, Eliphalet had fallen into *a habit* of detraction, and did it without thinking:—that is the best excuse that can be made for him. The old Federalists of Gabwrangle, and, foremost among them, his master, Theophilus Flam, soon corrected this unhappy proclivity, and gave him to understand that he was on a wrong scent. They peremptorily, to their great honor, insisted that from that day forth the Grimalkin must be decent. The consequence of this was fatal to Eliphalet Fox—fatal at least to his prosperity in Gabwrangle. Thenceforth the Grimalkin sunk into insignificance. As the poet says, Othello's occupation was gone. The subscribers grew testy and dropped off, under the influence of this uncongenial decency exacted from the editor. Eliphalet borrowed money, his habiliments grew shabby, he took up mean callings for the sake of pelf, he became a spunge; he grew bilious, atrabilious, patriotic and indignant. He went for REFORM—reform of the General Government, reform of the State Constitution, reform of private manners, reform of public observances. He took up an aversion to all kinds of respectability, became a deadly enemy to every man who laid up any money —made this sentiment a political question, talked of a division of property, called Nature a stepmother, said sundry hard things about the persecution of genius, and finally, one Sunday night, eloped from Gabwrangle, leaving his fiscal responsibilities in a state of as much perplexity as that into which these vile Whigs have brought those of the government. Alas, for Eliphalet! little did he dream that out of this desolation and dismay he was to pluck so bright a flower of prosperity as he now wears in his bosom. All the hounds of the law—as he so eloquently painted it to the New Light at our celebrated meeting—were set upon his track; but grace to his better destiny! he eluded them. To twenty writs placed on Monday morning in the sheriff's hands, that functionary made his return on Tuesday evening, "Eloped under whip and spur out of the bailiwick."—Oh, lucky Eliphalet!

In these straits the badgered patriot went to Washington; was recognized by our distinguished representative, who, knowing that we were in want of an editor fit to cope with The Whole Team, gave him a warm letter of recommendation to Nicodemus Handy, and forthwith was projected that famous movement, whereof I have already given the history, and which has so auspiciously resulted in the establishment of The Quodlibet Whole Hog.

CHAPTER VII.

ASTOUNDING EVENT—SUSPENSION OF SPECIE PAYMENTS—
PROCEEDINGS OF THE BANK OF QUODLIBET THEREUPON—RESOLVE OF
THE DIRECTORS AGAINST SUSPENSION—CONSPIRACY AND
THREATENED REVOLUTION HEADED BY FLAN. SUCKER—DIRECTORS
CHANGE THEIR MIND—THEIR CONSTERNATION AND ESCAPE—
REMARKABLE BRAVERY AND PRESENCE OF MIND OF THE HON.
MIDDLETON FLAM—HIS SPLENDID APPEAL TO THE INSURGENTS—
GENERAL JACKSON'S ORACULAR VIEWS IN REGARD TO THE
SUSPENSION.

Proh hominum fidem!

It falls to my lot, at this stage of my history, to be constrained to record an event the most astounding, the most awful, the most unexpected, the most treacherous, the most ungrateful, the most flagitious—yea, the most supereminently flagitious,—that the history of mankind affords. Notwithstanding that laudatory and political ejaculation which the Hero and Sage breathed out in the evening of his brilliant career, like the last notes of the swan, "I leave this great people prosperous and happy"—notwithstanding that flattering canzonet, with which he who pledges himself to walk in the Hero and Sage's footsteps, began his illustrious course, singing as it were the morning carol of the lark—"we present an aggregate of human prosperity surely not elsewhere to be found"—the echo of these sweet sounds had not died away upon the tympana of our ravished ears, before these banks—these gentle pet banks—these fostered, favored, sugar-plum and candy-fed pet banks, with all their troop of plethoric and pampered paragon sister banks, one and all, without one pang of remorse, without one word of warning, without even, as far as we could see, one tingle of a suppressed and struggling blush, incontinently suspended specie payments!! O curas hominum! Quantum est in rebus inane!

Shall I tell it? Even the Patriotic Copperplate Bank of Quodlibet was compelled to follow in this faithless path. Not at once, I confess—not off-hand, and with such malice prepense as the others—for Nicodemus Handy had a soul above such black ingratitude—but after a pause, and, let the truth be told in extenuation, because he could not help it.

The Hon. Middleton Flam was sent for upon the first tidings of this extraordinary kicking in the traces by these high-mettled institutions—tidings which reached Quodlibet, via the canal, about eleven o'clock one morning in May. The Directors were summoned into council. What was to be done? was the general question. Anthony Hardbottle, of the firm of Barndollar & Hardbottle—a grave man and a thoughtful; a man without flash, who seldom smiles—a lean man, hard favored and simple in his outgoings and incomings; a man, who has never sported, as long as I have known him, any other coat than that snuff-brown with covered buttons, and who does not wear out above one pair of shoes in a year; a man who could never be persuaded to give so far into the times as to put on a black cravat, but has always stuck to the white:—such a man, it may be easily imagined, was not to be carried away by new-fangled notions:—he was there at the Board, in place of Theodore Fog, who was compelled two years before to withdraw his name as a candidate for re-election. This same Anthony Hardbottle, speaking under the dictates of that cautious wisdom natural to him as a merchant, answered this question of What was to be done?—by another equally laconic and pregnant with meaning——

"How much cash have we on hand?"

"One hundred and seven dollars and thirty-seven and a half cents in silver," replied Nicodemus, "and five half eagles in gold, which were brought here by our honorable President and placed on deposit, after he had used them in the last election for the purpose of showing the people what an admirable currency we were to have, as soon as Mr. Benton should succeed in making it float up the stream of the Mississippi."

Again asked Anthony Hardbottle, "What circulation have you abroad?"

"Six hundred thousand dollars," replied Nicodemus, "and a trifle over."

"Then," said Anthony, "I think we had better suspend with the rest."

"Never," said the Hon. Middleton Flam, rising from his seat and thumping the table violently with his hand. "Never, sir, while I am President of this bank, and there is a shot in the locker."

"Bravo—well said, admirably said, spoke as a Quodlibetarian ought to speak!" shouted Dr. Thomas G. Winkleman, the keeper of the soda-water Pavilion; "I have fifteen dollars in five-penny bits; they are at the service of the Board, and while I hold a piece of coin, the Patriotic Copperplate Bank shall never be subjected to the reproach of being unable to meet its obligations. Anthony Hardbottle, as a Democrat I am surprised at you."

"I can't help it," replied Anthony; "in my opinion, our issues are larger than our means."

"How larger, sir?" demanded Mr. Snuffers, the President of the New Light, with some asperity of tone.—"Haven't we a batch of bran-new notes, just signed and ready for delivery? Redeem the old ones with new. Why should we suspend?"

"Gentlemen, I will put the question to the Board," interposed Mr. Flam, fearful lest a quarrel might arise, if the debate continued. "Shall this bank suspend specie payments? Those in favor of this iniquitous proposition will say AY."

No one answered. Anthony Hardbottle was intimidated by the President's stern manner.

"Those opposed to it will say No."

"No!" was the universal acclamation of the Board, with the exception of Anthony Hardbottle who did not open his lips.

"Thank you, gentlemen," said Mr. Flam, "for this generous support. I should have been compelled by the adoption of this proposition, much as I esteem this Board, much as I value your good opinion, to have returned the commission with which you have honored me as your President. Our country first, and then ourselves! The Democracy of Quodlibet never will suspend!"

At this moment confused noises were heard in the banking-room, which adjoined that in which the Directors were convened. Mr. Handy immediately sprang from his chair and went into this apartment.

There stood about thirty persons, principally boatmen from the canal. At their head, some paces advanced into the bank, was Flanigan Sucker. One sleeve of Flan's coat was torn open from the shoulder to the wrist; his shirt, of a very indefinite complexion, was open at the breast, disclosing the shaggy mat of hair that adorned this part of his person; his corduroy trowsers had but one suspender to keep them up, thus giving them rather a lop-sided set. His face was fiery-red; and his hat, which was considerably frayed at the brim, was drawn over one ear, and left uncovered a large portion of his forehead and crown which were embellished by wild elf locks of carroty hue.

"Nicodemus," said Flan. as soon as the Cashier made his appearance, "we have come to make a run upon the bank:—they say you've bursted your biler." Then turning to the crowd behind him, he shouted, "Growl, Tigers!— Yip! yip! Hurra!"

As Flan. yelled out these words, a strange muttering sound broke forth from the multitude.

"What put into your drunken noddle that we have broke?" inquired Mr. Handy, with great composure, as soon as silence was restored.

"Nim Porter ses, Nicodemus, that you're a gone horse, and that if you ain't busted up, you will be before night. So we have determined on a run."

Nim Porter, who was standing in the rear of the crowd, where he had come to

49

see how matters were going on, now stepped forward. Nim is the fattest man in Quodlibet, and besides, is the most dressy and good-natured man we have. On this occasion there he stood with a stiff starched linen roundabout jacket on, as white as the driven snow, with white drilling pantaloons just from the washerwoman, and the most strutting ruffle to his shirt that could have been manufactured out of cambric. In all points he was unlike the crowd of persons who occupied the room. "I said nothing of the sort—" was Nim's reply—"and I am willing now to bet ten to one that he can't produce a man here to say I said so."

"What's the odds!" cried Flan; "Nicodemus, we are resolved upon a run—so shell out!"

"Begin when it suits you," said Mr. Handy. "Let me have your note, and I will give you either silver or gold as you choose."

"You don't catch me that way," shouted Flan., with a drunken grimace. "Notes is not in my line—shell out anyhow. We have determined on a run—a genuine, dimmycratic sortie."

"Have you none of our paper?" again inquired Mr. Handy.

"Not a shaving, Nicodemus," replied Flan. "What's the odds?"

"But I have," said a big, squinting boatman, as he walked up to our Cashier, and untied his leather wallet. "There's sixty dollars, and I'll thank you for the cash.

"And I have twenty-five more," cried out another.

"And I twice twenty-five," said a gruff voice from the midst of the crowd.

All this time the number of persons outside was increasing, and very profane swearing was heard about the door. Mr. Handy stepped to the window to get a view of the assemblage, and seeing that nearly all the movable part of Quodlibet was gathering in front of the building, he retired with some trepidation into the Directors' room, and informed Mr. Flam and the Board of what was going on. They had a pretty good suspicion of this before Mr. Handy returned, for they had distinctly heard the uproar. Mr. Handy no sooner communicated the fact to them, than Mr. Flam, with considerable perturbation in his looks, rose and declared that Quodlibet was in a state of insurrection; and, as every one must be aware, that in the midst of a revolution no bank could be expected to pay specie, he moved, in consideration of this menacing state of affairs, that the Patriotic Copperplate Bank of Quodlibet suspend specie payments forthwith, and continue the same until such time as the re-establishment of the public peace should authorize a resumption. This motion was gratefully received by the Board, and carried without a division. During this interval, the conspirators having learned, through their leader, Flan. Sucker, that the Hon. Middleton Flam was in the house, forthwith set up a violent shouting for that distinguished gentleman to appear at the door. It was some moments before our representative was willing to obey this summons: the Board of Directors were thrown into a panic, and with great expedition got out of the back window into the yard, and made their escape—thus leaving the indomitable and unflinching President of the bank, a man of lion heart, alone in the apartment; while the yells and shouts of the multitude were ringing in his ears with awful reduplication. He was not at a loss to perform his duty, but, with a dignified and stately movement, stalked into the banking-room, approached the window that looked upon the street, threw it open, and gave himself in full view to the multitude.

There was a dreadful pause; a scowl sat upon every brow; a muttering silence prevailed. As Tacitus says: "Non tumultus, non quies, sed quale magni metus, et magnæ iræ silentium est." Mr. Flam raised his arm, and spoke in this strain: —

"Men of Quodlibet, what madness has seized upon you? Do you assemble in front of this edifice to make the day hideous with howling? Is it to insult Nicodemus Handy, a worthy New Light, or is it to affright the universe by pulling down these walls? Shame on you, men of Quodlibet! If you have a vengeance to wreak, do not inflict it upon us. Go to the Whigs, the authors of our misfortune. They have brought these things upon us. Year after year have we been struggling to give you a constitutional currency—the real Jackson gold——"

"Three cheers for Middleton Flam!" cried out twenty voices, and straightway the cheers ascended on the air; and in the midst was heard a well-known voice, "Yip! yip!—Go it, Middleton!"

"Yes, my friends," proceeded the orator, "while we have been laboring to give you the solid metals; while we have been fighting against this PAPER-MONEY PARTY, and have devoted all our energies to the endeavor to prostrate the influence of these RAG BARONS, these MONOPOLISTS, THESE CHAMPIONS OF VESTED RIGHTS AND CHARTERED PRIVILEGES, the WHIGS—we have been foiled at every turn by the power of their unholy combinations of associated wealth. They have filled your land with banks, and have brought upon us all the curses of *over-trading* and *over-speculating*, until the people are literally on their faces at the footstool of the Money Power. (Tremendous cheering.) Our course has been resolute and unwaveringly patriotic. We have stood in the breach and met the storm; but all without avail. Between the rich and the poor lies a mighty gulf. The rich man *has*, the poor man *wants*. Of that which the rich hath, does he give to the poor? Answer me, men of Quodlibet."

"No!" arose, deep-toned, from every throat.

"Then our course is plain. Poor men, one and all, rally round our Democratic banner. Let the aristocrats know and feel that you will not bear this tyranny."

"We will," shouted Flan. Sucker. "Go it, Middleton!"

"Gentlemen," continued Mr. Flam, "this bank of ours is purely DEMOCRATIC. It is an exception to all other banks; it is emphatically the poor man's friend: nothing can exceed the skill and caution with which it has been conducted. Would that all other banks were like it! We have, comparatively, but a small issue of paper afloat; we have a large supply of specie. You perceive, therefore, that we fear no run. You all saw with what alacrity our Cashier proffered to redeem whatever amount our respectable fellow-citizen, that excellent Democrat, Mr. Flanigan Sucker, might demand. (Cheers, and a cry of 'Yip!') Mr. Sucker was satisfied, and did not desire to burden himself with specie. Gentlemen, depend upon *me*. When there is danger, if such a thing could be to this New-Light Democratic bank, I will be the first to give you warning. (Cheers, and 'Hurrah for Flam.') Born with an instinctive love of the people, I should be the vilest of men, if I could ever forget my duty to them. (Immense cheering, and cries of 'Flam forever!') Take my advice, retire to your homes, keep an eye on the Whigs and their wicked schemes to bolster up the State banks, make no run upon this institution—it is an ill bird that defiles its own nest—and, before you depart, gentlemen, let me inform you that, having the greatest regard to your interest, we have determined upon a temporary suspension, as a mere matter of caution against the intrigues of the Whigs, who, we have every reason to believe, actuated by their implacable hatred of the New-Light Democracy, will assail this, your favorite bank, with a malevolence unexampled in all their past career. (Loud cheers, and cries of 'Stand by the bank.') But, Quodlibetarians, rally, and present a phalanx more terrible than the Macedonian to the invader. You can—I am sure you will— and, therefore, I tell you your bank is safe."

"We can, we will!" rose from the whole multitude, accompanied with cheers that might vie with the bursting of the ocean surge.

"Gentlemen," added Mr. Flam, "I thank you for the manifestation of this patriotic sentiment. It is no more than I expected of Quodlibet. In conclusion, I am requested, my good friends, by Mr. Handy, to say that having just prepared some notes on a *superior* paper, he will redeem at the counter any old ones you may chance to hold, in that new emission; and I can with pride assure you, that this late supply is equal, perhaps, to anything that has ever been issued in the United States. With my best wishes, gentlemen, for your permanent prosperity, under the new and glorious dynasty of that distinguished New-Light Democrat, whom the unbought suffrages of millions of freemen have called to the supreme executive chair, (cheers,) and under whose lead we fondly indulge the hope of speedily sweeping from existence this pestilential brood of Whig banks, I respectfully take my leave."

Having concluded this masterly appeal to the reason and good sense of the people, Mr. Flam withdrew under nine distinct rounds of applause.

The effect of this powerful speech, which has often since been compared to that of Cicero against Catiline, was completely to still the public mind of Quodlibet, and also to remove all apprehensions of the solidity of our bank. But its happiest feature was the vindication of the bank against that charge of treachery and ingratitude which so justly lies at the door of all the other banks of the country. The Patriotic Copperplate Bank of Quodlibet was, as Mr. Flam observed, *purely Democratic*—Democratic in its origin, in its principles, in its organization, in its management, in its officers, its stockholders, and its customers. Such a bank, of course, could not be unfaithful to the Democratic administration that fostered it—*infidelity or ingratitude to party is no inhabitant of a Democratic bosom.* If there be men upon earth who go all lengths, through thick and thin, for party, it is (I say it with pride) the genuine New-Light Quodlibetarian Democracy. Our bank, therefore, stands uncontaminated by that revolting perfidy which, at the instigation of Biddle and the Barings, brought all the other banks, in which there are Whig directors or officers, into the most wicked conspiracy recorded in history.

It was not long after this astounding event before the opinions uttered above were fully and most remarkably confirmed by a letter from the Hermitage; a letter which for its shrewdness of view, its perspicacity, its lucid style and Hero-and-Sage-like felicity of construction, is unequaled in the productions of the venerable Chief. I am happy to insert it here, as a most eloquent exposition of the causes of the suspension—feeling assured that its distinguished author had no reference to the Democratic banks, and especially none to ours of Quodlibet, but intended it entirely for the vile Whigs.

"*The history of the world*," says this immortal man, writing July ninth, to the virgin-minded, tremulously-sensitive, and unrewarded editor of the Globe, "*never has recorded such base treachery and perfidy as has been committed by the deposit banks against the government, and purely with a view of gratifying Biddle and the Barings, and by the suspension of specie payments, degrade, embarrass, and ruin, if they could, their own country, for the selfish views of making large profits by throwing out millions of depreciated paper upon the people—selling their specie at large premiums, and buying up their own paper at discounts of from 25 to 50 per cent., and now looking forward to be indulged in these speculations for years to come before they resume specie payments."*

Oracular old man! Sage and Seer! Priest and Prophet to lead thine Israelites beyond Jordan! Happy do I, S. S., Schoolmaster of Quodlibet, account myself that I have lived in this thy day!

CHAPTER VIII.

SIGNS OF DISCORD IN QUODLIBET—THE IRON-RAILING CONTROVERSY—
AGAMEMNON FLAG'S NOMINATION—REVOLT OF THEODORE FOG—THE
CELEBRATED SPLIT—CONSEQUENCES OF JESSE FERRET'S PERNICIOUS
DOGMA IN REFERENCE TO PUBLICANS—FIRST FRUITS OF THE SPLIT
MANIFESTED AT MRS. FERRET'S TEA DRINKING—GRAVE REFLECTIONS
BY THE AUTHOR—MORAL.

The exciting summer of 1837, with the special election of a member of Congress for the extra session—to which we returned our long-tried and faithful representative, Mr. Middleton Flam, almost without opposition—went by. All eyes were turned upon the proceedings of Congress at that extra sitting; and a great many speculations were afloat in Quodlibet, where, I am pained to disclose the fact, very serious contrariety of opinion began to spring up in reference to the Sub-Treasury. Our State election, for members of the Legislature, was to come on in October, and a convention, called for the purpose, had nominated Agamemnon Flag, at the head of the ticket, with Abram Schoolcraft, the nursery man in Bickerbray, and Curtius Short, Cheap store-keeper in Tumbledown, as the Regular New-Light Democratic Quodlibetarian candidates. Unhappily this nomination gave dissatisfaction to numbers of our friends. Agamemnon Flag, who was the only stump man on the ticket, (Schoolcraft and Short having expressly stipulated that they were not to be called on to speak in the canvass,) was a young member of the bar, comparatively a stranger to many in the Borough, (having within the last year removed from Bickerbray,) and, laboring under the infirmity of short-sightedness, wore a delicate pair of gold spectacles. I have observed that short-sighted persons in general are not apt to be popular in a Democratic government.

But there was another matter that operated against Agamemnon. Quodlibet had been made the county-seat of justice by an act of the last Legislature, and we were just finishing a court-house which, in anticipation of this event, we had commenced a year before. A question arose among the townspeople, whether the court-house square should be surrounded by a wooden or by an iron railing. This question created great agitation. Several Whigs of the Borough made themselves active in the debate, and went for the iron. The New-Light Quods were strong for wood. Agamemnon Flag, seeing that a great deal of ill blood was getting up between the parties, made a speech to a town meeting on this subject, and went in for a compromise—he was for wood on the *two sides* and *back* of the square, and iron *in front*. This proposition he advocated with great earnestness and ability, and finally carried his point by a close vote. The wooden party said that the vote was not a fair one, and that they could not regard it as a legitimate expression of the popular voice, because it was taken just as a shower of rain was coming up, when many persons present who had come without umbrellas had given no heed to the question, and voted as it were in the dark. However, the vote was not recalled, and the iron railing is now in a course of fabrication over at the Hogback Forge, which happens unluckily to be owned by Stephen P. Crabstock, one of the most bull-headed Whigs in this county, the job being given by the commissioners to him in consequence of there being no genuine New-Light Democratic iron works in this part of the county.

When Agamemnon Flag was brought out at the head of the ticket for the Legislature, nothing was said about the iron railing, and we had good reason to suppose that every true Quod would support the nomination; which in fact was made by the direction of our honorable representative in Congress, who had a great liking for Flag in consequence of a very beautifully written memoir of Mr. Flam, which appeared two years ago in the Bickerbray Scrutinizer, when Flag lived in that town. In point of principle, Agamemnon was altogether unexceptionable. He was an out-and-out Flamite of the first water, and an unadulterated Quodlibetarian in every sentiment.

Theodore Fog—I regret to be obliged to mention his name in any terms of disparagement, because he is unquestionably a man of talents and a true-bred New Light, and certainly we owe Theodore a good deal—had been very sour for some time past. He had never forgotten the making of Middleton Flam President of the bank. I have in a former chapter hinted somewhat of Theodore's unfortunate habits. Dolet mihi,—I grieve to repeat these things. But the truth must be told. His diurnal aberrations became at length so conspicuous that, after being twice elected a Director of the bank, his name was struck off the ticket and Anthony Hardbottle's substituted in his place. Theodore never had much practice at the bar, although he considers himself the founder of that fraternity at Quodlibet, being for a season the only lawyer in the Borough. That little practice had now pretty nearly left him; in consequence of which he thought himself badly used, and therefore entitled to a support from the public. These feelings operating upon his mind, induced him, soon after the nomination of Agamemnon Flag, to come out in opposition and declare himself an Independent Candidate.

The Whigs, taking advantage of this split in the party, brought out Andy Grant, son of old Michael of the Hogback; a young man of fair character, but wholly and fatally imbued with those dangerous opinions which have already brought so many misfortunes upon our country.

This was the state of things at the commencement of the month of September; and it will be seen in the sequel that very serious difficulties grew out of this division.

A meeting of the voters of the county, which included the three towns of Quodlibet, Tumbledown, and Bickerbray, was called at the Sycamore Spring, upon the Rumblebottom, about five miles below Quodlibet. This meeting was to be held on the eighth. A reference to these events is necessary to explain the scene which I am about to present to my reader.

Jesse Ferret, as my reader knows, had brought himself into some scandal by his indefinite political sentiments, and that most unquodlibetarian dogma that "a Publican should have no side." Now, Mrs. Ferret and her daughter, Susan Barndollar, were just antipodes to Jesse. Two truer women, more firm-set in the New-Light Democracy, more constant in opinion, whether in the utterance thereof or in its quality, and better able to hold their own, have I never chanced to meet, than this respectable mother and daughter. It is common to say women are not allowed a voice in our government. My faith! these two ladies had a voice in Quodlibet, allowed or not allowed—let the theory go as it may:—and Jesse Ferret knows that full well.

Mrs. Ferret is what we call a fleshy or lusty woman: she weighed two hundred and twelve, in Neal Hopper's new one-sided patent scale at the mill. She is amazingly well padded with fat across the shoulders, and has a craw-shaped bosom that in some degree encroaches upon her neck; and she is famous for wearing a large frilled and quilled cap with many blue ribbons, being a little given to finery. Although Susan Barndollar was grown up and married, Mrs. Ferret had a child in the arms at that time; and Jesse has even boasted, within the last five years, of running two cradles at one time.

It was on the evening of the seventh of September, the night before the meeting at the Sycamore Spring, when Mrs. Ferret had a tea drinking in the back parlor, at which I, the only one of the masculine, was present as a guest. Mrs. Younghusband was of the party, and Mrs. Snuffers, with her interesting fat female infant nine months old; the same dear child whose arrangements to appear in this world of cares procured me the honor of presiding over the New Light, on the memorable occasion of Mr. Flam's great speech at Christmas, whereof I have spoken in a former chapter: thanks to Mrs. Snuffers for that considerate favor! This good lady was there; and these two, with the addition of Miss Hardbottle, elder sister of Barndollar & Hardbottle, and Mrs. Susan Barndollar, who lived at home with her mother, made up the company.

"There is one thing," said Mrs. Ferret, as she rocked herself in a huge hickory arm-chair, which had been built on purpose for her, "that I *do* hold in despise; and that is, one of these here men who haint got no opinions. Ef you believe me, Mrs. Snuffers, that man Jesse Ferret—this woman's father, (pointing to

Mrs. Barndollar,) God forgive me that I should say anythink aginst my datur's own lawful flesh and blood!—but he's actelly afeard to go down to-morrow to the Sycamore Spring to hear the tongue-lashing which Theodore Fog, which is a man I always respected—they say he drinks, but there's many a man which don't drink, hasn't half his brains—Jesse's actelly afeard to go and hear how Theodore will use up Ag Flag and Andy Grant both at the same time, least they might be for making him take sides, which he hasn't the spunk to do. My patience! but it would be nuts to me to hear the speechification!—and, to think of it—that man hasn't the heart of a goose to go to the meeting!"

"Ah, Mrs. Ferret," said Mrs. Snuffers, talking as if she had a cold in the head, her voice being husky, in fact, from having taken a large pinch of snuff, "them politicks—them politicks! Poor Mr. Snuffers!—dear man: I 'spose you know he is President of the New Light; he's losing his naiteral rest upon account of that split. He put in his wote in the conwention for Ag, as innocent as a lamb, and here comes up that obstropolus iron railing, and smashes all the New Lights into outer darkness, with diwisions and contentions and all sorts of infractions. Mr. Snuffers says he shouldn't wonder if that unfortnate step should take the Hay Scales from him and leave me and this here innocent darlin' babe in a state of destitution. Oh them politicks!"

"Well, let people stand by their colors, says I," interposed Mrs. Barndollar, tartly, with a sharp shake of her head; "I go with my ma, although pa is pa. I think people ought to speak what they please, and mean what they please; and it's a mean thing not to do so, and that's gospel truth, or else this is not a free country. Ma is right; and if Mr. Snuffers is what Mr. Barndollar calls a Whole Hog, he'll not mind the people a jot, but go with his party; that's the law. And I don't agree by no means with ma, in going for Theodore against the nomination."

"Susan Barndollar, are you in earnest?" inquired her affectionate ma. "Who put it into your head to underrate and strangle down Theodore Fog, the oldest friend we have had sence we came to Quodlibet? and who brings more custom to our bar than the whole New-Light Club put together. Susan, Susan, I hope Jacob hain't been putting none of these ungrateful ideers into your breast. Ef this house of ours, commonly called and known by the name of The Hero, ought to go for any human, mortal, individual man, that man is Theodore Fog. Ef he is a little exintric in regard of his drinking, it won't be no new think in the Legislater, ef the tenth part of what I heerd is true. Ladies— tea," said the dame, as at this time a negro woman entered with a tray filled with great store of provender—"help yourself, Mrs. Younghusband—take a plate on your knee, and fork up one of them warfields—and take care of your gown, they're a dripping with butter. Mr. Secondthoughts, what under heaven has become of your perliteness that you can see Mrs. Younghusband a fishing up that briled dried beef without her fork no more sticking in it than if it was a live eel in the gravy!"

"Never mind me, Mrs. Ferret," replied Mrs. Younghusband, "and don't be a troublin' the schoolmaster on my account. They do say that there's some persons as hard to catch and pin down as hung beef crisped and floating in butter, and as you justly remarked, a while ago, one of these persons is not a hundred miles off from this house:" and here this good woman laughed heartily at her own joke.

"Oh Jesse Ferret, in course!" exclaimed the landlady.

"My pa!" said Mrs. Barndollar, joining in the laugh.

"As Mr. Ferret hasn't got many friends here," said Miss Hardbottle, "I'll be one. I think he is quite right, if he has no opinions, not to express them. Don't you think so, Mr. Secondthoughts?"

"Madam," said I in a very grave manner, "if I might be allowed to express myself freely, I would venture to remark, that it is very important to the ascendency of the New-Light Quodlibetarian Democratic party, that there should be no strife nor division in our ranks; and that, feeling the importance of this sentiment, it is one of our fundamental principles to go with the majority—whenever it can be ascertained. Now between Agamemnon Flag and Theodore Fog——"

"Theodore Fog is sich a *good* creature!" interrupted Mrs. Ferret.

"Ag is a *dear* young man," said Mrs. Barndollar.

"As for that, ladies," said Miss Hardbottle, "if you speak of goodness or beauty, Andy Grant can beat either, though he is a Whig."

"Hester Hardbottle!" shouted Mrs. Ferret.

"Hester Hardbottle!" shouted Mrs. Snuffers.

"Hester Hardbottle!" shouted Mrs. Younghusband.

"Hester Hardbottle!" shouted Mrs. Barndollar—all four at once.

"I do think so," said Miss Hardbottle, sharply, "and what I do think, I say."

"You have no right to say it, madam," said Mrs. Barndollar.

"Free country," said Miss Hardbottle.

"No such a thing for Whigs," quickly returned Mrs. Barndollar.

"Ladies! ladies! ladies!" said I, "peace, if you please:" but there was no peace, for these excellent females soon got into such a state of confusion in the attack and defense of Andy Grant, that I believe the tea-party would have broken up in a state of rebellion, if it had not been for the entrance of Mr. Ferret in the very height of the tumult. His appearance gave another turn to the conversation, for it all turned upon him.

"And so you are not going to the Sycamore Spring to-morrow," cried one.

"And I 'spose you won't vote for Theodore Fog," said Number Two.

"Nor for Ag Flag," said Number Three.

"But you will drop in a sly ticket for Andy Grant, may be, at last, ef no one should find you out," said Mrs. Ferret, who in this series counted Number Four. "Oh Jesse Ferret, ef you had a drop of blood in you that wasn't milk-and-water, you would be ashamed of sich shilly-shally conduct, that even the women makes you a laughing-stock!"

"Wife," said Jesse, taking a fierce stand in self-defense, "drop it! If my blood was milk-and-water, it would be curds-and-whey before this time. I tell you again, old lady, a Publican's got no right to have sentiments. The party's double splitted, and no man knows which way to turn himself. There's that cursed Iron Railing; and there's that infernal Suspension; and there's the Divorce of the Government from bed and board with the banks, that everybody's talking about; and there's Purse and Sword, and Specie Circlar, and Mint Drops, and the Lord knows what; that a poor, sinful, infallible tavern keeper doesn't know who's who, and what's what. I'm sure I can't tell whether I'm on my head or my heels; and if I was to go down yonder to the Sycamore Spring and hear all the palavering there, I should get so flustrated I wouldn't know which eend of me went foremost. So, I tell you I'll stay at home and stick to my motto:—that's as good as if I swore to it. Solomon Secondthoughts, ain't I right?"

"Jesse," said I, mildly, "have you any respect for the opinion of our distinguished representative, my former pupil, Middleton Flam?"

"Well, I voted for him," replied Jesse.

"Then," said I, "I admit there is a great perplexity about all these public measures and men, just at this time; and I am willing to allow that the New-Light Democracy do not as yet exactly understand their own minds; and therefore it is quite lawful to pause and look about you before you take your stand. This thing is certain, that the New-Light Democracy will undoubtedly go with the government, whatever line it chalks out for following the footsteps of its illustrious predecessor. Whether that line shall lead us North or

South, East or West, my poor skill is not able to instruct you. Whether we are *for* the banks or *against* them, is yet undecided, since we are pledged at least in favor of our own. In a Quodlibetarian sense, I do not scruple to affirm that we are *against* the banks and *for* the divorce; but in a private sense that opinion will require some reflection. Mr. Flam will be home from Congress before long, and until then we shall suspend our opinion. We are, at all hazards, real Flam men. Flam—I drop the mister when I speak of him as a principle—is our polar star—our cynosure in politics—our Pisgah, which gives us a view of the Promised Land. As a principle, our New-Light Democracy is all out-and-out Flam. Flam is our father, our guide, our Pillar of Cloud. Wait till Middleton Flam comes home."

Having thrown out these well-weighed and sententious remarks, both for the women and for Jesse, I was inwardly delighted to see how soothing was the effect upon my auditory; and as it is a precept inculcated by some sage observer of mankind, I forget his name, to leave your company when you have made an agreeable impression upon them, I did not tarry for further converse, but took up my hat and stick, and bade my worthy friends "good night."

Upon my return to my lodgings, I sat down and made the foregoing narration of what had passed in my presence, and I have incorporated the same into this history, with no little mortification; feeling myself compelled thereto by the consideration that the scene I have described, being, as it were, the first fruits of that unhappy dissension which grew up among the New Lights, and a significant commentary thereon, it may serve in the way of warning to all good Quodlibetarian Democrats who may chance to peruse these pages, against the folly of ever allowing themselves to have any individual opinions, when the leaders and marshals of the party shall have taken the trouble off their hands of thinking and determining for them. And, indeed, the moral may be carried further. For it is obvious, if Jesse Ferret had acted in the spirit and the intelligence of a true Quod, he would have ascertained the majority and gone with it; instead of which, he intrenched himself behind this fortress of neutrality, comprehended in the absurd dogma that a Publican ought to have no sides. Undoubtedly, the true precept should be in all cases of public servants, "Take the upper side." Thereon chiefly hangs the Quodlibetarian theory.

CHAPTER IX.

GREAT MEETING AT THE SYCAMORE SPRING—SOME DESCRIPTION OF THE ARRANGEMENTS—NICODEMUS HANDY CHOSEN TO PRESIDE ON THIS OCCASION—MOTION TO THAT EFFECT BY MR. SNUFFERS—THIS WORTHY GENTLEMAN'S MISFORTUNE—HIS ESCAPE—SUCCESSFUL ORGANIZATION OF THE MEETING.

The morning of the 8th of September, Anno Domini 1837, was cloudless and cool. The dust had been laid by a shower of rain a little before daylight, and the day therefore was auspicious to the wishes of all who proposed to assemble at the Sycamore Spring. By eight o'clock Ante Meridiem, Nicodemus Handy's barouche, with two beautiful bays, stood upon the gravel before Handy House on Copperplate Ridge. Agamemnon Flag, attired in a new blue coat with figured gilt buttons, white waistcoat, india-rubber watch-guard, snowy pantaloons of very fine drilling, and boots of drab prunelle, tipped at the toes with polished French leather, a watered-silk cravat, and gold spectacles, sat at the breakfast-table with Mrs. Handy and Henrietta, her daughter—the smallest, the neatest, and the best-shaped female, it is said by those who pretend to be judges, in Quodlibet.

Nicodemus was in a flurry. He had swallowed his breakfast with great dispatch, and four servants were busily in attendance upon him. Sam, the waiter, was beating time in the hall with a corn whisk alternately upon the person of his master and his left hand, after a very favorite and ingenious fashion of dusting a gentleman's coat, only known to and practiced by that musical race of colored dandies, of which Sam was a first-rate specimen. Sarah, a lady of Sam's complexion, Mrs. Handy's maid, was running up stairs to sprinkle some verbena perfume on Mr. Handy's cambric handkerchief; William was smoothing the nap of his glossy-black Brewster with a brush as soft as silk; and Mrs. Trotter, the housekeeper, was arranging a basket of sandwiches and a bottle of Rudesheimer to be stowed away in the box of the back seat of the barouche. The coachman, in a sky-blue frock, and hat with gold band secured by a huge buckle, was in his seat holding the reins, every moment speaking to the horses to make them restive, and then whipping them for not standing still. The whole scene was one eminently calculated to disprove that stale Whig slander which purports to affirm that "all the decency" was in their ranks:—nothing could be more striking than this refutation of it. And as I was myself present—having called in at that moment to deliver a message from the New-Light Club to Mr. Handy, apprising him of their intention to move that he should act as chairman of the meeting to be held at the Sycamore Spring—I witnessed with lively satisfaction the very decided impression of pleasure made upon an assemblage of New Lights, who stood looking on outside of the front gate, by this triumphant vindication of our party from the malevolent insinuations of the Whig press.

Agamemnon Flag seemed to be very much at his ease, and to be thinking but little about the meeting, while he sat uttering some pleasant things to Miss Handy;—at least I suppose they must have been pleasant to her, as she and her mother both laughed a good deal at what he said. By-the-by, there is a report in the Borough, that Ag is making up to this young lady, which will be a grand thing for him if she favors him, since she is an only child, and Nicodemus is amazingly rich.

"God bless me, my dear!" said Mr. Handy, breaking away from Sam's whisk, and speaking after the manner of a table of contents, (a habit which he has acquired since he has grown rich,) "past eight o'clock—I'm to be the chairman of that meeting—ought to be early on the ground—five miles off—no time for nonsense now—you and Henrietta and Ag—have to drive like lightning—barbacue, my dear—want to see the arrangements before the voters arrive—the schoolmaster will take a seat along side of Nace."

"Thank you kindly," said I; "I accept your offer with great pleasure."

"Shan't want William," he added, referring to the servant who generally rode with the coachman—"upon second thoughts, will put *our* Secondthoughts inside—ha! ha!—*must* have William—*shall* want him; you can sit (speaking to me) on the front seat—Ag and I behind—offer the other seat to Barndollar—want to be civil to *him*, my dear—come, hurry, hurry, hurry!—William, get on your livery and be prepared to mount beside Nace."

As it was very manifest that Mr. Handy was really in a hurry—as very opulent men are exceedingly apt to be—there was of course a great bustle to accommodate him, by getting off. Agamemnon immediately rose from the breakfast-table, and, taking up his superfine Leghorn hat, which was very chastely adorned with a light yellow ribbon band, the ends whereof hung a little over the rim, he put it gently on his head, and then standing before the ladies, asked them with very apparent complacency, whether they thought he was in good trim to appear before the Democracy—and having received answer that "he was exactly the thing," he signified his readiness to depart; whereupon we all bustled out to the barouche and took our seats. William clambered into his place, and away we went at full trot, down to The Hero to take up Jacob Barndollar.

When we arrived at the tavern door, we found there Nim Porter's trotting buggy with his stub-tailed gray. Nim himself appeared on the steps in a big broad-brimmed low-crowned Russia blue hat, set very knowingly over his right eye, with a long taper whip in his hand; and before we could take up Mr. Barndollar, this most good natured of bar-keepers, with an agility not to be expected in so fat a person, sprang up into his tub-shaped seat, which held him about as compactly as the shell of an acorn holds the nut, and spreading the skirts of his green coatee with steel buttons over the periphery of the same, darted off at a speed of about fifteen miles to the hour, down the Rumblebottom road. During this time Mrs. Ferret filled the front door, and Mrs. Barndollar was looking over her shoulder, while they both opened their batteries upon poor Jesse Ferret, in a contemporaneous objurgation of his mean-spiritedness, addressed to Mr. Handy in the barouche, but intended for the master of the hotel, who looked rather sheepishly through the window of the bar-room. Before he could say anything in his own defense, and even before the amiable ladies of his family were done talking, Jacob Barndollar came out, and got into the barouche; and as Mr. Handy was growing more and more impatient, he ordered Nace to lose no time, and so off we started. As well as I could judge, from looking back, until we turned down by Christy M'Curdy's mill, Mrs. Ferret was still arguing her case in the front door of The Hero.

All the roads leading to the Sycamore Spring were filled with persons on horseback, on foot, in gigs, buggies, barouches, and rattle-traps of every sort. It was obvious we were going to have a great meeting. Before nine o'clock, Mr. Handy was on the ground. About a hundred persons were already there. Booths were scattered along under the huge elms and sycamores which shaded a low flat upon the margin of the Rumblebottom. The fine, copious, old spring—where there has been many a barbacue in my time—was pouring out its crystal treasures, as some poet says, with prodigal bounty, and transferring them, as the Secretary does the deposits, by large draughts, from the living rock to the running Rumblebottom—in fact, taking them out of one bank, and distributing them between others. Not far from this spring, adumbrated by over-arching boughs—the reader will excuse this poetical orgasm—for fifteen years and upwards have I been visiting this fountain, sacred to Pan, (we used to have fish frys here,) and have ever grown poetical at the sight thereof—it is my infirmity: not far from the spring stood the tables —boards on trestles, and on the boards trenchers filled with cubic sections of beef, lamb, mutton, and ham, interspersed with pyramids of bread—a goodly sight! Upon skids, remote from the tables, stood a barrel of old Monongahela, and hard by in a cart, tumblers, pitchers, noggins, and bottles. Far off, at the opposite confine of this field of action, was a stage erected, with a chair for the President of the day, and benches of unplaned board for persons of inferior dignity. Everything was in order; and now that Mr. Handy had arrived he had nothing to do but wait for the gathering in of the people.

Presently Mr. Grant, mounted on a large bow-necked bay, arrived, with his four sons, all men grown, of a rustic, farmer-like complexion; they were attended by Augustus Postlethwaite Tompkinson, of The Whole Team, and some dozen Whigs from Thorough Blue, who had traveled as far as Mr. Grant's the night before, and now made a very solid and formidable troop. Andrew Grant, the candidate, a youth of good presence, and reputable, (bating his politics,) was of this party. Andy had been to college, and his father first intended to make a doctor of him, but the lad somehow took a dislike to physic, and turned in to this new business of engineering on canals and railroads, and was considered, I believe, a tolerably smart hand in that calling. But as he happened to catch a bilious fever in the Dismal Swamp, the old lady his mother, who always had made a pet of him, would not hear of his going back to that line of livelihood; and so he stayed at home helping to manage at the Hogback farm, and doing pretty much as *he* pleased; until, about a year before he was brought out, he married Stephen P. Crabstock's daughter; and ever since that event does as his *wife* pleases—spending his time one part of the year at the Iron Works, and the other at the old man's.

By eleven o'clock the company had pretty nearly got to its maximum. A large party came down in a wagon from Quodlibet with Abel Brawn—among them Neal Hopper, Sandy Buttercrop, Davy Post the wheelwright, and I can't tell how many more. Quipes, the painter, borrowed a horse out of Geoffry Wheeler's team, and was there studying human nature and the picturesque. Flan Sucker, one-eyed Ben Inky, and Jeff Drinker, with a squad of regular loafers, came on foot. The Tumbledownians were there in great force under Cale Goodfellow, to help Theodore Fog; and the Bickerbrayians with Virgil Philpot, the editor of The Scrutinizer, mustered a heavy phalanx in favor of Ag Flag. To swell the assemblage to its largest compass, there were about fifty laborers from the newly-begun Bickerbray and Meltpenny Railroad, a worthy accession to the New-Light Democracy, who had about a month before this meeting come into the State.

This is a hasty glance over the field of action, and will serve to show that the country was all alive to the importance of the occasion and duly estimated the nature of the crisis. Looking over this congregation I, as one having knowledge therein, may safely affirm, that the genuine Quods present fully outnumbered the Whigs three to one. Eliphalet Fox, who has been more accustomed to measure crowds, however, after a minute inspection of the various groups, judging by that tact which he says never failed him in discriminating between what he calls a Loco Foco and a Whig, (he does not pretend to say that he is so expert in pointing out a New Light, but as to a Loco he asserts he is perfect,) set down the number at nearer ten to one; and accordingly so reported it in the account of the meeting which afterwards appeared in The Whole Hog. Without, however, dwelling upon this topic, let us proceed to the business of the day.

At twelve o'clock dinner was announced; and this army of hungry politicians, with a unanimity of sentiment, an accord of principle, and a concert of action, which we might in vain seek for in other occupations of a political nature, combined, like a band of brothers, to devour the largest possible amount of the stores which lay before them. With somewhat less agreement they made their advances to the Monongahela; the more shy of the assemblage being rather kept at bay by the remarkable perseverance and adhesiveness of Flan Sucker, one-eyed Ben Inky, and a chosen body of troops under their command, who had constituted themselves the forlorn hope in this assault. Still, as the newspapers say when they are disposed to puff a popular play, the barrel went off very much to the satisfaction, and, indeed, the delight of the company.

These matters being dispatched, Nicodemus Handy, who during the repast had acted inimitably the part of a perfectly ravenous man, but who having an eye to the sandwiches and Rudesheimer, made his appetite rather a matter of "seems," rapped upon the table, and called upon every man to fill up his glass; which order was faithfully obeyed by Flan Sucker & Company, a firm that was in possession of all the tumblers—the remainder of the guests allowing the filling to be, as we say in grammar, "understood,"—and then offered the following toast, which, as he said, would speak for itself:—"The several candidates who are about to address the people—success to him who shall best deserve it!" Sucker & Company drained to the bottom, and then set up a shrill yell, very much in the style of the Winnebagoes, except that there was a running note of "Yip!" that was distinctively Suckerian.

"Now, gentlemen, to the stand!" cried out Mr. Handy.

But before the crowd obeyed this order, Mr. Snuffers had a motion to make. It was a matter of some importance, as the subject was considered in the New-Light Club, that our party should have the President of the day—and it was therefore determined that the moment dinner was over, and before the Whigs might be aware of it, Mr. Snuffers, the head of our club, should rise in some conspicuous place, and move that Nicodemus Handy be requested to preside over the meeting. Mr. Snuffers is a slow and nervous man, and was admonished to be on his guard, so as to make sure of getting ahead of the Whigs who we knew wanted Mr. Grant in the chair. He was in consequence very fidgety all the time of dinner; and now, when the moment for action arrived, the good old gentleman elbowed his way toward the center of the table, and without difficulty succeeded in clambering upon an inverted and empty flour-barrel, which had once been filled with bread. "I move, gentlemen," said he, with a tremulous and agitated voice—"I move, gentlemen, that Mr. Nicodemus Handy——"

Before the next word escaped from his lips, this worthy and respectable old gentleman broke in, and in an instant (I am shocked to tell it) was jammed up tight in the barrel—disappearing as a dip of twenty to the pound is apt to do when stuck into a black bottle—"be President of this meeting," said Mr. Doubleday, with a hurried utterance, taking up the word which was lost with Mr. Snuffers, and which, but for the admirable presence of mind of our Vice, might have been lost forever.

"Break the barrel to pieces!" cried out forty voices.

"Mr. Snuffers is blue in the face—he will die of apoplexy," cried out others.

"An ax!—knock the barrel to pieces!" shouted more, in great alarm at his precarious situation.

In a few moments our distressed and worthy President of the New Light was extricated from his unpleasant durance, and finding no harm done, we proceeded to take the question on the motion. Mr. Handy was thus called to the chair. Nine Vice-Presidents were appointed, and six Secretaries to record the proceedings. These matters being arranged, the whole assemblage moved toward the rostrum at the opposite end of the wood.

What followed we shall read in the next chapter.

CHAPTER X.

SCENES AT THE SYCAMORE SPRING—NICODEMUS HANDY'S SPEECH AS PRESIDENT—SKETCH OF ANDREW GRANT'S SPEECH—AGAMEMNON FLAG'S—ATTEMPTS AT INTERRUPTION—THEODORE FOG'S CELEBRATED SPEECH ON THIS OCCASION—ELOQUENT EXPOSITION OF PRINCIPLES—HIS TRIUMPH—HIS MISFORTUNE—QUIPES'S DISAPPOINTMENT OF HIS FRIENDS.

When the crowd had gathered around the stand appropriated to the President, the nine Vice-Presidents, and the six Secretaries, besides the speakers who were to address the meeting, and when every officer was in his place, Nicodemus Handy came forward with his pocket-handkerchief in his hand, wiping from his brow the perspiration, which naturally breaks out on a man of sensibility and wealth when called to discharge the honorable and responsible function of presiding over a vast concourse of freemen. By way of digression, I would take this occasion to remark upon the extreme appropriateness of the phrase which is now universally used in describing meetings of the people, and which always refers to them as *freemen*. Ever since the people have been drilled to walk in the way appointed for them by the leaders of their respective parties, and are so liberally told how they must think, speak, and vote; and when no man is allowed to walk out of that path without being threatened with condign punishment, it is extremely proper, in order to avoid odious imputations which malevolent observers might cast upon them, on all occasions to employ the phrase I have alluded to; since, if this were neglected, these malevolent observers might take it into their heads to call the people of our free Republic Tools, Instruments, Rank-and-File, and other names significant of a state of subserviency, which in the eyes of strangers might cast discredit on our free institutions: even the *officers* of our government might be branded with the name of *hirelings* and *servants*, and an opinion might thus be fostered that, instead of being the freest nation upon earth, we were a set of slaves governed by a set of hired servants—a most unwarrantable, unjust, and derogatory conclusion. For this reason, I am particular in the language above employed, and I think that every genuine Quod will see the value and the force of my vindication and use of this phrase.

Mr. Handy rose to his feet, wiped his brow, and made a graceful obedience to the assembled body of freemen.

"Gentlemen," said he, with a most laudable diffidence, in a voice which not more than fifteen persons, exclusive of the nine Vices and six Secretaries, could hear; "sensible of the great honor—endeavor to discharge with fidelity

—obvious incapacity—but exceedingly flattered by the testimony of your confidence;" then wiping his brow, still more vehemently, with his cambric handkerchief rolled up like a snow-ball, he continued: "It falls to my lot to introduce to you our distinguished friends, Agamemnon Flag, Andrew Grant, and Theodore Fog, Esquires, men of whom any land may be proud—they will speak for themselves. With such men to choose from, our country cannot fail to rise up to the very midnight of prosperity, honor, and renown. Thanks for your attention—rely upon your indulgence—Mr. Grant will lead off."

"Three cheers for Nicodemus Handy!" cried out several Quods, as soon as our distinguished townsman took his seat; and, thereupon, about twenty heads were uncovered, and the twenty throats appurtenant to the same gave the three rounds called for.

Andrew Grant now came forward, and made a discourse of about an hour's length. It was in the usual style of the Whigs, and began with an attempt to raise an impression that the country, notwithstanding General Jackson's express declaration to the contrary, given to the nation under the solemn sanction of a presidential message, and notwithstanding his successor's certificate to the same effect, was in a state of difficulty and distress. This young man, not more than twenty-five years of age, living in comparative obscurity, had the hardihood, in the face of a large and respectable body of freemen, to contradict the word of two Presidents of the United States! Then, after coloring this picture of adversity with all imaginable hues of shade, he did not scruple to affirm that the whole of these fancied embarrassments were brought on by the *folly*, as he termed it, of our rulers—charged the great Democratic majority of the nation with having carried bad measures through Congress—said the Whigs had warned us of the results of these measures— and even went to the point of asserting that the suspension of the banks was the consequence of the acts of the party in power. To make out this absurd proposition, he read extracts from the speeches of Whig members, against the removal of the deposits, to show what he called their prophecies of disaster to the people; then actually affirmed that the experiment of General Jackson upon the Currency had failed, and that all the Whig predictions had come true; and after sundry excursions into the Hard Money and State-Bank systems of the administration, finally wound up his remarks by a very fatiguing enumeration of the General's pledges to the people before his election, and his changes of opinion upon these subjects afterward;—in regard to which he produced and read certain long-winded documents from the President and Secretaries, to the great annoyance of our Quods, who, in fact, became so tired of this impertinent matter, that not more than half a dozen of them remained within hearing of the speaker, the great bulk of them having gone over to the spring to refresh themselves in a more agreeable manner.

Eliphalet Fox very aptly remarked, immediately after this long prosing was brought to an end, that the speech was a *perfect failure*: he had heard Andy Grant spoken of as a young man of talents, but he turns out to be a miserable take-in. "Nothing in him, sir!" said Eliphalet, in his terse way; "nothing in him, sir!"

The Whigs, as is usual with them, affected to be hugely delighted. Augustus Postlethwaite Tompkinson took pencil-notes and announced his purpose to publish the speech entire. "A great speech that," said he to Mr. Snuffers —"extraordinary young man!—great speech."

Mr. Handy now lost no time in presenting Agamemnon Flag, who came forward with a confident, self-possessed air, smiling through his gold spectacles, and apparently very much delighted at the opportunity of presenting himself before his fellow-citizens.

"I see before me," said he, in a clear, fine-toned voice, and with an affable manner, "a vast concourse of——"

"Put on your hat," cried out three or four from the crowd, upon observing that a sunbeam had straggled through the foliage and lit up Agamemnon's yellow, curly locks, likening them to golden wire.

"Thank you, my friends," said the orator, stepping one pace to the right and thus bringing himself into the shade, "in the presence of the sovereign people, I always stand uncovered, regardless of the exposure of my person."

This happy sally brought forth a long and loud clapping of hands from the great multitude of Quods, who, the moment Andy Grant had finished speaking, had crowded back to the stand.

"Take off your goold specs, Ag; let's see your Dimmycratic phiz out and out!" said Flan Sucker at the top of his voice, from the outskirts of the assemblage.

A loud laugh that shook full one hundred diaphragms, followed this demand, and Agamemnon good-naturedly took off his glasses.

"Anything to oblige you, gentlemen," said he; "but as I am very short-sighted, I deprive myself of the pleasure of a better view of my worthy fellow-citizens."

"Put on your specs, Ag," said Nim Porter—"never mind Flan Sucker!"

"Put on your specs!" cried out the whole of the convention who had nominated the ticket, backed by a number of their friends."

"Blast his eyes!" said Cale Goodfellow, turning to his Tumbledownians, who were all friends of Fog, and of course opposed to the nomination. "Let's have a representative who can *see* what he is about—none of your goold daylights!"

"Specs or no specs, go it!—Yip!" shouted Flan. Sucker, with a voice that rang like a trumpet.

"Or-der!—Or-der!" said Mr. Handy, rising from his seat and coming forward beside the speaker, and waving his hand to the crowd, greatly concerned to see these manifestations of dissension in the ranks of the party. "Gentlemen, it is but fair that every man should be heard, and the chair takes occasion to say, that it is mortified at these interruptions. If the gentlemen opposed to the nomination—the chair alludes to those who have unfortunately allowed themselves to be influenced by the iron railing, a subject which has nothing upon earth to do with the pending election—if these gentlemen are not disposed to give Mr. Agamemnon Flag an opportunity of delivering himself, the chair would invite such persons to reflect upon the obvious impropriety of such a course. The chair is persuaded that this disturbance results from mere want of reflection, and hopes it shall not be required again to remind gentlemen of the courtesy due to Mr. Flag."

As Virgil describes in that notable passage, the subduing of the rage of popular commotion by Æneas, and likens it to the mandate of Neptune quelling the waves of old ocean, so fell Mr. Handy's timely reproof upon the Anti-iron Railings, and, in a moment, all was still. Agamemnon then began again in his original track.

"I see before me a vast concourse of free citizens—the solid, substantial, durable, permanent, everlasting pillars of free government. The honest, upright, pure, hard-handed, horny-fisted, Democratic yeomanry of the country are here—not the flesh and blood of the country, for that is the pampered aristocracy—but the bone and sinew surround me. It rejoices my eyes to behold these honest, sturdy, independent, intelligent, invincible tillers of the soil—these brawny, unconquerable, liberty-loving working-men—I say, sir, I delight to look upon them; my feeble vision, sir——"

"Put on your specs, Ag!" shouted Ben Inky and Flan Sucker again, at the same instant;—and the cry was echoed from various quarters.

Some moments of disorder again prevailed, which required the second interposition of Mr. Handy, who, in the most spirited manner, proclaimed his positive determination to resign, unless the order of the meeting could be preserved. "I will never consent," said he, with a most laudable energy, "to hold any post, executive or representative, for one moment after I shall have discovered that I do not possess the confidence of the people; the chair must feel itself compelled, by every sentiment which, as a friend of the New-Light Democracy, it holds dear, to resign the moment it finds that it has fallen into a minority." Then followed these remarkable words:—"Sustain me, Quodlibetarians, or let me go!"

For full five minutes after this, the uproar was tremendous. The Iron Railings and Anti-iron Railings almost came to blows. The Tumbledownians and Bickerbrayians took their appropriate sides in the contest, and, for a space, nothing was heard but shouts of Fog!—Flag!—Fog!—Flag! over the whole field. When both parties had bawled themselves perfectly hoarse, and for mere want of wind ceased the clamor, Theodore Fog mounted the hustings, and made a special request of his friends to keep the peace and hear Mr. Flag to an end. He put this request upon the ground of a personal favor to himself, and promised them that, at the proper time, they should hear his sentiments very fully upon all the agitating questions of the day.

This appeal was conclusive, and Mr. Flag once more presented himself. But the interruptions he had suffered seemed most unhappily to have thrown him entirely out of gear; and becoming very much embarrassed, he struggled for some moments to regain his self-possession, as I thought, without success— although Fox thought otherwise,—and, after less than half an hour's speaking, sat down, rather crest-fallen and mortified.

I may unwittingly do Mr. Flag injustice in this remark; for, in truth, my mind was greatly occupied with the tumult, and I confess I was, therefore, not a very attentive listener. Fox, on the contrary, was minutely observant of the speech, and did not scruple to pronounce it a masterly effort of eloquence, calculated to place Mr. Flag beside the first statesmen of our country. This was his opinion at the time, and it was even more warmly and eulogistically expressed subsequently, in The Whole Hog, where the speech appeared in nine closely-printed columns on the following Saturday.

Theodore Fog was always a great favorite at our public meetings, and the moment now approached when the field was to be surrendered to him. The New Lights, including the members of the nominating convention and the friends of the Iron Railing Compromise, backed by Virgil Philpot of The Scrutinizer, and a large force of Bickerbrayians, were determined that Agamemnon Flag should not want a very decisive token of applause; and they accordingly called out for "nine cheers for the regular candidate!" Responsive to this call, their whole party lustily set about the work; and, for some minutes after the conclusion of Agamemnon's speech, the air resounded with huzzas for "Flag and the Constitution!" "New Light and Regular Nomination!" This was answered by a round for "Fog and Reform!" "Retrenchment and no Iron Railing!" and Fog, in the midst of this acclamation, appearing on the speaker's stand, all cries were lost in the most violent clapping of hands.

Theodore Fog's figure is about six feet, lean and bony, and with a stoop which inclines a little to the right, so as to bring his left shoulder somewhat higher than its opposite. His arms are unusually long, his head small, his face strongly furrowed with deep lines, his eyes of a greenish luster, his nose decidedly of the pug species, his mouth large, his complexion of that sallow, drum-head, parchment hue that equally defies the war of the elements, and the ravages of alcohol. Although short of fifty years of age, his hair is iron gray, and spreads in a thick mat over his whole cranium. At no time of life has he been careful of dress, but now has declined into an extreme of negligence in this particular. On the present occasion, he wore a striped gingham coat, rather short in the sleeves, and cross-barred pantaloons; his shirt collar was turned down over a narrow, horsehair stock; and a broad black ribbon guard crossed his breast and terminated in the right pocket of a black bombazet waistcoat, where it was plainly to be seen from the external impression, lodged a large watch. He presented himself to the multitude, holding in his hand a rather shabby straw hat, which he, nevertheless, flourished with the air and grace of one who had known better days than his habiliments seemed to denote.

He stood for some time bowing and waving his hat in return for the clamorous approbation with which he was greeted; and when, at length, silence was restored, he began his speech.

"Countrymen and friends: you of Quodlibet, Bickerbray, Tumbledown and the adjacent parts, hear me! I am an old, tried and trusty, unflinching and unterrified Quodlibetarian New-Light Democrat—Flan Sucker, bring us a tumbler of water—tangle it, Flan: no hypocrisy in me, gentlemen,—I go for the ardent. You all know I am, and was from the first, opposed to the iron railing—(here arose a cheer from the Anties)—but I don't come to talk to you about that. You know, moreover, that I am an anti-nomination man—I'm out on independent grounds—every man for himself, as the jackass said to the chickens—(a loud laugh.) I want to say a word about Agamemnon Flag—commonly called Ag Flag. Who's he? Look at them gold spectacles, and you will see what he is at once. When the plastic hand of Dame Nature set about the fabrication of that masterpiece of human mechanism, a genuine, out-and-out thorough-stiched New-Light Democrat, she never thought of sticking upon him a nose to be ridden by two gold rings hung over it like a pair of saddlebags—(loud laughter.) We have other uses for our gold; we want it for mint-drops—old Tom Benton's mint-drops—to be run up into them, to give the honest, poor man something better, when his week's work is done, than Copperplate Bank rags, signed Nicodemus Handy—(loud shouts and cheers from Flan Sucker's squad and the Tumbledowns; and groans and hisses from the Convention men and Bickerbrays.) Friends, I tell you, our party is split; emphatically split. I have seen this coming for some time. We have three sets of New Lights among us, and it is time we should know it. There are THE MANDARINS, our big bugs, and I could name them to you. You will find them on Copperplate Ridge—('Bah! bah!' from the New-Light Club—'Go it The! go it, old fellow!' from the Anties.) You will find them at Popular Flats—('That won't do!' cried fifty voices; 'three cheers for the Hon. Middleton Flam!'—loud cheering for Flam: 'Walk into them, Fog!' from the Anties—great laughter and rubbing of hands among the Whigs.) You will find them in the Forwarding and Commission Line—(great uproar on all sides.) After the Mandarins, come THE MIDDLINGS; and after the Middlings, THE TRUE GRITS—the hearty, whole-souled, no-mistake Quods. I'm a TRUE GRIT!—(great applause.) We are nature's noblemen—give me that water, Flan. I call myself one of the Royal Family of the Sovereign People—(renewed laughter and applause.) I am no kid-glove-MANDARIN-Democrat: I am no milk-and-water, flesh-and-fowl, half-hawk-half-buzzard-MIDDLING-Democrat: I am, to all intents and purposes, toties quoties, in puris naturalibus, a TRUE GRIT, a whole TRUE GRIT, and nothing but a TRUE GRIT.—(Here Theodore was obliged to pause a full minute on account of the cheering.)

"Now this brings me," he continued after drinking off the potation which Flan Sucker had assiduously placed upon the stand for his use, "to Andy Grant. Andy Grant has told you a great deal about General Jackson's pledges, and his changes and whatnot. Well, sirs, he *did* change—what of it? Is Democracy like the laws of the Medes and Persians? Is that great sublime truth which vivifies the patriot's heart, resuscitates his ambition and sparkles in the human breast, like a stone in the bottom of a well, for toads to sit on? or is it the divine rainbow spanning the earth with its arch, and changing with the sun, now in the east, now in the west? Is it a post set up in a stream for the liquid element of human policy forever to roll by and leave behind? or is it the mighty mass of steam power that not only floats upon that element, but flies onward across the great ocean of mortal things forever changing in its career? Is not Democracy itself the march of intellect? and does not marching consist in change of place? I hear you all answer, with one accord, Ay, ay, ay!—(Taking the word from the orator, there was a loud affirmative response to these questions.)

"Well, then, Jackson did change. He was *for* the single term—he was *against* it: I confess the fact. He was *for* the Protective System—he was *against* it: I agree to it. He was *for* a National Bank—he was *against* it: what of that? He was *for* the distribution of the surplus, and again he was *against* it; I know it. He was *for* Internal Improvements;—he changed his mind—he was *against* them. Then again, sirs, he was *against* the interference of officers in the elections;—he was sorry for it, and took the other tack. He was *against* the appointment of members of Congress—in theory;—in practice he was *for* it.

He was *against* this Sub-Treasury—and perhaps he is now *for* it. It is all true, as Andy Grant has told you:—it is in the documents, I don't deny it. Sirs, it is the glory of his character that he has been *for* and *against* everything;—and as Mr. Van Buren promises to follow in his footsteps, he, of course, will be for and against everything—I know him. He would not be a genuine New Light, if he were not. We are all (and here Fog raised his voice to the highest key, and struck the board sharply with his hand) FOR and AGAINST everything! How else can we be with the majority? What is the New-Light Quodlibetarian Democracy, but a strict conformity to the will of the majority? Against that and that only we never go!—(tremendous applause.) As Levi Beardsly said, Perish Commerce, Perish Credit!—and I say, Perish Currency, Banks, Sub-Treasury, Constitution, Law, Benton, Amos, Van—I had almost said perish Old Hickory—but *always* go with the MAJORITY!"

After this burst, which may be said to be truly eloquent, Theodore made a very happy hit in touching upon the natural hostility between the *rich* and the *poor*, showing, with great point of remark, how impossible it was for these two classes to have any Christian feelings toward each other; and arguing from that the great New-Light Democratic principle, that in every department of the government any man who holds property ought to be deprived of all influence, and that it was the poor man's right to legislate away the rich man's possessions. "Do we not know," said he, "that in every community the majority are poor? that there are two men without property for every one man with it? Of course then, it follows logically, that, as two heads are better than one, the sole right, as well as the sole power of legislation is in the poor, and that they may make laws for the government of the rich; but the rich cannot make laws for the government of the poor. Besides, who would be the most impartial in such a matter, the man legislating for his *own* property, or the man legislating for his *neighbor's*? This requires no reply."

Upon the subject of the Sub-Treasury, Fog avowed boldly his non-committalism. "I am not sure, at this moment," said he, "how the land lies. I wait to ascertain the sentiment of the majority, which, without taking sides, I rather incline to think is against the measure. I judge from the vote of the New Lights two years ago—although, I confess, that two years are a long period for a New Light to look back, and that it is rather over the usual time in which custom requires we should change. *I shall wait for events.*"

There were other subjects embraced in this speech, upon which my memoranda are imperfect; but there was one part of it, toward the conclusion, which was very pathetic.

The orator turned to those strangers among us who had come over from the Bickerbray and Meltpenny Railroad. "Gentlemen," said he, "you stand in a peculiarly interesting relation to the New Lights. You are strangers, and, as the poet says,

'Stranger is a sacred name.'

Therefore, it is our wish to take you in. You have not been over sixty days in our State: you are separated, many of you, from your sweethearts—some of you from your wives—all of you from your homes:—wife—sweetheart—home! Affecting words!

'Where is the man with soul so dead
Who never to himself hath said,
   This is my own, my native land?' and so forth."

Here Theodore took up his red pocket-handkerchief, which was already well saturated with the sweat of his brow, and feelingly wiped his eyes for some moments, manifestly overcome by his emotions. At length he proceeded.

"Do not despond, gentlemen—do not despair. The New Lights are your friends, and not only shall you find wife, sweetheart, home—ay, and children, in Quodlibet, but if you are here next month, we will see if some of you are not entitled to a vote—that's all.—I have no doubt a large portion of your respectable body are better voters than you think you are. And at all events, if you are not, it becomes us as a Christian people to extend to you that privilege. I go for the repeal of all laws which tyrannically require a year's residence in the State, before a stranger is allowed to vote."

"Hurra for Fog—hurra for Fog!" burst forth in loud chorus from the new-comers.

"But," said Theodore in continuation, "as I scorn concealment, I must be frank with you. The stranger should be grateful to his friends; and I, therefore, for one, never can consent to extend the invaluable privilege of suffrage to an unworthy man. He must be a New Light, an ardent, unblenching Quodlibetarian Democrat, ready to go in whatever way we who take the trouble to do his thinking for him, require;—it is but reasonable. We think, study, burn the midnight lamp, and toil, when he sleeps, and all for the good of the man who has no time to do these things for himself—what is his duty in return? Why, to stand by *us* who make these sacrifices for his welfare—clearly—undoubtedly—incontestably."

"Hurra for Fog!" again rose in hoarse reduplications on the air.

"And now, fellow-countrymen, one and all—men of Quodlibet, men of Bickerbray—and especially men of Old Tumbledown, long my home, and never absent from my heart—I have exposed to you frankly, freely, unhesitatingly my principles and professions.—You see me as I am—naked,

76

guileless, and robed in the simplicity of my nature.—Flan, another glass of that stuff, my boy. I do not imitate my friend Andy Grant—for he *is* my friend —we can differ in politics and break no scores!—I do not, like him and the Whigs, entertain you with frothy declamation, appealing to your passions or your prejudices—I scorn such stratagems.—No, I address myself solely and severely, sternly, without a flower, prosaically, without a figure, soberly, without a flight, to your cool, temperate, and unseduced capacity of logical deduction. Yes, gentlemen, I, a poor man, do battle against the hosts of the rich. I, the friend of honest labor, struggle against the huge monopoly of hoarded wealth, hoarded by grinding the faces of our sterling but destitute laboring men—alone, I strive against these banded powers—will you desert me in the strife?"

"Never!" cried Flan Sucker, Ben Inky, and six more of Fog's principal men —"Never, never!"

"Then I am content. Come weal, come woe, here is a heart that will never—or rather, gentlemen, let me say in the words of the poet—(it now became quite obvious that Theodore was beginning to be very seriously affected by the frequent refreshment which Flan Sucker had administered during his speech,)

'Come one, come all, this rock shall fly
From his firm base as soon as I.'

"In conclusion, all I have to say is this—We are about to part.—When you go to your homes, and with hearts enraptured by all a father's and a husband's failings—feelings—you take your seats beside the old family firesides, and with the partners of your bosoms getting supper, and your interesting progeny clustering on your knees,—in the midst of all these blessings pause to ask yourselves, what are they? Your hearts will answer, they are *our Country*! How then, you will inquire, is that country to be preserved, as a rich inheritance to these cherubs?—who by this time have climbed as high as your waistcoat pockets, into which they have, with the natural instinct of young New Lights, thrust their little fingers—the response will be ready—Go to the polls in October—go, determined to sustain the everlasting principles of the New-Light Quodlibetarian Democracy—go, with a firm resolve to support no Mandarin, no Middling, but to sustain an unadulterated True Grit:—go, to vote for Theodore Fog, and your country shall be forever great, prosperous and happy."

A wave of the hand and a bow showed that Theodore had uttered his last words—upon which several rounds of applause, resembling the simultaneous clapping of wings and crowing of an acre of cocks, more than anything else I can imagine, shook the firmament, and, as the old song has it, "made the welkin roar." A party of Tumbledownians, instigated by Cale Goodfellow—(a wag who follows sporting, and keeps a bank—I mean a faro bank—at Tumbledown, a most special friend of Theodore's)—rushed up to the platform, and, seizing the orator in their arms, bore him off in triumph to the spring, where they fell to celebrating their victory, in advance of the election, over a fresh supply of spirits produced by Cale Goodfellow for the occasion. The result was that Theodore was obliged to be taken home to Quodlibet in a condition which Mr. Handy, who is President of the Temperance Society, pronounced to be perfectly shocking.

Some speaking took place after this by several volunteers: but from the agitated condition of the assemblage, and the prevalence of uproar, nothing worthy of notice transpired, and by sundown nearly all who could get away had retired.

Quipes had been an attentive observer of the earlier scenes of the day, and as he had his drawing-book with him, we had reason to expect some spirited sketches of the crowd; but the poor fellow, being fatigued and thirsty, and of a singularly weak head, was overtaken by his drought, and was laid away in the afternoon in Abel Brawn's wagon, in which he was brought to Quodlibet, Neal Hopper undertaking to ride his horse back to the Borough.

The result of this day's proceedings was unfavorable to the regular nomination, and highly auspicious to Theodore Fog. It was very evident that The Split was going to do us a great deal of harm, and this gave much uneasiness to the club. The Whigs seemed to consider it a good omen, and old Mr. Grant and his party left the field in high spirits.

CHAPTER XI.

THE DIVISION OF THE PARTY BECOMES MORE DISTINCT—ADMIRABLE ADDRESS OF ELIPHALET FOX AT THIS JUNCTURE—RESULT OF THE ELECTION—REJOICINGS OF THE TRUE GRITS—JESSE FERRET'S DIFFICULTIES—IS TAKEN TO TASK BY HIS DAME—CANDID AVOWAL OF HIS EMBARRASSMENTS—THEODORE FOG'S EXPOSITION OF TRUE GRIT PRINCIPLES—HIS GOOD-NATURED ENCOURAGEMENT OF JESSE FERRET —DABBS'S TREAT.

The proceedings at the Sycamore Spring furnished melancholy evidence of the serious character of the split which had taken place in our ranks. This was a source of anxious and painful reflection to the New Lights. But the assiduity with which we endeavored to heal this dissension only made matters worse. The Whole Team, which, although not within the county, claimed to take a deep interest in this election, on the score of being within our congressional district, noticed our divisions with much self-gratulation, and made the best of them, by attacking Agamemnon Flag as "the creature" (to use its own unscrupulous language) of the Hon. Middleton Flam; while, at the same time, it opened the flood-gates of its abuse upon Theodore Fog, as a man of "bad habits, loose manners, and objectionable morals." The Bickerbray Scrutinizer was devoted to Flag and the regular ticket, and therefore defended Agamemnon against The Whole Team, and let fly several arrows against Theodore Fog; thus unhappily fomenting the differences among our friends.

The course pursued by Eliphalet Fox, at this difficult juncture, was one calculated to raise him in the esteem of every true Quod, and to place him on a pinnacle among editors. He took none of those middle grounds which scarcely ever fail to bring a politician into contempt with both parties—but, with a boldness entirely peculiar to himself, and in the highest degree illustrative of the New-Light theory, stoutly advocated each of our candidates, as the course of the canvass seemed to encourage their respective chances of success. Thus, when Theodore Fog first announced himself as the independent candidate, and when every one appeared to regard this step as an act of presumption which could not but result in defeat, Eliphalet put forth the following paragraph:—

"*Mister* Theodore Fog, of this Borough, an old practitioner at *more than one bar*, having waked up one morning with the idea that he was born to fill the measure of his country's glory, as well as he fills that of his own every night, has conceived the sublime project of running on an independent ticket, in the approaching election. We would whisper in our friend The.'s ear, that he has barked up the wrong tree. Independence is not a word to be found in the New-Light dictionary. The voters of this county can never be seduced from the support of the regular nomination; especially when it is headed by such a man as Agamemnon Flag, whose eloquence, accomplishments, and remarkable Democratic simplicity of manners, as well as his perfect surrender of himself to the cause of his Party, give him the highest claim to the consideration of every right-minded and unadulterated Quod. Verb. sap. sat."

Now, after the meeting of the Sycamore Spring, a new view of matters broke upon Eliphalet's vision. He was certainly taken by surprise at the demonstration which that meeting afforded of Theodore's strength with the voters; and in the account of that event, which appeared in The Whole Hog on the succeeding Saturday, one scarcely knows whether most to commend the sincerity of the writer, or the justness of the tribute paid to the masterly effort of Mr. Fog. Speaking of that effort, the editor employs this language:—

"In regard to our esteemed fellow-townsman, Theodore Fog, the public expectation was more than realized. This unstudied orator, with all the freshness impressed upon his mind by the mint of nature herself, contemning the aid of tinsel show, and presenting himself in the homely habiliments of an unvarnished, and, as our adversaries scoffingly add, of an unwashed New Light, poured forth a resistless flood of native oratory, remarkable for that massive vigor of thought, and that felicity of expression, which are the rare endowments only of genius, trained *among* the people, and whose soul is *with* the people. He descanted upon the brilliant career of our never-sufficiently-to-be-flattered administration, with an effect that thrilled in the pulse, glowed in the countenance, and broke forth in the reiterated shouts of every warm-hearted, straight-out, lead-following, unagainst-the-wishes-or-commands-of-the-luminaries-of-the-party-rebelling New-Light Democrat on the ground. We are happy to add our decided conviction that the election of this staunch champion of the *real* New Lights is placed beyond a doubt."

The intrepidity of this paragraph will strike every one who reflects that the canvass, at the time this appeared, was far from being brought to a close; and that the result, whatever Eliphalet might have thought of it, was deemed exceedingly doubtful. Indeed, we had subsequently a proof given to us, in The Whole Hog itself, that very serious opinions began to prevail against the possibility of Mr. Fog's carrying the day, in opposition to Flag.

The New-Light Club, with some few and unimportant exceptions, had determined, as they thought themselves in duty bound, to sustain the regular ticket, and for this purpose, when matters were running very strong for Fog, and when, indeed, they began to entertain a well-grounded fear that Andy Grant might slip in by the aid of these divisions, resolved upon having a night procession in the Borough. This expedient we have always resorted to with the happiest effects whenever we have found the hopes of the New Lights beginning to ebb; it serves to animate our friends, by throwing, as it were, a glare over their minds, and to render them more docile to the word of command from those who take upon themselves the labor of judging for the multitude. We now had recourse to this device with a very flattering, though as it turned out in the end, a deceptive manifestation of its influence upon the election. The procession was made; paper lanterns in abundance, bearing a variety of inscriptions of the most encouraging exhortation to the friends of Flag and the Ticket, were procured for the occasion. Every lantern and every banner had written upon it FLAM, in the hope thus to identify the ticket with our distinguished representative in Congress, and bring in the aid of his great name to our cause. Mottoes, having reference to "the Old Hero of the Hermitage," were also profusely used, and even the Hickory Tree was reared aloft in the procession, covered with small cup lamps in imitation of its fruit. Every one in Quodlibet supposed that this stroke of the procession settled the matter. It undoubtedly converted the Borough and brought it into the utmost harmony on our side. But the Tumbledownians, among whom Fog's great strength was found, were not there; and from Bickerbray the delegation was not as large as it ought to have been. Still, the evidence of popular support to the ticket was deemed conclusive; so much so, that Eliphalet Fox's next editorial referred to it as "indicative of the stern resolve of the New Lights, once and forever, to crush the insubordinate and rebellious temper with which certain factious and discontented pretenders to the name of Democrats had endeavored to sow discord in the ranks of the faithful, by setting up the absurd doctrine of independent opinion—a doctrine so fatal to the New-Light Democracy wherever it has been allowed. Agamemnon Flag," the editor proceeded to remark, "was not a man to be put down by the frothy, ginger-pop eloquence engendered in the hot atmosphere of cock-tail and julep manufactories. Mr. Fog may now perceive that his secret perambulations to spread dissension in the New-Light ranks, and his hypocritical boast of Independence will be scowled upon by every honest eye and spurned by every honest tongue which are to be found among the high-minded New-Light yeomanry of Quodlibet, Bickerbray, Tumbledown, and the adjacent parts."

The election soon after this took place, when, greatly to the astonishment of our club, and in fact of the whole party, the result was announced to be as set forth in this table:—

Quods.		*Whig.*
Theodore Fog,	1191.	Andrew Grant, 1039.
Abram Schoolcraft,	1084.	
Curtius Short,	1063.	
Agamemnon Flag,	758.	

Thus it appeared that Theodore Fog far outran the rest of the ticket, and that Agamemnon Flag fell considerably below the Whig vote.

Eliphalet Fox, greatly delighted at the triumph of this election, lost no time in publishing a handbill announcing the issue. It was headed

"GLORIOUS VICTORY! QUODLIBET ERECT!"

and proceeded to descant on the event in this wise:—

"We have never for a moment permitted ourselves to doubt that our estimable fellow-townsman Theodore Fog, one of the purest, most disinterested and ablest Democrats of the glorious New-Light Quodlibetarian School, would lead the polls; and, indeed, we took occasion to insinuate as much after his celebrated speech at the Sycamore Spring, which it was our good fortune to hear, and which, as an exposition of sound New-Light principles, gave us such unmixed delight. We cannot but feel regret that Mr. Flag's friends should have so inconsiderately consented to place his name on the ticket, before they had ascertained Mr. Fog's views in regard to the election. An understanding upon this subject would have saved them the mortification of presenting a name which, from the first, we felt a presentiment was destined to incur defeat; and it would have spared Mr. Flag the pain he must suffer in the present event. The youth of this gentleman, his want of acquaintance with the people, arising, doubtless, from the imperfection of his vision, and his unfortunate espousal of the Iron Railing Compromise, very obviously stood in the way of his success. A day will, however, come around when, in our judgment, the people will do justice to his pretension, which we undertake to say is considerable."

From these extracts, the reader is already prepared to exclaim with me, Oh, excellent Eliphalet Fox—mirror of editors—pillar of the New-Light faith! What exquisite address, what consummate skill hast thou not evinced in these editorial effusions! Methinks I see Eliphalet, a tide-waiter on events, watching the ebb and flow of popular opinion; ever ready, at a moment's warning, to launch his little boat of editorship on the biggest wave, and upon that wave to ride secure beyond the breakers, out upon the glassy ocean of politics and then, after taking an observation of the wind, to trim his sail with such nautical forecast as shall make him sure to be borne along with the breeze toward whatever haven it shall please the higher powers to direct him; sagaciously counting in such haven to find the richest return on his little stock of ventures. I see his meager, attenuated, diminutive person, elevated on a footstool six inches above the floor, behind a high but somewhat rickety desk, in the northwest corner of his lumber-filled office, where scissor-clipped gazettes are strewed, elbow deep, over an old walnut table, and where three dingy caricatures of Harry Clay, Nic Biddle, and John C. Calhoun, are tacked against his smoky walls; there I see him quiet, but at work, with pen in hand, ever and anon darting his cat-like eye at the door, upon each new-comer who comes to tell the news of the canvass. I hear his husky, dry, and querulous voice, tisicky and quick, asking, how goes it in Bickerbray? What from Tumbledown? and as he receives his answer *pro* or *con.*, Fog or Flag, he turns to his half-scribbled sheet to remould his paragraph, with the dexterity of an old and practiced Quod, in such phrase as shall assuredly earn him the good-will of the winner. Rare Eliphalet! Admirable Fox! Incomparable servant of an incomparable master!

It is with a sad and melancholy sincerity I record the fact, that this election left behind it much heart-burning in Quodlibet. The New-Light Democracy were now broken into three parts, the Mandarins, the Middlings, and the True Grits; and Theodore Fog, in command of the True Grits, had evidently got the upper hand. The defeat of Agamemnon Flag was a severe blow to our distinguished representative, the Hon. Middleton Flam, and no less galling to Nicodemus Handy; for these three worthy gentlemen were undoubtedly at the head of the Mandarins, and their overthrow on the present occasion led to unpleasant consequences which I shall be called upon to notice hereafter.

The first unhappy fruit of this election was of a domestic nature, and wrought very seriously against the peace of our friend Jesse Ferret.

For three days and nights after the publication of the polls, all Quodlibet was alive with the rejoicings of the True Grits at the success of Theodore Fog. The bar-room of The Hero was full all day with these energetic friends of the prosperous candidate; and it is worthy of remark that their number was vastly greater than was shown by the ballot box, many more individuals claiming the honor of having voted for him than the return of the polls would authorize us to believe; all night long bonfires blazed, drums and fifes disturbed the repose of the Borough, and processions, not remarkable for their decorum, marched from house to house with Theodore mounted in a chair, borne on the shoulders of sturdy True Grits. A hundred torches in the hands of thirty men and seventy boys, flared on the signs and flickered on the walls of Quodlibet, and fifty negroes, great and small, ragged and patched, hatless and hatted, slip-shod and barefoot, leaped, danced, limped, and hobbled in wide-spread concourse around black Isaac the Kent bugle player, and yellow Josh the clarionet man, who struck in with the drum and fife to the tune of Jim Crow, about the center of the column. Flan Sucker was installed grand marshal of this procession, and was called KING OF THE TRUE GRITS; while Ben Inky, Sim Travers, Jeff Drinker, and More M'Nulty, served along the flanks as his lieutenants; the whole array huzzaing at every corner, and stopping to refresh every time they came into the neighborhood of Peter Ounce's, Jesse Ferret's, or the smaller ordinaries which the rapid growth of Quodlibet had supplied in various quarters to relieve the drought of its inhabitants.

This state of things, as I have said, continued for three days after the election. At the end of that period, Jesse Ferret, somewhere about noon, was in his bar casting up his accounts. He wore a serious, disturbed countenance—not because his accounts showed a bad face; for so far from that, the late jubilee had very considerably increased his capital in trade, but because his rest had been broken—and Jesse never could bear to lose his sleep. While he was engaged in summing up these recent gains, his worthy spouse entered the bar and quietly seated herself in a chair behind him. The expression of her face showed that her thoughts were occupied with matter of interesting import: a slight frown sat upon her brow, her lips were partially compressed, and her fat arms made an attempt to cross each other on her bosom. The chair was too small for her; and, from her peculiar configuration, one looking at her in a full front view would not be likely to conjecture she was seated, but rather that she was a short and dumpy woman, and leaned against some prop for rest— the line from her chin to her toe being that of the face of a pyramid. Her posture denoted an assumed patience. So quietly had she entered the inclosure of the bar, that Jesse was altogether ignorant of her presence, and therefore continued at his occupation. It was not long, however, before his attention was awakened to the interesting fact that his wife was behind him, by the salutation, conveyed in a rather deep-toned voice, "Jesse Ferret, how long are you agoing to be poking over them accounts?"

Jesse turned short round, in some surprise at the sound of these well-known accents so near him, and, surveying the dame for an instant, replied—

"Bless me, Polly! how came you here? You go about like one of them church-yard vaporations that melts in thin air and frightens children in the dead of night. What did you want with me, my love?"

"I want to know," said Mrs. Ferret, "who's master of this house—you or me? Ef I'm the master, say so—but ef you're the master, then act as sich. It ain't no longer to be endured, this shilly-shally, visy-versy politicks of yourn. Here you are casting up of the accounts this blessed day, and please Heaven, if there's one cent got into the till in the three days that have gone by, the last person in the world to thank for it is yourself, Jesse Ferret. Theodore Fog's *in* —got in by a vote that one might say's almost magnanimous, and he's got all the thirstiest men in this Borough under his thumb—and he's been pouring 'em in here in shoals, which he wouldn't have done, one man of 'em, ef it hadn't a been for my principles, which goes the whole hog—and you so contrairy, constantly a giving out your no sides—it's raly abominable! and time you should change, Jesse Ferret, it is."

"Why, my dear, don't you see the good of it?" said Mr. Ferret, in a mild, good-natured tone of expostulation. "The very best thing we can do is for you to go on as you are doing, and me to go on as I am. Here's come up a great split in the party; and presently, as sure as you are born, they'll be having their separate houses and making party questions out of it: then, my dear, you know Theodore Fog and his people counts you as a sort of sun-dial to their side, and goes almost by your pinting. And then the others, you know, can't have nothing to find fault against me upon account of my sentiments: so, in this way we shall get the custom of the thorough-stitchers, the half-and-halfs, the promiscuous, and of every kind of stripe that's going. Can't you see into it, Mrs. Ferret?"

"No, I cannot see into it," replied the landlady. "In the first place, them Mandarins, as The. Fog says, is not worth the looking after in our line—they drink nothing but Champagne and Madeery, and ef they do sometimes send down to our bar for ourn, they are sure to turn up their noses at it, and say it's sour. Didn't Nicodemus Handy tell me to my face that my Anchor Brand, which you've got on the top shelf, and which cost you six dollars a basket at auction, was nothing but turnip-juice?—and did you ever know Middleton Flam to call for as much as a thimbleful of your liquors, with all his preachings and parleyings in this house? No, you did not: and it's your duty to cast off your bucket o' both sides, and go in for The. with the True Grits, as he calls them; and true enough they are in the drinking line!—that, nobody who knows them, will deny. I'm tired, Jesse Ferret, and fretted down to the very bone, at being put upon in this here way, having to keep up the politicks of this house, which I don't think you haint no right to do, I don't. I'm been a talking to you about this tell I'm tired, and I wonder you can be so obstinate, considering I take it so much to heart."

"Now, Polly," interposed our landlord with an affectionate remonstrance, intended to soothe Mrs. Ferret's feelings, "many's the struggle I've had on this here very topic with my own conscience; I may say I have wrestled for it at the very bottom of my nature. But the case is this, and I'll explain it to you once for all. I've got a sentiment at the core of my heart, which is a secret in regard of these here politicks. I wish to go right—you know I do—but if I only knowed what sentiments *to* take up:—there's the mystery. If I knowed *that*, I should feel easy; but I never could keep any principles, upon account of the changes. Before a plain, simple man can cleverly tell where he is, everything has whisked away in the contrairy direction. One year we are 'all tariff,' and the next, 'down with it as an abomination.' Here we go 'for canals and railroads!'—a crack of the whip, and there we are all t'other side. 'No electioneering of officers!' cries out the captain of the squad. 'Turn that fellow out, he don't work for the party!' cries the very same captain in the very next breath. 'Retrenchment and reform!' says every big fellow there at Washington; and the same words are bawled all the way down among us, even to Theodore Fog;—'Damn the expense!' (the Lord forgive me for using such words,) says the very same fellows in the same breath, 'stick on a million here and a million there—the more the merrier!' And so we go. Here, t'other day, this here Sub-Treasury was monarchy and revolution to boot, and treason outright; and now, what it *is*, every man's afeard to say—some's for, some's against—some's both, and all's in a state of amalgamation, perplexity, and caterwauling unaccountable. What between specy circlars, anti-masons, pocketing of bills, (Lord knows what that means!) vetoes, distribution, fortifications, abolition, running down Indians, and running up accounts, politics has got into a jumble that a Philadelphy lawyer couldn't steer through them. A poor publican has a straining time of it, Polly. He can't get right if he tries—and if he does blunder upon it, he can't *stay* right six months, let him do his best—morally impossible! That's where it's a matter o' conscience with me; and my conclusion is, in such a mucilaginous state of affairs, a man who wants to accommodate the public must be either all sides or no sides; and, therefore I say, my motto is, a publican should—leastways I speak in regard to these times—have no sides. And there's the whole matter laid out to you, Polly, my wife."

"All sides, any day, before No sides!" replied Mrs. Ferret. "As Susan Barndollar says, stick to your colors and they'll carry you to sides a plenty, I'll warrant you. Don't Theodore Fog tell us the Democracy's a trying of experiments—and, Lord bless us! ef they haint carried you on sides enough, then you *are* an unreasonable man. Principle isn't principle—it's following of your party:—you change when *it* changes, whereby you are always right. Now, these here True Grits is two to one to the Mandarins and Middlings both, and they devour, yes, ten times as much liquor. Ef you had an eye in your head, you'd come out a True Grit—it's a naiteral tavern-keeper's politics."

"'Spose, my dear," said Jesse, waxing warm, "things takes a turn off hand. 'Spose these True Grits are upset—as I shouldn't wonder they would be, as soon as Middleton Flam comes home from Congress, and winds up the people right again—as he has often done before—am I going to run my head against a post by offending the whole New-Light Club, which meets at our house, and make enemies by having sentiments of my own? You don't know me, Polly Ferret."

"Well, and ef things does take a turn?" replied the wife, "is there anythink new in that, in this Borough? Haint we had turns before? Theodore Fog will turn with 'em—that's his principle—that's my principle, and it ought, by rights, to be yourn. Doesn't the schoolmaster tell you to stick to the upper side? Doesn't our member, Middleton Flam, tell you the same thing, and Nicodemus Handy, and Liphlet Fox? There's your own barkeeper, Nim Porter, that's asleep in yander winder, who's got more sense than you have; he knows what side his bread's buttered—and even your own child, Susan Barndollar, though she stuck out for the nomination, isn't such a ninny as to have no principles. We're Dimmycrats, and always counts with the majority; and that's safe whichever way it goes; and, as I said before, no mortal man can find out a better side than that for a tavern-keeper. But it's the Whigs your're a courting, Jesse Ferret—the Whigs, neither more nor less—and it's pitiful in you to be so sneaking."

"Polly, if you aint got no better language than that to use to me," exclaimed Ferret, under considerable excitement, "I'd advise you to hold your tongue."

"My tongue's my own, Mr. Ferret," replied the landlady, "and I don't want none of your advice what I'm to do with it. I have used it long enough to know how to keep it a running, and how to stop it, without being taught by you."

"I've got no right to listen to you, if I don't choose," retorted the landlord. "Women has their milking and churning to look after, and, to my thinking, they'd best attend to that, instead of skreiking out politics in public bar-rooms—that's my opinion, Mrs. Ferret."

"Women, indeed!—for *you* to talk about women!—You're the laughing-stock of all the petticoats of our Borough," said the wife, in a high key of exacerbation. "Mrs. Younghusband, and Mrs. Snuffers, and Mrs. Doubleday makes you a continual banter, and it hurts my feelings as the mother of your children, it does."

"Seize Mrs. Younghusband, and Mrs. Snuffers, and Mrs. Doubleday, all three!" exclaimed Ferret in a sort of demi-oath.

"What's that you said, Mr. Ferret?"

"I said seize 'em! and I don't care the rinsings of that glass if you tell 'em so, —a set of mandrakes."

"Oh, Jesse Ferret, Jesse Ferret,—as a man who sets up to be an example, what are you coming to!" exclaimed the landlady, with uplifted hands. "Ef your children could hear such profanity. I declare to patience, you'd try the quarters of the meekest mother in the universe."

How far this conjugal outflash might have gone in its natural course, it is impossible for me to say; although Nim Porter, who pretended to be asleep all the time, and who heard every word of it, and related it with much pleasantry to me, says he has often witnessed these breezes between this worthy couple, and always found that they made up as soon as Mrs. Ferret got out of breath —which, by-the-by, she being short-winded, generally occurred in about half an hour from the first rising of her anger; but, on the present occasion, it was happily interrupted by the entrance of Theodore Fog, Dabbs, the foreman in Eliphalet Fox's printing-office, Flan Sucker, More M'Nulty, and Sim Travers, who all marched directly up to the bar. I had entered upon the heels of this party, and having taken up "The Whole Hog" for my perusal, in one corner of the room, was myself a witness to the scene that followed.

Nim Porter, who was seated in an elbow-chair, resting the back of his head against a window-sill at the opposite end of the bar-room and counterfeiting sleep, was now roused up to attend to the customers.

"My dear Mrs. Ferret—paragon of landladies," said Fog, "Pillar—yes, bolster of our cause—some drink! Dabbs owes a treat, and we have resolved that the libation shall be made under the eye of our own queen. Dabbs, say what the mixture shall be; I'm not particular—my throat is a turnpike traveled by all imaginable potations. A mint julep, Dabbs? gentlemen! Flan, a julep? Yes? A julep, a julep all round. Agreed to, nem. con. Mrs. Ferret, five juleps; charge Dabbs—Dabbs's treat."

Mrs. Ferret's anger against her spouse gradually faded under this accost; a slight glimpse of sunshine began to break over her visage as she addressed herself to the task of preparing the required compounds, and Nim Porter busied himself in picking sprigs of mint from a large bouquet of that invaluable plant, which flourished in native verdure over the rim of a two quart tumbler, in which it seemed to grow as in a flower-pot.

Ferret had retreated from the bar toward the door which looked upon the street; and Theodore Fog, who, as the truth must be spoken, was at this hour very considerably advanced toward his customary zenith of excitement, thrust his hands under the skirts of his striped gingham coatee, and strutted with the air of a prime minister in a farce, around the room.

"Nim," said he,

> "'Bid thy mistress, when my drink is ready,
>
> She strike upon the bell.'

Ferret—glorious turn out, Ferret. True Grits all alive. Pound that ice fine, Nim —no water, recollect. First-rate fellows, Ferret—go the whole—real Quods— diamonds."

"Hope you'll mend matters now, Mr. Fog, since you've got in," said Ferret. "I'm for giving every one a chance; wish you success."

"Of course you do, Ferret," replied Fog; "and so you would have wished Ag Flag success if he'd got in."

"Or Andy Grant, either," said Mrs. Ferret; "my husband's not partikler."

"You're right, Ferret—you're right!" interrupted Fog, "always go with the current—that's sound philosophy—that's my rule. Dabbs, isn't that metaphysics? Flan, don't you call that the true theory of the balance of power? Gentlemen, I submit it to you all."

"Real True-Grit doctrine," said Flan; "find out how the cat jumps—then go ahead."

"Fundamental, that," said Dabbs; "principles change, measures vary, names rise and fall, but majority is always majority."

"Bravo, Dabbs!" ejaculated Theodore Fog; "*Tempora mutantur et nos mutamur cum illis*—that's our True-Grit motto. The nominative case always agrees with the verb; the people are the verb, we're the nominative case. That's logic, Mrs. Ferret. Nim, how have you made out in these illustrious 'three days?'"

"Cursed sleepy," answered Nim Porter, who was now brewing the drink by pouring it from one tumbler to another; "haven't had three hours rest in the whole three nights. No right to complain though—won four bets—had two to one against Andy Grant with Tompkinson—and even against Ag with three of the New-Light Club. I knew d—d well how it was going, ever since the meeting at the Sycamore Spring. Fog, you touched them fellows that work on the Bickerbray and Meltpenny Road 'twixt wind and water."

"Didn't I?" exclaimed Fog; "I opine I did; unequivocally, I fancy I did. I venture to add, with all possible energy of asseveration, that I did that thing, Nim. That's what I call walking into the understanding of the independent, electoral constituent body; and the best of it is, we got them their votes, you dog!"

"You didn't lose no votes that I could bring you," said Mrs. Ferret, "although you didn't get Jesse's. But that wa'n't much loss—for Jesse's of little account anyhow, and hasn't the influence of a chicken in this Borough—as no man hasn't, whose afeard of his shadow."

"Well, we don't want to hear no more about that," interrupted the landlord. "Mr. Fog knows it wasn't ill will to him—but only my principle, that publicans had best not take sides."

"And who has a right to object to that?" exclaimed Fog. "Give us your hand, Jesse—I'd do the same thing myself, if I were in your place."

"Well, ef you aint the forgivingest creature, Mr. Fog!" said the landlady.

"Mrs. Ferret, your health!—gentlemen, take your respective glasses—Dabbs, your health—Jesse—Flan—all of you—Success to the True Grits! Top off, boys."

They all drank.

Fog applied the tumbler to his lips; looked straight forward, with what might be called a fixed stare upon vacancy, his eyes expressing the deep emotion of sensual pleasure which the icy compound inspired as it slowly flowed over his palate, and for a full minute employed himself without pause in draining the contents of his glass—gradually and slowly arching back his head until the last drop trickled from the bottom.

"Amazing seductive beverage, Mrs. Ferret!" he said as he smacked his lips, and set the tumbler down upon the board. "Fascinating potation! If I were not an example of consummate prudence, and the most circumspect being not yet gathered within the pale of the Temperance Society, my virtue would have fallen a victim before this to that enticing cordial, Mrs. Ferret. But I'm proof —I have been sorely tried, and have come out of the furnace, as you see me, superior to the temptations of this wicked world. Dabbs, poney up—we must go to the raffle, which begins in five minutes at Rhody M'Caw's stable—that pacing roan, Nim—you'll be there, of course:—in your line. Come, gentlemen—don't wipe your mouths with your sleeves—let the odor exhale.

As some poet somewhere says, speaking of a mint julep,

> 'Sweet vale of Ovoca, how calm could I rest,—
>
> If there's a drink upon earth
>
> It is this—it is this.'

Not the words exactly—but something in that run. Jesse, the Flower of Quodlibet—Mrs. Ferret, Queen of the Spear Mint—good-by. Nim, you rascal —after the raffle is over, expect to see me as dry as an oven."

When Fog had delivered himself of this rhapsody—which, no doubt, has impressed the reader with the conviction that this noontide glass had done its work upon the brain of our new representative in the Legislature—the whole party made their exit; and Jesse Ferret, anxious to avoid another conference with his dame, professing a wish to witness the raffle, followed in their footsteps.

CHAPTER XII.

THIRD ERA—DIVISIONS IN QUODLIBET CONTINUE—FOMENTED BY THE
WOMEN—FOG RATHER DISAPPOINTS HIS FRIENDS BY HIS COURSE IN
THE LEGISLATURE—PROSTRATION OF BUSINESS IN THE BOROUGH—
TRACED TO THE MERCHANTS—MR. FLAM'S OPINION OF THEM, AND
THE CONSEQUENCE THEREOF—INDIGNATION OF THE NEW LIGHTS
AGAINST THEM—FOG'S EULOGIUM UPON THEM—MOVEMENTS OF THE
TRUE GRITS—FOX'S SKILLFUL MANAGEMENT—THE TIGERTAIL AFFAIR
—MYSTERIOUS TERMINATION OF IT—NIM PORTER'S INDISCRETION.

The design of this little book forbids that I should do more than cursorily touch upon many incidents in the history of Quodlibet, which, although abundant of interest to the curious reader, are not so immediately connected with the main purpose of this work—that purpose being to unfold the operation of the great principle of the New-Light Quodlibetarian theory.

Whenever the time shall arrive, as I would fain persuade myself it must, in which the public shall feel such concern in the affairs of Quodlibet as to demand of me a full disclosure of the treasures of my MSS., I shall greatly delight in spreading before it many particulars which I have collected, having reference to the private concernments and domestic transactions of our people and their sundry ways in regard to many matters which do not fall within the scope of my present undertaking. For, truly, the history of Quodlibet will be found, when impartially narrated, to yield a plentiful fruitage of ethical, moral and social instruction, as well as political—to which latter aspect are my labors at this time confined.

In conformity with my plan, and being desirous to hasten forward to a more modern epoch in these annals, I pass over the intervening space, and bring my reader almost a year in advance of the events narrated in the last chapter.

It was now approaching the fifth year of the Removal:—the long session of Congress had closed in July, 1838. The Hon. Middleton Flam had once more returned to his constituents, and temporarily mingled in the walks of private life. Greatly was his return desiderated at this epoch. We had got all wrong—we lacked information—we wanted this great man's advice.

The split at this time—if I may use a metaphor—was green and wide; or, in plainer language, our dissensions ran high. If the men might be said to be at sixes and sevens, the women were twice as bad—they were at twelves and fourteens. Mrs. Ferret had become inveterate, and headed a party of Feminine True Grits; Susan Barndollar, who had a temper of her own, of course became inveterate too, and, as Barndollar & Hardbottle were accounted a rich firm, she headed, or strove to do so, a party of Feminine Mandarins. Hester

Hardbottle, under a similar impulse, took command of the Female Middlings. Thus marshaled, the New-Light women manifested a very high degree of political corruscation, and kept the Borough in perpetual hot water. Every tea-party was a scalding concern, and it was lamentable to see what a foothold the serpent of discord had gained in our little Eden of Quodlibet.

The men were not so ferocious; in part because they had their business to look after; but chiefly, because the stronger, when they failed in argument, could drub the weaker—and that drubbing system is a great moderator of political opinions. The women, having neither of these motives to keep quiet, took the bits in their mouths and ran off as fast as, and whenever, they chose.

Theodore Fog's conduct in the Legislature, during the past winter, had in some degree rather weakened the cause of his friends. He had disappointed them—although they were unwilling publicly to allow as much—on two points: First, because he had not got them all provided with offices, as he had, it appeared, secretly promised; but, on the contrary, came home without having accomplished that desirable object for a single individual of the party; and, secondly, because he had been exceedingly irregular in his habits during the whole session, and had consequently made but four speeches, of three hours each, during the winter, when it was confidently expected that he would have made at least thirty-four, and have completely silenced the opposition. The irregularity of his habits they could forgive; but the matter of the offices sunk deep in their hearts—they began to suspect his Democracy.

A change had also taken place in the business affairs of Quodlibet. All improvements had ceased:—many persons were out of employment; industry was declining; trade was at a low ebb; the mechanics were grumbling, and four mercantile houses had failed. Immediately after the suspension Nicodemus Handy had issued a great amount of small notes. Dr. Thomas G. Winkelman, actuated by patriotic emotions, also issued a batch payable in soda-water, soap, or physic. Zachary Younghusband, the tinplate-worker and postmaster, reflecting on the crisis, and being determined to contribute his mite toward the regulation of the currency, followed the example of Dr. Winkelman, and put out a ream, redeemable in Copperplate Bank notes when presented to the amount of five dollars at his tinplate shop. Sim Travers, who had a drinking shed at the lower end of the canal basin, with equal public spirit, uttered his paper in fips, "Good for a Drink." Many others imitated these precedents, whereby it fell out that no part of the Union was better supplied with a currency than Quodlibet.

Still the Borough languished and pined under a gradual decay of its prosperity; and it was long before our wise men could ascertain the real source of this decline. The cause was at last discovered. We are indebted for its development to the astuteness of our distinguished representative. There were eight of the principal mercantile houses of the Borough which had been established by Whigs: in fact, throwing out Barndollar & Hardbottle, all the merchants of Quodlibet might be said to be opposed to the administration. It was very apparent, after the Hon. Middleton Flam drew the attention of the club to this fact, that these houses had combined to produce an utter prostration of business, solely for political effect, and that the malevolence of four of the most thriving among them had gone so far as even to render themselves bankrupt, and to break up, for no earthly purpose but that of making the administration unpopular. "This is a specimen of the gratitude," said Mr. Flam, speaking with great emotion upon the subject, "this is the gratitude of these commercial vultures—(he always called them commercial vultures after the Suspension, and when speaking to the people)—for all the manifold favors and bounties which, for five years past, the government has been so assiduously heaping upon their heads. This is their acknowledgment of the extraordinary kindness shown them by the Secretary of the Treasury when he directed our bank to lend these vipers the public money! Biddle and the Barings are at the bottom of this conspiracy; and the merchants of the United States, yes, and the manufacturers and all the moneyed men, would gladly beggar themselves and their families rather than allow us to regulate their currency and make them the happiest people on earth. What unparalleled perfidy!"

After this, the New Lights of course became indignant against the merchants, and held them up, as they deserved, to public execration, as the authors of all our misfortunes. From Quodlibet, this sentiment became general among the New-Light Democrats everywhere. Mr. Van Buren caught the idea; the Globe expatiated upon it; the Stump rang with it; and it soon took its place as one of the cardinal maxims in the New-Light creed. Such is the supremacy of one commanding intellect!

Never was there a topic equal to this in the elections. "The merchants," Theodore Fog very pertinently remarked, "are a first-rate subject for a stump speech: they are a monstrous *little* knot of fellows, anyhow—and, comparatively speaking, of no sort of account, in the way of voting. Having the handling of a good deal of cash, and plenty to do in the way of giving and taking of promissory notes, you can slap upon them the argument of The Money Power with tremendous effect: you can tickle them with the whip of Aristocracy in perfection; and you can run 'em down with the text of the money-changers in the Temple, and all that sort of thing, to a nicety. Besides, there are so few of them that either *can* make a speech before the people, or, if they can, will take the trouble to follow a man about for that purpose, that you are not likely to be pestered with their replies. Capital animals for *an opposition*, they take a lathering so quiet! Then, sir, for every *one* merchant you lay upon his back, you gain *five* True Grits to your side. I've studied that out. Our people, I mean the New Lights, can be made to hate a merchant like snakes—because if he does get on well with his business, and makes a little fortune, we can call him a Rag Baron, a Ruffle Shirt, a Scrub Aristocrat,—and that's equal to sending him to the deserts of Arabia: and if he fails, as the greater part of the poor devils do, we can get up a still worse cry against him for turning the humble and honest laborer out of employment, grinding the faces of the poor, depriving the widow and the orphan of their bread, and coining the sweat of the Bone and Sinew's brow to feed Usurers, Brokers, and Shavers. And, by-the-by, these arguments are quite good against manufacturers and Whig master-mechanics. But a merchant, sir, can't hold up his head one moment before them. Every which way, sir, he's a prime scapegoat. Then, sir, when we want to make an EXPERIMENT,—why, of course, we go to the merchants. Here's all this *currency* business, especially the tail of it, the Sub-Treasury—fine thing to stir up the people with—sounds well in theory, though a little mischievous in practice. Well, sir, we test it on the merchants: *we* get the popularity, *they* get the damage. The approved philosophical mode to try a dangerous experiment, is to attempt it on a cat:— sir, *The Merchants are our cats.*"

Mr. Flam, seeing the state of our divisions, took a great deal of trouble to restore harmony into our ranks, and certainly did much to overawe the True Grits, who, now fancying themselves in the ascendent, became very dictatorial. Eliphalet Fox, although he took every occasion to speak in his paper greatly in commendation of Mr. Flam, was, nevertheless, an active upholder of the True-Grit division. "Our worthy representative," he said, "was happily stationed above the influence of these little *family quarrels*; and it was undoubtedly a subject of congratulation with that distinguished gentleman, that every section of the great Democratic household of Quodlibet could cordially unite the testimonials of their confidence in his talents, his patriotism, and his fidelity to the interests of his constituents."

This paragraph was considered a master-stroke of New-Light Democracy in Eliphalet, because its tendency was to keep him and his paper on good terms with all parties supporting the administration, while it left him free to pursue the paramount objects which the True Grits steadily kept in view.

These objects were the attainment of all the lucrative offices in our district,— a striking exemplification of which now occurred in the celebrated Tigertail affair. That affair my duty as a chronicler requires me to notice.

A secret meeting of the True Grits had been lately held in the Borough. The subject in discussion was a weighty one. It was reported to this conclave that

Ferox Tigertail, the marshal of this district, who resided and kept his office in Bickerbray, had in his employment two individuals of suspicious principles. The first was Washington Cutbush, a clerk, who had been overheard to say, at the Sycamore Spring, in a confidential conversation with his brother-in-law, Lemuel Garret, that he began to think Tom Benton's gold currency a HUMBUG! The second was Corney Dust, the porter and firemaker of the office, who, there was reason to believe, had voted at the last election for Agamemnon Flag. Upon these facts being vouched to the meeting by Magnus Morehead, the True Grit shoemaker in the Borough, and Sandy Buttercrop, the express-rider, message-carrier, baggage-porter, and follower of sundry other visible means of livelihood, it was resolved that a committee of three, to consist of Eliphalet Fox, Dr. Winkelman, and Nim Porter, should wait upon Mr. Tigertail, communicate to him the full extent of the charge, and require him, in the name of The Exclusive, New-Light, True-Grit Democrats of Quodlibet, forthwith to dismiss Washington Cutbush from his office, and substitute Magnus Morehead in his place; and also to supersede Corney Dust by the appointment of Sandy Buttercrop.

The committee, in pursuance of these instructions, visited the marshal, and explained the object of their mission in respectful but firm language. Tigertail, being a choleric man, and an old Federalist to boot,—who had been converted to the New-Light faith about eight years ago, at the date of the renewal of his commission,—heard the committee with exemplary composure; and then setting his eyes, with a fixed glare, upon Eliphalet Fox, he waited about ten seconds—at the end of which brief period of deliberation, he kicked the said Eliphalet clean out of his office:—and this being done to his entire satisfaction, he rather testily invited Dr. Winkelman and Nim Porter to follow their chairman. It is due to these two gentlemen to say, that like good committee men, they did so,—even anticipating the marshal's invitation to the adoption of that course of conduct.

This incident being faithfully reported by the committee to the meeting of True Grits, convened for the express purpose of learning the result, it was unanimously resolved,—First, that Tigertail's demeanor was mysterious, equivocal, and unexpected; secondly, that it was unpolite to Eliphalet Fox; and, thirdly, that it was against the principles and usages known to the New-Light Democracy. Another resolution was adopted to lay the whole matter before the President of the United States, and to instruct him, as the Representative of the People, to dismiss Marshal Tigertail, without delay, from his post; and confer it upon the injured Eliphalet Fox, whose kicking entitled him to the deepest sympathy of the party, and gave him, according to a well-established maxim of the New Lights, a right to immediate preferment.

These resolutions imparted great satisfaction to the meeting, and no doubt was entertained that the President would act upon the subject with that promptitude which distinguishes his character. Marshal Tigertail was looked upon as a doomed man, and no better than a Whig; and indeed he was already considered as having joined that party. Dr. Thomas G. Winkelman, Nim Porter, and Dabbs, the compositor, were intrusted with this embassy of instruction to the President;—Eliphalet Fox being left out of the deputation from obvious considerations of delicacy—a sentiment which it must be allowed has ever characterized the proceedings of the True Grits on all occasions, and which many of the most observant and sagacious of that sect have asserted has been the principal cause of the failure of their schemes.

The new deputation lost no time in setting forth upon the execution of their duty. They were attended to the stage coach by a large number of True Grits, who, to use the language of Theodore Fog, "signalized their departure with indignant pomp." Great expectations were indulged on this appeal, or rather this mandate to the President. Day after day passed by without bringing news from the mission:—the Globe was taken from each mail with increased avidity, in the hope of seeing some official announcement of the removal of Tigertail. A provoking silence on that point reigned throughout its columns. Ten days rolled on without a letter from the committee:—a fortnight wore away, and yet none had returned. A traveler at last reported that he had seen Nim Porter at the White Sulphur Springs. It was ascertained that Dr. Winkelman was in the City of New York purchasing drugs for his shop; and upon investigation it was discovered that Dabbs had been at his work in the printing-office, unknown to the Borough, for more than a week. By a singular coincidence of feeling among the True Grits, all curiosity as to the fate of the mission suddenly subsided. The subject was treated with indifference; and in the course of a few days, after both Dr. Winkelman and Nim Porter had returned home, when the Thorough Blue Whole Team put forth a paragraph inquiring after the Tigertail Embassy, the Whole Hog came out with a petulant and snappish reply, affirming that the report of such a mission was a mere Whig lie, coined with a view to political effect, and uttered in the Whole Team simply because "that mendacious and filthy sheet delighted to revel in falsehood, and had never been known to stumble upon the truth, even by accident." Dr. Winkelman studiously avoided all reference to his absence from the Borough, and Nim Porter was equally cautious for about a month; at the expiration of which period Neal Hopper happened to say, in his presence, he had good reason to know that Marshal Tigertail was no favorite with the President, and would be removed from office before the end of the next Congress;—whereupon Nim, very unguardedly and under a sudden, uncontrollable impulse, planted himself before the miller and said,—

"I'll bet you one hundred dollars to ten upon that."

"Well, I 'spose you know?" said Neal, struck by Nim's peremptory manner.

"Conclusively and distinctly," replied Nim with some heat. "If you think Liphalet Fox is going to be the marshal you're mistaken: I know Martin Van Buren," he added with some display of self-importance, "considerably—and I can tell you that he goes the whole figure against rotation in this individual and identical case. He's a Mandarin from snout to tail—trained up from the gum, and wouldn't touch a True Grit with a forty-foot pole. Martin has defined his position emphatically. There can't be a possibility of mistake upon the subject."

"Do you mean to say that you heard him say so?" inquired William Goodlack, the tailor, a strenuous member of the True Grits, looking angrily at Nim.

"That's neither here nor there," replied Nim. "But I'll stand to the bet of one hundred dollars to ten, that Tigertail's not turned out of office this year: you are welcome to take it yourself, Billy Goodlack, if you're a mind for a bet."

"Whoever said Tigertail ought to be turned out?" asked Goodlack, peevishly, "'cepting Neal Hopper, who picked up such a story out of the nine thousand lies of the Whole Team?"

From this little brush with Nim Porter, and from the looks that passed between the parties engaged in it, there was room for the inference that the President didn't give much encouragement to the committee who went to him with instructions to turn out the marshal: and this is nearly everything that has ever transpired in Quodlibet upon that subject. It is very certain that, for some time after this date, the True Grits were not so bold as a party as they had been before. Eliphalet Fox was undoubtedly much chop-fallen during all the following winter.

CHAPTER XIII.

A POLITICAL DISCUSSION AT ABEL BRAWN'S SHOP—ABEL'S VIEWS OF THE SUB-TREASURY—IMPORTANT COMMUNICATION MADE BY THEODORE FOG—THE NEW LIGHTS TAKE GROUND AGAINST THE BANKS—THE HON. MIDDLETON FLAM RESIGNS THE PRESIDENCY OF THE COPPERPLATE BANK—SNUFFERS ASPIRES TO THE SUCCESSION.

Toward the latter end of August, in the year referred to in the last chapter, about five o'clock in the afternoon, a much larger collection than usual of work horses were seen around Abel Brawn's shop, waiting to be shod. The shop stands a few rods below Christy M'Curdy's mill, and immediately upon the bank of the Rumblebottom. The mill is just outside of the compactly-built portion of the Borough; and from the door, Neal Hopper, the miller, could see along the road, on his left hand, into the principal cross street of Quodlibet, and on his right, directly into Abel Brawn's smith-shop. This advantage of position was much prized by Neal, because it enabled him to observe everybody going either from the town-side or the country-side to the blacksmith's. And as the shop was a famous ground for political discussion and newsmongering; and as Neal had an insaturable stomach (insaturabile abdomen) for that sort of gossip, a glance from the mill door gave him the means of knowing who was either at or on the way to the shop. Then, if the company suited him, he was in the habit of confiding the temporary government of the mill to a mealy-headed negro called Cicero, who could turn out a grist as well as himself, and so allow himself the chance of a brush at argument with Abel Brawn's customers.

On this evening in August, as I said, there were more horses than usual at the smithy. Six or seven men were lounging about the door or in the shop, talking very loud, with every now and then a word from Abel, who was busily employed alternately hammering out shoes on the anvil, and fitting them to the horses' feet; while squinting Billy Spike, a rather ungainly lad, an apprentice to the smith, was keeping off the flies with a horsetail fastened to the end of a stick. I had been taking a walk that evening with some of my boys to look at the ruins of the old school-house, and, seeing this little gathering about Abel Brawn's, I stopped to hear what was going on. Being somewhat fatigued by my exercitation, I sat down on the bench under the shed, having sent my boys home by themselves, and remained here a quiet though not an inattentive spectator of the scene before me. It is by cultivating such opportunities that I have been enabled to impart that interest to these pages which, without vanity, I may say my reader cannot fail to discover in them. Such have ever been my choicest and most profitable moments of observation—subseciva quædam tempora, quæ ego perire non patiar.

Neal Hopper was engaged in repairing a bolting-cloth up stairs in the mill, and, for some time after this assemblage had gathered about the smith's shop, did not hear or seem to know what was going forward, until there came a loud, sharp laugh and a whoop which aroused his attention. As soon as he heard this, he pricked up his ears, listened a moment, and upon a repetition of the laugh, stepped to the window, looked down toward the shop and saw who were there, then called Cicero to finish the repair of the bolting-cloth—and went straight to the blacksmith's.

"Well, what's the fraction," said Neal, "that you're all a busting out in such a spell of a laugh about?"

Hearing Neal's voice, Abel Brawn put down the horse's foot which he was then shoeing, from his lap, and standing upright, replied,—

"There seems to be a sort of a snarl here among these brother Democrats of yours, concerning of this here Sub-Treasury. Some of them say it's against the banks, and some of them say it's for the banks. They have got it that Cambreling should have give out in Congress that it was going to help the banks and keep them up; and others, on the contrary, say that Old Tom Benton swears that it won't leave so much as the skin of a corporated company 'twixt Down East and the Mississippi. And they say, moreover, that little Martin lays dark about it."

"What does the Globe give out concerning of it?" inquired Neal.

"Well, the Globe," replied Sam Pivot, the assessor of our county, who was out for sheriff, and who was very cautious in all his opinions, "is, as I take it, a little dubious. Sometimes he makes this Sub-Treasury a smasher to all banks; and then again he fetches it up as a sort of staff to prop the good ones and to knock down the cripples. Last fall, just before the New York election, he rather buttered the banks, seeing that the Democracy in that quarter hadn't made up their minds to run as strong against the laboring people as they are willing to do over here in the South. But in April, when the Virginny elections was up, he was as savage as a meat-ax;—and I rather expect, from what I see in the President's message, that it isn't yet fairly understood whether the Sub-Treasury is to kill or cure the banking system."

"It's a pig in a poke, to make the best of it," said Abel Brawn; "and is flung before the people now because Van hasn't got nothing better to offer us, and not because he values it above an old shoe. To my thinking, when the people have decided against a law, as they have done now against this Sub-Treasury, as you call it, twice in Congress, a President of the United States ought to have that respect for the will of the people to let it drop. That's what I call

Whig Democracy—though it mayn't be yourn."

"Never!" exclaimed Tom Crop, the constable of our Borough. "If the people go agin the Dimocracy, the Dimocracy ought to put them down. We go for principle; and it's our business to try it over and over again, until we carry it. Truth is mighty and *will* prevail, as the old Gineral says."

"I have never been able," said Neal Hopper, "rightly to make out what this Sub-Treasury is, anyhow. If any man knows, let him tell me."

"What does that signify?" answered Crop. "Some calls it a divorce—but betwixt who I don't know, and what's more, I don't care. It's for the poor man we are a fighting, against the rich. The Whigs are for making the poor poorer, and the rich richer—and I say any man who goes against the Sub-Treasury, can't have no respect for Dimmicratic principles."

"I'll tell you what it is," said Abel Brawn; "ever since the old Federals took hold of General Jackson's skirts, and joined him in breaking down the banks, they have been plotting to keep their heads above water—and so they set about making experiments right and left, to see if they couldn't hit upon something new to please the people. But, bless you—they don't know no more about the people than they do about making horseshoes; and that's the reason why they have been such bunglers in all their works: and the end has been to bring us into such a pickle as no country ever was in before. They have teetotally ruinated everything they have laid their hands on—and now they come out and say 'the people expect too much from the Government,' and by way of making that saying good, they have got up this Sub-Treasury, which is nothing more nor less than a contrivance to get all the money of the country into their own strong box, knowing that when they have *the money*, they have got *the power*, for as long as they please. That's an old Federal trick, which they understand as well as any men in the world. Now the people, who see into this scheme, don't like it, and so they vote it down in Congress. Well, what does these Federals do then? Submit? No—to be sure not—that's not their principle. They go at it again; set to drilling of Congress, and by promising this man, and buying off that one with an office, and setting their papers to telling all sorts of lies, they get the country so confounded at last that it doesn't know whether it is on its head or its heels. But the worst of it is, these very Federals—some of them real old Blue Lights—go about preaching about rich and poor, and sowing enmity between them; and they work so diligent upon this heat, that many a simple man at last believes them. It's all a trick—a mean, sneaking deceit, which I am ashamed to think any honest poor man in this happy country of ours could be taken in by for one minute. But we never had this talk until we got Federal measures and Federal men at the head of the Government. Who are the rich that they talk about? Why, it is every man who has sense enough to know that they are imposing on him, whether he be worth a million or worth only five hundred dollars—unless indeed it be one of their own rich men, and then they can't praise him too much. Is industry a sin in this land, that when it has earned a little something for a wet day, the man who has thriven by it must be held up as an enemy to his country? Does it hurt a man's patriotism, when he sends his children to school, and works until he can buy a tract of land to start them well in life—or when he rents a pew in church, and carries his family there to teach them to fear God and keep his commandments? Is it to be told *against* a man, that his neighbors count him to be frugal and thrifty, and that he is considered respectable in the world? Yet that is your new fashioned Democracy, which wants to put every one in the dust who doesn't idle away his time and squander his substance, and let his family go to rack, whilst he strolls about the country bawling Democracy. Thank God! the Democracy I've larnt in my time has taught me to do to others as I would have others do to me; and which has imbibed into my mind the principle that I am a freeman, and have a right to think for myself, to speak for myself, and to act for myself, without having a string put through my nose to lead me wherever it suits a set of scheming, lying, cunning politicians to have me for their benefit. Democracy's not what it used to be, or you would never find the people putting up with this eternal dictation from the President and his friends to Congress and to the nation, what he will have, and what he won't have:—that's what I call rank monarchy, and I will fight against it to my latest breath.

"You will have a chance to judge for yourselves whether the President dictates to the people or not, in this very matter of the Sub-Treasury:—wait till the next session of Congress:—the bill has just been rejected a second time. You will see that Martin isn't a going to give it up, but will bring it forward again and again—until at last, I make no doubt, he will get a Congress shabby enough to do his bidding, and pass it;—and many of the very men who are against it to-day, will abandon their own opinions and go for it, for no other reason in the world but that they will be afraid of their nose-leaders, who will tell them they are no Democrats unless they support the President. It is nothing more nor less than *enlisting* men in the service, and marching and countermarching them whichever way the *officers* choose; besides bringing every man to a drum-head who dares to disobey orders."

"What's Tom Benton's notion?" inquired Neal Hopper.

"He goes for the Sub-Treasury out and out," said Pivot.

"In course, he does, all hollow," interrupted Tom Crop, with rather a fierce frown and an angry tone, designed to express his indignant feeling at the sentiments uttered by Abel Brawn, and which sternness of countenance had been gradually gathering during the whole time occupied by the Blacksmith's discourse. "There's none of this slang in him. He's agin all Monypolies, and for the rale Constitutional Currency—and them's the genuine Dimmicratic principles:—leastways, they've come about so now, whatever they might 'a been in times past. Old Tom's the first man what ever found out what the Constitutional Currency raly was, and sot the Dimmicrats a goin' on the Hard-Money track! And, besides, don't I know these banks?—they're nuisances in grain, and naturally as good as strikes a poor man in his vitals. I've seed it myself. Here was Joe Plumb, the cider-press maker, got a note from Jerry Lantern down here at the crossroads, for settin' up his cider-press, and he heaved it in the bank for them to collect it—and what does the bank do, but go and *purtest* it! That's the way they treat a poor man like Joe Plumb, what's obliged to work for his livin':—would they 'a sarved a Big Bug so? No—don't tell me about the banks! I'm sick a hearin' on 'em."

This discussion was now interrupted by the approach of Theodore Fog, Flan Sucker, and Sim Travers. By this addition to the company, the New Lights gained an overwhelming preponderance of numbers over their adversaries. Indeed, Abel Brawn, and Davy Post, the wheelwright, were the only Whigs in the assemblage; and the consequence was that Abel, who fought them all pretty manfully at first, was obliged to give in so far as to remain silent—with the exception of a random shot, which now and then he let off by way of repartee—Abel not being bad at that. Davy Post was naturally a silent man, and, therefore, did not pretend to be a speaker on this occasion.

As soon as Theodore Fog was informed what was the topic in debate, and especially of the doubts which seemed to be prevalent regarding the Sub-Treasury, he took a station against the door-post, where the whole company gathered around him; and, being now in an oratorical mood, he began to address the auditory in something like a speech:—

"Gentlemen," said he, at the same time drawing, with a jerk, his neckcloth away and flaunting it in his hand, "in a free government we have no secrets. Freedom of Opinion and its twin-sister Freedom of Discussion are chartered libertines that float upon the ambient air consecrated to the Genius of Universal Emancipation——"

"Hurra for old The!" shouted Sim Travers.

"Ya—hoop—halloo—go it!" yelled Flan Sucker, with a wild and deafening scream, which sufficiently manifested the fact that he was most noisily drunk.

Several of the company interfered by remonstrating with Flan against this unnecessary demonstration of fervor, which Flan, on the other hand, insisted upon as his right.

"Whenever old The. Fog comes out high flown," said he, "I yells as a matter of principle. It's encouragin' to youth. Nebuchadnezzar, the King of the Jews, couldn't beat him at a speech: he's the butt cut of Democracy."

"Flan, hold your tongue," said Theodore. "Gentlemen, we have no secrets. Abel Brawn and Davy Post are welcome to hear all I have to impart. I know —everybody knows—that we have been in a state of suspense on the great question of the Sub-Treasury. The INDEPENDENT Treasury, as we are going to call it since Congress rejected it—we'll try what a new name will do. I say we have been in suspense. Like honest New Lights we have waited to see how the cat would jump. Some men imagined that Martin would bow to the judgment of the people and give it up. They did not know the stern, uncompromising, footstep-following principles that dwell at the bottom of his heart. He will *never* give it up—the people *must* take it: he has got nothing else for them. Hasn't he tried everything else? And isn't this the *last* thing he could think of? Why, then, of course, the people *must* gulp it down, or the party is broke. Where is the slave that would desert his party? Who's here so base would be a turncoat? The Whigs call the President the *servant* of the people—we call him the Ruler, the Great Chieftain,—and when a man deserts him he is a TURNCOAT—that is sound New-Light doctrine.

"Sirs, it has been developed in the recent demonstrations of contemporary history——"

"Yip!"

"Silence, Flan Sucker, and don't make a fool of yourself. It has been discovered that bank influence has defeated the Sub-Treasury bill. Every member who voted against it has received a large bribe from the banks. The Globe man has lately discovered this astounding corruption: the President is aware of it; and for this reason, in addition to that which I have already mentioned, he is determined to run it as the INDEPENDENT Treasury again. Every New Light is expected to toe the mark."

"Three cheers for that!" cried Pivot.

"We have heretofore *partially* denounced the banks," continued Fog; "we are now to open upon them like hounds—worry them like rats. From this day forth, the Quods will take a new turn;—they will dismiss all pity from their bosoms, and cry aloud for strangling the banks—not even excepting our own. Patriotism demands the sacrifice. Down with paper money! will be the word. Turn the tables on the Whigs, and call the whole bank system the spawn of aristocracy—remember that. At the same time, gentlemen, be not afraid. No harm will be done to any bank you have a liking for—the essence of the thing is in the noise. We shall have perhaps to kill the banks in the District of

Columbia—but that's nothing;—it will be an offering to consistency. All experiments require an exhausted receiver—and the District is ours;—a snug little piece of machinery to play upon. So keep it in mind—Treasury Notes and no Paper Money!—down with Credit, and up with the Independent Treasury!"

"Ain't that first-rate?" said Sim Travers. "The., who sot that agoin'?"

"Who?" replied Fog. "Why, some of the highest men in this nation—the Lights of the age. Middleton Flam has just received letters from Washington, laying open the whole plan of operations. He has accordingly determined to put himself in position for ultimate action, by resigning the presidency of the bank. Middleton Flam, gentlemen, I am free to say it, although we have differed on some questions, is a great man and an honor to the New Lights. He has already sent his resignation to Nicodemus Handy. The Board meet to-morrow to act upon it. You may imagine, gentlemen, who is looked to as his successor. But I here announce to *you*, the conglomerate essence of my constituency at large, that on no consideration can I be persuaded to accept the vacant place. No, gentlemen, the whole tenor of my life renders that impossible. I have defined my position years ago; and every man must see, that president of that, or any other bank, I can never be. Simon Snuffers is the man. If he can make it agreeable to the Democratic principle upon which he holds the Hay Scales—and that it is for you to say—I have no doubt he will accept. Simon has no ulterior objects;—and men without ulterior objects may do as they please. But I trust that this responsible post will never be pressed upon me. Upon that point I cannot indulge the wishes of my friends."

The importance of this speech was duly appreciated by those to whom it was addressed; and as every man was anxious to know what everybody else thought about these matters, there was an immediate adjournment to the Borough. The consequence was, that Abel Brawn's shop was left in a few moments without a customer; and in the course of the next half hour the news communicated by Theodore Fog was in every man's mouth. The movement at Washington was held to be decisive. The Independent Treasury, from that moment, became a leading test of the allegiance of the Democrats of Quodlibet.

CHAPTER XIV.

LETTER FROM A CABINET OFFICER TO MR. FLAM—DIRECTIONS TO THE
DEMOCRACY—THE CABINET OFFICER'S MODE OF PRODUCING AN
IMPRESSION—THE PRESIDENT'S DETERMINATION IN REGARD TO THE
INDEPENDENT TREASURY—WARNING TO DESERTERS—CANDIDATES
FOR MR. FLAM'S PLACE IN THE BANK—HARDBOTTLE ELECTED—
THEODORE FOG'S OUTBREAK—HE COOLS DOWN AND STANDS UPON
PRINCIPLE—HARDBOTTLE UNPOPULAR.

The fact was as Theodore Fog had stated it. Mr. Flam had received a letter
from a member of the Cabinet, apprising him that it was deemed absolutely
necessary to the preservation of the New-Light Democratic Party to become
extremely pointed in their assault against the State Banks, and that the
misdeeds of those institutions should be exaggerated as much as possible, and
then charged upon the Whigs.

"This attack," said the letter, "must be made with more than usual clamor, and
followed up with unremitting industry, that, by force of the first word and
incessant repetition, we may get the people to believe that we have had
nothing to do with the creation of these corporations; but have, in fact, been
inveterately hostile to them from the first, and that our opponents have been
their sole patrons and friends. Our recent outcry on this subject has succeeded
so well with the people, that we are determined now to make the denunciation
of the banks our chief topic, by way of preparation for the Independent
Treasury which we are resolved the people shall swallow. We cannot too
strongly impress upon our friends the propriety of charging upon the Whigs
that we have repeatedly warned them against increasing the number of banks
in the States. By this device we shall put upon their shoulders all those
mischiefs of *over-banking* and *over-trading*, which *they* used to talk about.
We must impute to them all the evils of the paper system—except the
Treasury notes, which it would be well for us to praise, as an admirable
Democratic scheme to give the country a METALLIC currency. It has also
been deemed important," continued the writer, "that we should prove that the
government has lost more money by the State banks than by any other agents
it has ever employed. This idea was hinted to the Secretary of the Treasury,
who has, in consequence, very recently been at work upon the subject, and
has produced a report altogether conclusive against the banks. He will
continue these labors with a view to the instruction of Congress and all our
other inquiring friends; being, in no respect, daunted by that unlucky report
made by him in 1834, which, singularly enough, proves the opposite side of
the case; for, as he remarks, the specific gravity of his State papers is so great
as to sink them too deep for the perception of the present generation,—and

that consequently his report of 1834 must be pretty well forgotten by this time, which, indeed, I think quite likely;—it was so long-winded, dozy, and prosy, (a note in the margin marked this as 'confidential,') that I should not wonder if more than ten men in Congress ever read it, and of those, perhaps not a single one retains any distinct impression of its meaning." The letter exhorted Mr. Flam to make these views known to the drill sergeants and corporals of the party in Quodlibet, and to stimulate them to active exertions in the part assigned to them. "Pound it into public mind," said the writer, "that the Whigs are the authors of the present evils; continual pounding will inevitably, at last, do the business. Many a time have I riveted, by diligent hammering, a politic and necessary fabrication upon the credulity of the people—so fast that no art of my adversary could tear it away to make room for the truth: therefore, I say to you and our Democratic friends—hammer without ceasing."

A letter also from the Secretary, at the same time, informed Mr. Flam, that as the people had so contumaciously rejected the Independent Treasury bill, by their representatives in Congress, the President was now determined to carry it at all hazards; and consequently it was expected that no New-Light Democrat would be so false to the glorious principles of the Quodlibetarian theory as to interpose any opinion of his own between the will of the President and the appropriate duty of the people. "If such should be the case," said the Secretary, "Mr. Van Buren can have no alternative—the individual so recreant to the eternal principles of the New-Light Democracy must be denounced by the Globe as an enemy to freedom, and, what is worse, a traitor to his party."

Mr. Flam reflected upon these communications with grave attention; and having shown them to some of his intimate friends, among whom I count it my highest honor to be ranked, he announced his purpose to resign his post in the bank. For this step he had two good reasons: the first was the necessity of disencumbering himself of a connection which might have impeded his usefulness—to use his own words—in his public relations; the second reason was, that he had borrowed so large an amount from the bank, as to circumscribe its bounty greatly to the prejudice of sundry of the directors who were, in consequence, beginning to complain of his management of the institution, and were even threatening to run an opposition against him in the election which was but a few months off. It was whispered also that Nicodemus Handy had given him a mysterious but friendly hint to resign, without explaining his reasons. Upon these considerations his mind was made up; and accordingly the resignation was laid before the Board at the time indicated by Theodore Fog.

This event produced great sensation in Quodlibet; not less from the curiosity to know why our distinguished representative should relinquish so lucrative a post, than from the interest felt in the measure of selecting his successor. Fifteen of our most strenuous New-Light Democrats were candidates; and notwithstanding the speech made at the blacksmith's shop, Theodore Fog was the first who wrote a letter to the Board to apprise them that, in consequence of the eager importunity of his Democratic friends to confide the bank to his management, he found himself compelled to forego his objections to having any concern with the banking system, and therefore would not feel himself at liberty to decline the Presidency in case it should be offered to him. He said he wished it to be distinctly understood, that emolument was not his object: but that he was actuated solely by his attachment to that New-Light Democratic principle which taught him on all occasions to seek preferment, as the means of widening the sphere of his usefulness, and to increase his worldly fortune only for the sake of the good it enabled him to dispense to the people. On no other terms was he willing to accept the government of the bank.

Some two or three days were spent in canvassing this matter; when the choice ultimately, upon the twenty-fifth balloting, fell upon Anthony Hardbottle, who had not been previously thought of for the place, and was only brought forward when all attempts to elect others had failed. The fifteen original candidates became greatly incensed at this choice. Theodore Fog was furious: he said Hardbottle could scarcely be called a Democrat:—if anything, he was half Whig—nay, he believed, whole Whig:—and to elect a Whig to a great responsible post like that—a post connected with the national fisc, allied to the money power, so intimately related to the important concerns of the currency!—it was not to be tolerated. The Genius of New-Light Democracy should array herself in steel, indue herself in panoply, buckle on her armor, shake her lance against it, or, in other words, he deemed it incompatible with free institutions to allow a Whig, or, at least, a man who never attended political meetings, and who held the Whigs in respect—to preside over such a Democratic institution as the Copperplate Bank of Quodlibet. Theodore continued raving in this strain until he drank nine juleps, interspersed with numberless other potations, and became so incapable of motion as to render it necessary for Mrs. Ferret to have him carried to bed. As he cooled, so cooled his competitors. Indeed, in the course of a few days, Theodore Fog, in commenting upon the pretensions of the several defeated candidates, found so many objections to them individually and collectively, as to bring himself into an excellent temper upon the subject, whereby he was able to make merry with the whole election; and thus, by degrees, he fell back into the state of mind which he had manifested at the smith's shop, and declared that no consideration could possibly induce him, professing the principles he did, to accept any post connected with a bank. He expressed himself in sharp and censorious terms against what, he said, he had constantly observed: namely, that he never knew a post in a bank to be vacant, from the President down to the porter, including Directors and all, in regard to which he didn't find half a dozen Loco Focos, to say nothing of New-Light Democrats, applicants to fill the vacancy: he thought it inconsistent with principle, now that orders had come for the Democracy to abuse the banks, to seek or accept such places; and he did not care who knew his sentiments upon the subject.

Mr. Hardbottle was a strict man of business, and did not, it is true, greatly interest himself in politics. Yet, nevertheless, he was a decided supporter of the New-Light cause, and was always esteemed a useful member of the Borough. One thing that made against him in the Board was, that he had never been a very active customer to the bank, except so far only as keeping his commercial account there. He was often urged to accept accommodations with a view to the improvement of the Borough, but almost invariably refused, from an aversion to indulging in these useful speculations. His brother Directors, in consequence, rather regarded him as a man who was deficient in public spirit; and they imagined that he might be inclined to depreciate the value of the services they had rendered the bank by the liberal employment they had given to its funds. Mr. Hardbottle, therefore, might be said to have entered into the government of the bank under inauspicious circumstances, and was likely not to be a very popular President. He was, however, determined upon one thing, and that was to make a thorough examination of the bank for the purpose of bringing about a resumption of specie payments at the earliest possible moment; for some complaints had gone abroad against the Bank of Quodlibet for not resuming when the other banks of the country affected to be anxious for that measure.

In consequence of this determination of the new President, the bank was kept in perpetual bustle for the whole fortnight succeeding the election. What then occurred will be told in the next chapter.

CHAPTER XV.

UNHAPPY EVENT IN THE LIFE OF NICODEMUS HANDY—CONSTERNATION OF QUODLIBET—DISASTERS AMONG THE DIRECTORS—EXPLOSION OF THE BANK—CONVERSATION BETWEEN THEODORE FOG AND MR. GRANT—FOG'S VIEWS OF THE QUESTION OF DISTRESS—COMPLIMENT TO JESSE FERRET.

I know not which way to turn. Auribus teneo lupum. I can scarcely compose myself to write. Such an event! Many things have happened in this world to excite wonder, many grief, many indignation, many wailing, lamentation, and moans; but we have had an incident in the Borough which overmasters all these emotions by the height and the depth, the length and the breadth, the stupendous magnitude of the amazement which it has spread through all minds.

The investigation of the affairs of the bank, under the direction of Mr. Hardbottle, lasted more than a fortnight. They were not yet brought to a close, when—— Let the following paragraph from an extra Whole Hog, issued on the spur of the moment, tell the rest. I have no nerve for such a disclosure.

"ASTOUNDING WHIG DEFALCATION.

"Our Borough has just been thrown into a state of stupefaction by an event which completely eclipses every other act of crime and villainy with which the annals of Whiggery abound. Nicodemus Handy, the Whig Cashier of that extortionate, swindling Whig rag-factory, the Patriotic Copperplate Bank of Quodlibet, left this Borough yesterday morning in the People's Line, which runs through Thorough Blue. As this journey was undertaken with the pretense of business, it attracted no attention until this morning, when the indefatigable Democratic President of that institution, Mr. Anthony Hardbottle, who was recently elected for the purpose of a thorough investigation into its concerns, (suspicions having been long indulged of its rottenness; and, in fact, our worthy representative, the Hon. Middleton Flam, an unterrified and incorruptible New Light, having retired from the head of the institution on account of the disgusting irregularities which fell within his view,) laid a statement before the Board which showed that the Cashier had secreted upwards of $160,000, the greater part of which funds there is reason to believe he has made away with in the course of the last three months. Measures were taken to pursue the offender, and as far as possible to secure the bank by attachments upon his property, which is supposed to be considerable. For the present, we forbear all comment, except so far as to remark, that we look upon this atrocious fraud but as the natural fruit of that system of Whig measures which has cumbered the land with mushroom banks, filthy rags, and swarms of scrub aristocrats in the shape of presidents, cashiers, directors, and clerks. We may speedily expect to hear of many more Whigs following the example of our absquatulating Cashier."

The sensation produced in the Borough by this intelligence is not to be described. The flight of Mr. Handy was the only topic of conversation for a week. An officer followed him to Thorough Blue, whence, it was rumored, the fugitive had shaped his course for Texas: other reports assigned Canada as his place of refuge—all was uncertainty. Legal measures were taken to secure his property. This consisted of his elegant mansion on Copperplate Ridge, sundry rows of warehouses, and other buildings in Quodlibet, a large number of which had been left for two years past in an unfinished state. Upon investigation it was ascertained that the whole of this estate had been converted into money; our worthy representative, the Hon. Middleton Flam, having an absolute conveyance for Handy House, its furniture, and appurtenances, and certain political friends, connected with the custom-house in New York, rank Whigs, having mortgages on all the rest of the property. The consequence was, the bank was able to secure nothing.

One of our first proceedings, after the flight of the Cashier, was to call together the New-Light Club, where resolutions were passed denouncing his fraud as the necessary consequence of his Whig principles, censuring the bank, in the strongest terms, as a swindling Whig concern, and avowing an unalterable devotion to the Independent Treasury, as the only sound, genuine, New-Light Democratic experiment which it was proper for the government to make, in the present condition of affairs—unless the President should change his mind and find out something still more Democratic; in which event the New-Light Club pledged itself to give that other measure their cordial and patriotic support.

In the course of a fortnight, the inhabitants of the Borough were surprised to read from a New York paper, in the list of passengers who sailed for Liverpool by the packet of the first of October, among the names of sundry fashionables, those also of Mrs. and Miss Handy; and we were, not long afterward, relieved from all doubt as to the Cashier's destination, by seeing it publicly announced that he had gone to Havre, from which point, as soon as he could be joined by his interesting and distressed family, he designed making the tour of Europe.

From the period of the elopement of Mr. Handy, we had a series of convulsions. The first incident of importance that followed it, was the failure of the whole Board of Directors; each of whom, according to his own showing, had lost so much money by the absconding Cashier as to be totally unable to pay up his liabilities to the bank. The next disaster was the explosion of the bank itself. The abduction of so large an amount of its funds, as well as its unfortunate list of bad debts from the Directors, rendered this inevitable. Then came riots among the holders of its paper, who besieged the door for several days, and even threatened to pull down the building. Never was a community in a more unhappy commotion than ours at this eventful epoch.

Mr. Grant visited the Borough frequently during the prevalence of these disorders. One day he met Theodore Fog, who seemed to be rather pleasurably excited by the events which occupied and engrossed the public attention—for Theodore, as he was in the habit of remarking, had nothing to lose by these domestic convulsions, and everything to gain. The election was at hand, and he was again the True-Grit candidate; but on this occasion there was no opposition from his own party, and the chance of electing a Whig was deemed hopeless. That side made no nomination; and Fog, therefore, with his two colleagues of the last year, was in a fair way to walk over the course without a contest. The interests of the election, consequently, were altogether absorbed in the other incidents of the day. Still, Theodore was not inattentive to the voters, and was, as usual, loquacious and voluble.

"A pretty considerable upheaving of the elements of social life, Mr. Grant," said he, upon encountering the old gentleman on Ferret's steps at the front door of The Hero.

"I think so," replied Mr. Grant; "you have brought your pigs at last to a fine market."

"*Our* pigs!" exclaimed Fog, with an excellent representation of surprise:
—"well, that beats M'Gonegal, and he beat the devil. The whole litter comes from a Whig mother: it is the spawn of that aristocracy, against which the intelligence, the honor, and the virtue of the nation have been waging war ever since the Reign of Terror;—but, sir, it is down; the intelligence and firmness of the people have triumphed at last."

"You allude, I suppose, to your Democratic bank here," said Mr. Grant.

"No doubt," replied Fog, "the Whigs will attempt to shuffle the bank off *their* shoulders and buckle it on the Democrats. But that won't do, sir; that's too stale a trick to deceive the people. The Whigs, sir, are men of property; the

Democrats are poor, sir. Banks are not made by poor men, Mr. Grant; there's the logic of the case."

"And this Patriotic Copperplate Bank of Quodlibet was not set on foot by Nicodemus Handy and Theodore Fog?" returned Mr. Grant.

"By Nicodemus Handy," replied Fog, "not by me. Sir, Nicodemus was always a Whig; and, what's more, attempted to beguile me into his scheme. He took advantage of my unsuspecting temper—endeavored to lull into security my artless, confiding nature; essayed, sir, but in vain, to seduce me from my allegiance to the Democratic faith, by tempting offers of the presidency of the bank—but, sir, my virtue was too stern for his treacherous arts. I saw the gilded bait and spurned it. It was—I say it myself—a rare example of successful resistance to the fascinations of the tempter. Many a Democrat has fallen into the snare of the Whigs under less allurement. I pride myself on this evidence of self-command. I have reason to be proud of it."

"You have a short memory," said Mr. Grant.

"Why as to that, old friend," replied Fog with a good-natured laugh, at the same time laying his hand on Mr. Grant's shoulder, "you can't call *that* a fault. Every politician has a short memory—he'd be no politician without it. Mine's no shorter than the rest. Sir, let me tell you, the great secret of the success of the immutable, New-Light, Quodlibetarian Democracy, is in the shortness of the memory. Still, I would like to know what you mean by the remark."

"I mean to say," replied Mr. Grant, "that when you and Nicodemus Handy were endeavoring to persuade me to take an interest in your bank, you didn't think it so undemocratic as you seem to do to-day."

"It is impossible for me to remember what I said on the occasion to which you allude, sir," returned Fog; "but my principles have always been the same. I could not have gone against them, sir; morally impossible."

"And I told you that your bank was a humbug," continued Mr. Grant.

"Ay, ay," rejoined Fog; "that's the old song. You Whigs are monstrous good at prophesying after the result is known."

"You admit, I suppose," said Mr. Grant, "that this Bank of Quodlibet has exploded?"

"Burst, sir, into a thousand tatters," replied Fog.

"You admit that there is a large amount of paper money afloat?"

"A genuine Whig crop," answered Fog: "enough to make a stack as large as the largest in your barnyard."

"You admit the derangement of values all over the country?"

"Yes, and of the people too, if you make it a point."

"The failures of traders and of banks?"

"Yes."

"This is reasonable, Mr. Fog. Now, you shall judge whether the Whigs prophesy *before* or *after* the result," said Mr. Grant, as he thrust his hand into his skirt pocket and drew forth a pamphlet. "I expected to meet you to-day, and I have brought you a document for your especial perusal. It is the speech of a Whig member of Congress, made in 1834, upon the Removal of the Deposits;—you will find the leaf turned down at page 32; and, as you are a good reader, I wish you would favor this company by reading it aloud, where you see it scored in the margin."

"Not I," replied Theodore; "that's four years ago. The statute of limitation bars that."

"He's afeard to read it," said Abel Brawn to some five or six persons, who had collected around the steps during this conversation. "Mr. Grant's mighty particular with his documents, and ain't to be shook off in an argument."

"The., you ain't afeard, old fellow?" said Flan Sucker. "Walk into him, The. Read it."

"Give me the book," said Fog, "and let's see what it is. Speech by Horace Binney—eh? Who's he? I think I have heard the name. Well, for the sake of obliging a friend, I'll read.—*Conticuere omnes*—which means listen." Fog then read as follows:—

"It is here that we find a pregnant source of the present agony—it is in the clearly avowed design to bring a second time upon this land the curse of an unregulated, uncontrolled State-Bank paper currency. We are again to see the drama which already, in the course of the present century, has passed before us, and closed in ruin. If the project shall be successful——"

"What project?" inquired Fog.

"The destruction of the Bank of the United States, and the refusal to create another in its place," answered Mr. Grant.

Theodore read on—

"If the project shall be successful, we are again to see these paper missiles shooting in every direction through the country—a derangement of all values,—a depreciated circulation—a suspension of specie payments;—then a further extension of the

114

same detestable paper—a still greater depreciation—with failures of traders and failures of banks in its train—to arrive at last at the same point from which we departed in 1817."

"A rank forgery," said Theodore Fog, "printed for the occasion."

"That won't do," replied Mr. Grant; "I have been the owner of this pamphlet ever since 1834 myself."

"Then Binney is a Dimmycrat," said Sim Travers, "and you are trying to pass him off on us for a Whig. Sound Dimmycratic doctrine and true prophecy."

"Huzza for Binney!" shouted Flan Sucker, "a tip-top Dimmycrat, whoever he is!—I never heard of him before."

"Yes," said Mr. Grant, "one ounce of his Democracy is worth a ton weight of the best you will find in the Globe. But read on, a little further below, where you see it scored."

"I have an innate and mortal aversion to reading," returned Fog.

"It must be gone through," said Flan Sucker,—"because them sentiments is the rale Dimmocracy, and we want to hear them. So, go it, The!—Yip—listen boys, to the doctrine."

"Well," said Fog, "if you will have it—as the pillory said to the thief, 'lend me your ears.'"

"I thank the Secretary," he began with a discreet voice, reading where Mr. Grant appointed for him, "for the disclosure of this plan. I trust in God it will be defeated: that the Bank of the United States, while it is in existence, may be sustained and strengthened by the public opinion, and interests of the people, to defeat it: that the sound and sober State banks of the Union may resist it—for it is their cause: that the poor men and laborers in the land may resist it—for it is a scheme to get from every one of them a dollar's worth of labor for fifty cents, and to make fraud the currency of the country as much as paper. Sir, the Bank of the United States, in any other relation than to the currency and property of the country, is as little to me as to any man under heaven; but after the prime and vigor of life are passed, and the power of accumulation is gone, to see the children stripped, by the monstrous imposture of a paper currency, of all that the father's industry had provided for them—this, sir, may well excuse the warmth that denounces this plan, as the precursor of universal dismay and ruin."

"I'll read no more," said Fog, giving back the book, with a theatrical flourish of his arm, to Mr. Grant; "it is nothing more than stealing our principles from us, and then bringing them up to break our heads."

"It is good Whig prophecy, four years before its fulfillment," said Mr. Grant, "and which has come true to the letter. It shows you that we set our faces against your increase of banks in the very beginning; gave you warning of what was to come; painted the very evils of this day so plainly before your eyes that nothing but willful blindness prevented you from seeing them; and now, when it has all fallen out as it was foretold, you attempt to make us responsible to the people for your measures."

"Sir," said Fog, rather evading the argument, as it is an admirable part of the New-Light system to do when it pinches, "the New-Light Democracy changes its measures, but never its principles. We go, sir, for the will of the people— that's the principle which lies at the bottom of all our actions. If the people are for new measures, we frankly come out with them. Now, sir, the people are *against* the banks—they are *for* the Independent Treasury: of course, then, you know where to find *us*. You can't get round us—there we are."

"I'll not dispute that point with you," replied Mr. Grant; "you have been changing from bad to worse ever since you have had the control of affairs. I only wanted to remind you that the present distress of the country is the work of your own hands, and that you have brought it about with your eyes open."

Saying these words Mr. Grant walked off toward the stable, where he mounted his horse and rode out of the Borough.

As soon as the old gentleman was gone, Theodore Fog remarked that he had not had as dry a talk for some years, and proposed to the company a general visit to the bar.

"They talk of *distress*," said he. "Mr. Grant has gone off with his head full of that notion of distress; it's a famous Whig argument, that. But what distress is there? Drinking's as cheap; eating's as cheap as ever; so is lying. Eating, drinking, and lying, are the three principal occupations of man. Lying *down*, I mean, metaphorically for sleeping. Where's the distress, then? Mere panic— false alarm—a Whig invention! The country is better off than it ever was before. Not for men who trade upon credit, I allow—not for merchants and shippers in general—not for your fellows that go about for jobs—not for farmers—not for regular laborers—not for mechanics, with families on their hands, and perhaps not for single ones neither;—but first-rate for lawyers, bar-keepers, and brokers, for marshals and sheriffs—capital for constables— nonpareil for postmasters, contractors, express-riders, and office-holders; and glorious for fellows that are fond of talking and have nothing to do:—these are the very gristle of the New-Light Democracy, and make a genteel majority at the elections."

"Mr. Fog," said Jesse Ferret, "I am so well pleased at your reading for Mr. Grant this morning, that I'm determined to give you a treat;—help yourself and your friends. Gentlemen, walk up."

"Glad you liked it, old buck," replied Fog. "Bless your heart, I'm used to such things. A political man must always be ready for rubbers; never would get a gloss if it wasn't for brushing. That Binney's a smart fellow; but every word of that speech was whispered into his ear by Benton; I know the fact personally. He and Benton sit up every night of their lives together in Washington, playing old sledge and drinking cocktail: that accounts for Binney's Democracy. Gentlemen, our friend Ferret's treat—we'll drink his health—a worthy, persuadable, amenable man—so here's to him. Wait for the word—Jesse Ferret, a gentleman and a scholar, an antiquarian and a tavern-keeper—long life to him!"

CHAPTER XVI.

A RAPID REVIEW OF ONE YEAR—WHAT THE AUTHOR IS COMPELLED TO
PRETERMIT—THE PRESIDENT'S "SOBER SECONDTHOUGHT" MESSAGE
RECEIVED AT QUODLIBET WITH GREAT REJOICING—THE AUTHOR
COMMUNES WITH HIS READER TOUCHING NEW-LIGHT PRINCIPLES—
ILLUSTRATIONS OF THEM—REMARKABLE DEXTERITY OF THE
SECRETARY—INTERESTING LETTER FROM THE HON. MIDDLETON FLAM
—DAWNING OF THE PRESIDENTIAL CANVASS—THE NORTHERN MAN
WITH SOUTHERN PRINCIPLES AND HIS MANNIKIN.

Time held his course. Another year went by, and brought us to the sixth since
the Removal. The year which I pass over was marked by many public and
domestic incidents worthy of note in the history of Quodlibet. Gladly would I
have tarried to entertain my reader with some of these; but I am admonished
of the necessity of bringing these desultory annals to a close. Especially might
I find much to interest many of those who will peruse these pages, in the
private and personal affairs of the Borough; some of the events of the bygone
year being of a nature to kindle up pathetic emotions in their bosoms. The
blank despair of Agamemnon Flag when he first heard of the flight of
Nicodemus Handy; his melancholy visits of consolation to the bereaved
family; the disinterested avowal of his long-smothered and smouldering love
to the heiress apparent; and his offer of his hand and fortune—consisting of a
new suit of clothes, and a horse and gig, purchased on credit—to this dejected
lady; his still blanker despair, his disappointment and vows of revenge when,
after listening to his suit, he found it announced that she had sailed without
him, to make the grand tour of Europe; and finally, the stoical philosophy
with which he renounced all claim to the reversionary interest in the one
hundred and sixty thousand dollars taken from the bank, as well as the net
proceeds of Handy Place, and the rows of buildings, finished and unfinished,
in Quodlibet—these incidents would furnish an episode of tenderness and
passion without a parallel since the Medea of Euripides.

But these excursions are foreign from the purpose of this book, and I am sure
would be disallowed by the respectable committee at whose instance I have
entered upon this task. Indeed, they have explicitly enjoined that I divulge
nothing under their sanction, touching the concerns of Quodlibet which in any
manner borders upon the romantic. Upon these subjects their caution is, Nulli
tacuisse nocet, tutum silentii præmium. I must, therefore, reluctantly pretermit
all such matter—reserving for some other occasion the gratification of the
public curiosity therein.

In looking back upon the public events of this interval, I deem it necessary, in
passing, merely to notice the fact that the New Lights were greatly rejoiced to

find in Mr. Van Buren's message to Congress a complete justification of the Secretary's promise to Mr. Flam, the import of which was to assure our representative that the President had made up his mind, after the rejection of that measure, to carry the Independent Treasury in spite of the people. Our uncompromising, fearless, and *unshakable* Quods, true to the dictates of their creed, were, I repeat, greatly rejoiced at the manly perseverance and unquenchable self-will with which the President delivered over that question to the "Sober Secondthoughts" (a pest upon the unlucky coincidence of that phrase with my patronymic!—it hath given license to the tongues of the wags, to my annoyance) of the people. Every good New-Light Democrat in the land understood the hint—and a presidential hint is no small matter to a Democrat now-a-days. Truly delightful was it to see how it acted upon the New Lights. Not a man among them who had hitherto halted on a scruple of conscience, but became thereupon, in the twinkling of an eye, a devoted champion of the Independent Treasury; and that, too, without knowing, or caring to know, what it was. It was hoisted in capitals, at the head of Eliphalet Fox's Weekly, and became forthwith, as it were, a word written on our banner. We were, one and all, converted into milites subsignani, and became the Maccabees of this new kind of Independent Treasury.

It has doubtless often occurred to the reader of this irregular history to inquire how it comes to pass that the historian has ventured to relate with such composure, nay, with such complacency, what superficial thinkers, at least, might deem to be the *changes* in the political principles of the New Lights. Superficial is a good word, and truly explains the case. Our *principles*, as every one who is gifted with sufficient astuteness could not fail to have observed throughout this narrative—and as, in fact, we have more than once insinuated—are much deeper than the *measures* we, from time to time, find it convenient to adopt. We hold a change of measures, a change of opinions, a change of doctrine, and even a change of established facts, as nothing. But a change of men we totally abhor; a change of office, unless in the way of promotion, we utterly discountenance; and a change from a majority to a minority we execrate as wholly abominable, detestable, and in nowise to be endured. Now, in our creed, men, officers, and majorities make up the complex idea of what we denominate *principle*. The whole scope of the New-Light philosophy is, by the vigor of this thing *principle*, as I have defined it, to keep the Whigs down and our modern school of New-Light Democrats up. We proudly appeal to our past history to sustain our consistency in this pursuit. Let any dispassionate observer trace our meanderings through the last ten years: he will see the efficacy of our system manifested in the wonderful, the almost miraculous conversion of Old Blue-Light Federalists, and Federalists of every hue, into the Born Veterans of Democracy, and in investing these worthy relics of ancient patriotism with the most profitable offices in the gift of the government. He will see it in the merciless war—bellum ad internecionem—waged by our forces in the name of the people, against credit, commerce, and industry: he will remark how abundantly, and, as it were, by magic, it has fed the nation upon the economical, and therefore republican food of promises, relating to a sound currency—especially those referring to the gold and silver, while it was stealing along into the cheap and convenient system of a government paper in the shape of Treasury notes; and he will observe, with unfeigned surprise and redoubled admiration, how effectually it has secured to us the services and the money of the most opulent individuals in the land, and of the largest corporations created by the States—in a most signal degree those concerned in public works—while it preaches against wealth, chartered privileges and monopolies, and, by its zeal against them, has enlisted almost every penniless man, every wasted bankrupt, and every cracked reputation in the Union upon our side. But we have a still more illustrious exemplification of the practical value of our philosophy in the address with which affairs are managed by the head of the Treasury.

The letter of directions to the Hon. Middleton Flam, with which my readers have been favored in a previous chapter, it will be remembered, required the New Lights to support the Independent Treasury, and as necessary thereto, to take ground against the State banks, as altogether unsafe depositories of the public money. It further intimated, supposing we might be diffident about this, that the Secretary of the Treasury had already furnished evidence of this fact, and would, at the proper time, make it manifest that the Government had lost more money by the banks than by any other agents it had ever trusted. Our club had never before been aware that the Secretary had reversed his old opinions on this grave question, and we, therefore, lost no time in making a call upon our member for information. Great anxiety was felt to possess the Secretary's views. A substantial vindication of the Independent Treasury in this aspect, by the overthrow of the banks on the authority of the man who had built them up, was a desideratum which we all acknowledged; and its success we were prepared to regard as the greatest triumph of the New-Light principle, to be accomplished through the influence of that matchless Secretary, "whose mind," as Theodore Fog once remarked, "was endued with a radiating faculty sufficiently intense to light up the bottom of a bog, impart a vitreous translucency to the home of the frog, and illuminate the abode of the bat with a luster more brilliant than that which glittered through the boudoirs of the palace of Aladdin." We were aware that in 1834 his duty required him to prove that the State banks, while unmolested by the vexatious presence of a bank of the United States, were the safest of all possible custodiaries of the people's money; and that it was the Monster Bank alone which incapacitated them to fulfill their engagements to the Government—thence deducing the fact, that when the monster was dead, the public funds could be no otherwise than safe in their keeping. We were aware that at that time it was more particularly his duty to praise the State banks, because the unprincipled Whigs denied the fact of their safety, and opposed the scheme of giving them the public treasure, on the very ground that the Government had been a heavy loser by them from the period of the war up to the date of the charter of the bank. We had read carefully his report of the 12th of December in that year, and remembered these words:—

> "It is a remarkable fact connected with this inquiry, though often represented otherwise, that not a single selected State bank failed between the expiration of the old charter and the grant of the new one; and that none of our losses included in our unavailable funds happened until some time in 1817, after the United States Bank was in operation."

This, and some other facts culled from the same report, constituted the armory of weapons by which our club so manfully fought and prostrated the croaking and factious Whigs of Quodlibet, when, in their ravings, they predicted loss from our employment of the pet banks. But the New Lights being now ordered to take another tack, and being promised a good fabrication of facts to fortify our position, we rested on our arms like soldiers confident in the talents of their general to intrench them in their new camp, secure against every charge of the enemy. Mr. Flam lost no time in providing us with the Secretary's report of February 27th, 1838. That officer did not deceive our hopes. This luminous paper carried demonstration on its wings and refutation in its footsteps. Prodigious man! Enormous functionary! Brightest of ministers! Samson of the New Lights! Aaron and Moses both in one, of our Democratic, Quodlibetarian, Golden-calf-worshiping Israelites, (I speak symbolically, and not in derogation of the anxiously-looked-for and long-desired Bentonian coin.) He but touched the rock of New-Light faith, and forth gushed the facts like water—yea, and arguments like milk and water. With what gratulation did we read,—

> "The loss to the Treasury by taking depreciated notes, in 1814, '15, '16, and '17, is estimated at quite five millions five hundred thousand dollars; and there is now on hand of such notes then received and never paid away, or collected, about eighty thousand dollars more."

There was a conclusive argument to all that the Whigs might have urged in favor of the safety of State banks, if they had thought proper to defend them; and, in truth, it was some little mortification to us that our adversaries did not come out in favor of the banks, when we were so well provided with facts to put them down. But they, with that remarkable obstinacy which has ever characterized them, and which is altogether behind the age, stuck to their old opinions, and left us without anything to controvert, except, indeed, our own facts of 1834.

This instance, however, serves to show with what majestic bounds the New Lights have passed over the broad field of measures, and with what facile and graceful dexterity they have refuted that antiquated and vulgar adage which stigmatizes facts as stubborn things. Thus the beauty of this unrivaled philosophy consists in the harmony with which it reconciles past times with the present, with which it dovetails discordant principles, with which it brings into brotherhood elements the most repulsive, facts the most antagonistical, men the most variant, and contingencies the most impossible; which converts every man into a Janus, every highway into a labyrinth, every beacon into a lighthouse—giving to falsehood the value of truth, to shadow the usefulness of substance, and to concealment the estimation of candor. Truly is it the great discovery of modern times! My reader, I trust, will not, now that I have opened his understanding to the perception of this sublime spell-working philosophy, allow himself henceforth to question the laudable sentiment of approbation with which I have developed the practical operation of this theory in the history of Quodlibet.

There was another matter worthy of remark in the events of the year, which I must cursorily notice before I proceed to the era with which I propose presently to occupy my readers. The Presidential election was now in view, and received that grave consideration from the members of Congress which they are in the habit of giving to everything in Washington except the trifling business of making laws. Our diligent and watchful representative, some time before the close of the short session, wrote to our club a letter full of important advice for our guidance in the affairs of the approaching canvass for the Presidency.

Among other valuable disclosures, "the Whigs," said he, "are to hold a Convention at Harrisburg. Harry Clay, or, as they term him, Harry of the West, is to be their man;—at least, so we suspect. Whoever he be, we have made up our minds as to our course—*he is to be run down in the South as an Abolitionist.* Abolition is the best hobby we have had since the death of the Monster. We have already broken ground; and if Kendall and Blair can't prove Clay or anybody else to be an abolitionist, the deuce is in it: their right hand will have forgotten its cunning. The Globe is full of the matter already. Tell Eliphalet Fox to begin at once and bark in the same key:—all the little dogs are expected to yelp after the old hound—or, as Pickens calls him, the

Galvanized Corpse: many of them are at it lustily now. In 1836, Van's principles were luckily Northern;—so we have resolved to let them have full swing beyond the Potomac, and to put him in masquerade for the South. We rely implicitly on the stolidity of Pennsylvania; and shall secure New York by a concession to her banks, which for the time we mean to treat amiably. Our chief aim is the South. Van, being thoroughly imbued with the New-Light Quodlibetarian Democracy, has consented, for the benefit of our cause south of Potomac, to be dubbed 'The Northern man with Southern principles'— remember that, and tell Fox to ring the changes on it in every paper. We have hired a New Hampshire man to play clown to Van; and he somersets when his master does. This has a most striking effect. We call him the mannikin of the North with Southern principles—Van's mignonette. Our contract required him to bring in the anti-abolition resolutions touching the petitions; and although he could not venture against *the reception*, he has bolted down all the rest, *totidem verbis et syllabis*, as we wrote them for him;—*the reception* we struck out to accommodate the Democratic abolitionism of his district. The effect of this coup d'état was magical; and having gagged Wise and the rest of the Whigs with the Previous Question, we have left them in a state of unnatural retention which threatens to prove fatal. It is universally considered here a most lucky hit—Van and the Mannikin; and we shall, with these performers, play 'The Northern man with Southern Principles,' to crowded houses. Keep it going!—and don't forget, Clay is an Abolitionist. If the Harrisburg convention nominates anybody else—the same paragraphs will suit *him*;— Mutato nomine de te fabula narretur. Get the Secretary to translate that. Be discreet, and show this letter only to the faithful."

It may readily be imagined that our club was thrown into ecstacy by this confidential missive. Being the custodiary of the letter, I have ventured, without the permission of the club, to incorporate it in these annals; taking upon myself the risk of their displeasure rather than withhold so fine a specimen of the New-Light Quodlibetarian Democracy;—and indeed I can see no reason why the world shouldn't have it. We have no secrets among the New Lights.

I proceed now to the Fourth Era in these annals.

CHAPTER XVII.

FOURTH ERA—THE HON. MIDDLETON FLAM RE-ELECTED—THE NEW LIGHTS DETERMINE TO STIGMATIZE THE WHIGS AS FEDERALISTS—MR. FLAM'S INSTRUCTIONS IN REGARD TO THE PRESIDENTIAL CANVASS—NOMINATION OF HARRISON AND TYLER—COURSE OF THE NEW LIGHTS—FORMATION OF THE GRAND CENTRAL COMMITTEE OF UNFLINCHING NEW-LIGHT QUODLIBETARIAN DEMOCRATS—ITS PRESIDENT, SECRETARY, AND PLACE OF MEETING.

In the autumn of 1839, the Hon. Middleton Flam was again our candidate for Congress. He was opposed by the celebrated John Smith, of Thorough Blue. This contest was marked by one conspicuous feature: we had completely succeeded in appropriating to our party the name of Democrats—at least we had labored very hard to do so;—our next move was to get up the old hue and cry of Federalism against the Whigs. This required great boldness; but Middleton Flam entered upon the endeavor with the intrepidity of a hero. Eliphalet Fox walked in his footsteps, and from all quarters, simultaneously, and by a well-managed concert, the cry of Federalist was poured forth upon our opponents; and Henry Clay especially—as we counted on him for the Presidential candidate—was proved to be tainted with Federalism beyond all hope of bleaching it out.

We had now two great points settled with reference to the canvass for the Presidency: the Whig candidate was to be brought into disgrace, first, as an Abolitionist, and, secondly, as a Federalist. Mr. Flam gave our club every assurance that these two charges combined would destroy the purest man that ever lived; and that it was only necessary to drive these spikes with a sledgehammer every day, and the Democracy in the end could not fail to believe in the existence and in the enormity of these offenses, no matter who should be brought out by the Whigs—whether Scott, Clay, Harrison, or Webster.

But we had pretty conclusively made up our minds that Clay was to be the man; and our club in consequence immediately set about procuring the materials for a biography of that statesman, designed to demonstrate that he had all his life been a Hartford Conventionist in sentiment, and an unsparing enemy of Southern institutions. This task was consigned to Eliphalet Fox, who very soon amassed a wonderful amount of matter exactly to our purpose. In this, Eliphalet gave evidence of his usual skill; and his facts were so contrived that they might be used with equal success against either of the four above named, or indeed any one else who might be brought forward: but as Eliphalet had a particular hatred for Mr. Clay, and was more accustomed to defame him than any other great man in the nation, the compilation was imbued with a spirit that would have been much more effective in breaking down Mr. Clay's reputation than that of either of the others.

Great was the sensation produced in Quodlibet, great was our mortification, and great our surprise upon receiving the news in December from Harrisburg. The convention actually passed by Mr. Clay, passed by the great claims of Scott and Webster, and brought out General William Henry Harrison, together with John Tyler for the Vice-Presidency;—thus, by a perversity which, on all important occasions, distinguishes the Whigs, putting the two old horses of 1836 upon the course.

Mr. Flam was now at Washington. Our club met and immediately opened a correspondence with him for advice. "Keep your eye on the Globe," was his first admonition. His second was, "Open upon Harrison your Abolition batteries;—swear that the nomination was procured by Garrison;—charge Tyler with being a slaveholder, and send that off to New Hampshire;—prove that Harrison was a stark Federalist by accepting an ensigncy from the hands of Washington;—but, above all, turn him into derision for his poverty and plain habits."

It was wonderful to see the zeal with which Quodlibet set about the task assigned to it by its distinguished counselor. Eliphalet Fox, with a degree of magnanimity uncommon in an editor, took the field in behalf of Mr. Clay. "That persecuted patriot," said he, "who deserved more of his party than any man in the nation, has been treated with absolute contempt. It was due to his great claims to offer him the Presidency; but the spirit of abolition swayed this factious convention, and Mr. Clay was rejected solely on account of his well-known and deep-rooted attachment to the slave-holding interests of the South. As to General Harrison," the same article continued, "his humble station as the clerk of a county court, his insignificance and poverty, will leave the Democrats but little to overcome. Well has an enlightened and patriotic contemporary press, a distinguished pillar of the New Lights, remarked, in reference to the habits of General Harrison's life and the lowness of his associations, that two thousand dollars a year, a LOG CABIN, and a barrel of HARD CIDER would induce him to resign all claims to the honors his inconsiderate friends have proffered him."

The same paper propounded a series of interrogatories skillfully addressed to John Tyler, inquiring of him—what number of slaves he employed on his plantation, what was the ratio of their increase in each year, and how many he had disposed of at various intervals to Southern traders:—which interrogatories were admirably drawn up in language so equivocal in its import as to infer, what it did not directly assert, an extensive traffic in a commodity which could not but excite great indignation against him among the large mass of voters of all sides in the North.

How beautiful are these evidences of the operation of our New-Light philosophy! What a master in this science is the unrivaled Eliphalet Fox!

It was soon discovered that our club had fallen into a slight mistake touching the Log Cabin and Hard Cider, and the charge of poverty brought against General Harrison. The audacious Whigs had even the effrontery to adopt the LOG CABIN and HARD CIDER as the emblem of their party, and to ask the aid of those whom we had inconsiderately derided for living in those humble cabins and using this cheap luxury of cider, to make war against our New-Light Democracy. The Log Cabin instantly became the representative of a sentiment and a word of power; and, in a perfect tornado of enthusiasm, was raised in every village, hamlet, and meeting ground in the land.

Truly did this sudden uprising of the emblem strike dismay into our ranks! Quid consilii capiemus? was our universal question in Quodlibet. What should we do? Recourse was had to Mr. Flam. "Drop," said that ready-witted man in reply, "the charge of poverty against Harrison: say he is rolling in wealth. Bring out your Federalism against him with new vigor. Call the Log Cabin banner senseless mummery—and declare your disgust against it, as lowering the tone of public sentiment and morals. If that doesn't do, get some New-Light Democratic preacher to say that Hard Cider produces more intoxication than all the liquors the Democrats ever drank: let him rail against Whig meetings as Hard Cider orgies—remember the word;—and if we can only identify the New-Light Democracy with Temperance, its twin sister, we shall produce an unheard-of effect. Meantime, ply the Abolition battery with all possible diligence—and vamp up anew that old charge of hiring out criminals to service; but be careful to make no mistake—describe it as 'selling poor white men into slavery for debt.' To prove that Harrison is *against* slavery and at the same time *in favor* of it, will be a most happy stroke of our New-Light Quodlibetarian philosophy. Don't fail to do this with all possible industry. Tell Eliphalet Fox that the endeavor is worthy of his genius, and if he ever expects to become a great man, now is the opportunity presented to him."

These counsels gave us great encouragement, and we set ourselves to work in earnest. The New-Light Club was confined in its operations to the Borough of Quodlibet. Our whole Congressional district, including Thorough Blue, Tumbledown, and Bickerbray, required the supervision of a body which might be organized to regulate the affairs of the canvass within that limit. This gave rise to the Central Committee. A convention was called to meet in Quodlibet, where every portion of the district should be represented. That convention resulted in the appointment of a Committee of Twelve of the staunchest and most active of the New Lights. It was called "The Grand Central Committee of Unflinching New-Light Quodlibetarian Democrats." The name was sonorous, euphonious, and, in a certain sense, magnificent—but being too long for ordinary use, we reduced it for working purposes to "The Great New-Light Democratic Central Committee of Quodlibet." Eliphalet Fox was made President; and the humble author of these chronicles, in consideration of his fidelity in the discharge of his duty to the New-Light Club, was chosen to be Secretary also of the committee—an honor which, with due reverence and thankfulness, he hath assumed.

From the date of its organization, the committee, a majority whereof are inhabitants of Quodlibet, meet once a week with most commendable punctuality, and, as we have reason to believe, with signal usefulness to the glorious cause in which we have embarked. Zachary Younghusband, who is a member, gratuitously and generously, out of his mere zeal in the cause, proffered the use of his room up stairs above the tin-plate workshop, for our sessions—an offer which we were reluctantly obliged to decline, after one trial, on account of the noise created by the workmen below. I mention this praiseworthy offer as due to Zachary, in favor of whom the committee passed a vote of thanks. We found a more quiet place of meeting in the back room of the cabinet store of Isaiah Crape, the Undertaker, for which we agreed to pay fifty cents a week and find our own lights. In this secluded spot much is done to shape and direct the destinies of this Great Republic.

CHAPTER XVIII.

PROCEEDINGS OF THE GRAND CENTRAL COMMITTEE—VINDICATION OF THE SEVERITY PRACTICED AGAINST GENERAL HARRISON—TACTICS OF THE NEW LIGHTS—ABOLITIONISM—SELLING WHITE MEN FOR DEBT— HARRISON A COWARD—CONSIDERATIONS WHICH LED TO THE NAMING OF THE OPPOSITION BRITISH WHIGS—STRATAGEM AGAINST HARRISON, AND THE CLAMOR AGAINST HIM FOR NOT ANSWERING—HOPE OF THE NEW LIGHTS CONFIRMED BY THE CONNECTICUT, RHODE ISLAND, AND VIRGINIA ELECTIONS—BALTIMORE CONVENTION A FAILURE— IMPORTANT LETTER FROM MR. FLAM—AMOS KENDALL'S PURPOSE TO RESIGN—EXCITEMENT OF COMPOSITION PRESCRIBED BY HIS PHYSICIAN—CENTRAL COMMITTEE SANCTION THE COMPILATION OF THESE ANNALS.

The Grand Central Committee having been thus happily organized, devoted itself with exemplary diligence to the important concerns of the Presidential election, which, from this time forth, became the engrossing subject of all men's thoughts. A volume would not suffice to develop the multifarious labors of the committee. I could not in less space recount the resolutions, with long argumentative preambles, linking by means of Whereases, like rings, whole newspaper loads of facts, invented for the purpose;—the addresses, the speeches copied from the Globe, and extracts from private letters—to say nothing of the paragraphs, the sole offspring of editorial brains, and all the other machinery employed by the committee to defame, traduce, and vilify General Harrison, for the unpardonable sin of being thought by the Whigs a fit man to preside over this vast Republic. It was our duty to render, if possible, his very name offensive in the nostrils of the people. In this endeavor it may easily be imagined that we found abundance to do in rummaging up old scraps of history, the falsification of public records, the oblique interpretation of equivocal laws, and in practicing all the other customary arts of warfare known to the New-Light tactics.

Admirable is that wisdom of the New Democracy which has provided such an ordeal of punishment for the man who, in opposition to their wishes, dares to make claim to the favor of the people. What better chastisement can be inflicted upon such rash aspirant, than this preliminary gauntlet which it is ordained for him to run before he can be made sensible of the insolence of his pretensions? Thrice tormented is it his lot to be, in the fiery furnace of hatred, malice, and all uncharitableness, before he shall see the end of his vain probation. As certain tribes of Indians have a custom of torturing, to the verge of stoutest human endurance, the candidate for the honor of being accounted a Brave; so in imitation of this commendable usage did we determine, in no less degree, to torture the man whom the hardihood of the Whigs had placed before the nation for the like empty and unavailing honor.

It did truly seem to the New Lights no small insolence of those men who call themselves Whigs, to propose any individual for the Presidency, while the people were already favored with a chief whose whole life was lustrous with the radiance of the Quodlibetarian Democracy. The very idea of a New Light presupposes an innate, inherent, and intuitive fitness to fill any station of any kind or degree whatever; and here was one distinguished as the very fountain of New-Light principles already at the head of the nation, dispensing the favors and wielding the power of his great office to the supreme content of all Quodlibetarians—the only persons in this Republic whose interests deserve to be held of any account in the concerns of government. Nothing but the rankest faction could originate an opposition to his beneficent administration. Acting upon this conviction, the Central Committee certainly did not spare General Harrison.

It was, however, soon perceived that the General was a little stronger with the people than we supposed him to be; and sundry were the changes to which we were consequently obliged to resort in our mode of attack. The *abolitionism* we never lost sight of: the *selling of white men into slavery for debt* was also a steady topic; and some of the more ingenious of the committee fell upon the device of proving the old General *a coward*: but our great effort was to convert him and all his friends into old Blue-Light *Federalists*. This was always considered our master-stroke; and I may appeal to all the New-Light papers of this day for evidence, that in that department of our labors we plied our task with an industry that has never been surpassed. The Jersey election, also, we turned to great account in Congress, and certainly blew our trumpet on that question both loud and long. It was a noble illustration of our zeal for State Rights, which all the world knows is one of the favorite articles in our present faith. With an eye to this same question of State Rights, we succeeded in getting up a tolerable good commotion in Congress on the subject of State debts; holding it our duty, as friends of the sovereignty of the States, to do all in our power to break down their credit, and to warn the world against placing any confidence in their pledges—although, upon this subject, I am bound to confess that our success has not answered our expectations.

There was one movement upon which our committee placed great reliance. Mr. Van Buren, and indeed the whole New-Light Democracy, had so often changed their course upon public measures, as I have already shown, that the nation had been by degrees brought into a belief that every public man was, of necessity, and from the very nature of his organization, bound to certify, at least once a year, the state of his principles and the character of his opinions on all questions of policy whatever. Now Mr. Van Buren, in 1836, came to the

Presidency upon a very summary, and to himself, very comfortable profession of faith. All that he professed at that time was to follow in the footsteps—which said footsteps had scope and variation enough to allow him to take any path he thought proper. General Harrison, in that contest of 1836, did not enjoy this advantage, but was compelled to be somewhat specific in the indication of the grounds upon which his election claimed to be based. He had, consequently, not only been very full in this exposition, but had likewise referred his interrogators to a vast amount of written and printed opinions, which on divers occasions, in the course of his public career, he had found reason to express.

In the present canvass it was determined by our committee, and in fact by our New-Light friends in general, that he should reiterate afresh everything he had ever said or written on public matters, and that we should, by no means, be content with mere references to past declarations. Indeed, it seemed to our New-Light Democracy that, inasmuch as *our* President kept no opinions more than three years old, at the outside, it was impossible that General Harrison could be so antiquated as to stick to his for a longer term. Confiding in this impression, plans were laid by the New Lights to write letters to the General in the guise of friends, and in case he should refer the querists to his former expositions, without full and ample repetition of all he had said before, to bring a whirlwind of indignant reproof about his ears as a man who was afraid to trust the public with his sentiments. This stratagem succeeded beyond the most sanguine expectation of the New Lights. The General was caught in the trap; and such a clamor as was raised has never before been known in any part of the world.

"He won't answer questions!" exclaimed the Globe. "Gracious Heaven! what an insult to the intelligence of a nation of vigilant, truth-seeking, anxiously-inquiring freemen! A silent candidate! What contumely to the people! What contempt of the fundamental principles of free government!"

"Gracious Heaven! what contempt of the people!" re-echoed the Quodlibet Whole Team.

"Gracious Heaven! what contumely!" shouted the Bickerbray Scrutinizer.

"Gracious Heaven!" etc. etc., ejaculated two thousand patriotic, disciplined, footstep-following papers of all dimensions, from six by twelve to three feet square, from one end of the Union to the other. Never was there such a Gracious Heavening carried on in this country!

In the midst of all this successively came on the Connecticut, Rhode Island, and Virginia elections. The results everybody knows. Although ostensibly and to outward appearance against us, we saw in them what our infatuated opponents could not see, the certain token of our success. It was evident to us, from the returns of these elections, that a great reaction must occur; and Mr. Doubleday now very sagely remarked, "that there was no longer room to doubt that we should beat the Whigs in the fall." But the Whigs, instead of desponding at these events, began to take heart, and straightway set about getting up a Convention in Baltimore. Well, that convention was held on the Fourth of May. I was present, and I pronounce it to have been a *thorough failure*. The Whigs have represented that at least twenty thousand persons were assembled on that occasion. According to the accurate system of computation adopted by the New Lights, and which is infallible in regard to the numbers attending Whig meetings, the whole assemblage, including boys and blacks, did not quite reach two thousand, and of those a large number were New Lights.

Still it is due to truth that I should say there were some timid men in our committee who were not altogether satisfied with the appearances of the day. We found it difficult to make them comprehend how the late elections had operated in our favor. Yet it is a fact that we never were thoroughly convinced of the *certainty* of our success until we saw the returns in these elections. Connecticut and Rhode Island we had before considered doubtful: we now had no doubt. And as to Virginia, we became at once fully persuaded that our success there was actually "brilliant:"—such is the beautiful operation of the New-Light philosophy in bringing consolation to its votaries under apparent disaster, and suggesting encouragement where others would despond.

Yet it must not be concealed that these incidents produced some slight sensation in our committee. Mr. Flam wrote from Washington a letter of grave reflection. "Although," said he, "our success in Virginia has transcended our expectations, yet we are not quite certain that our *abolition* battery has been altogether *very effective*. Indeed, it is questioned here whether it would not be as well to abandon it, and even point the guns in the opposite direction. *Martin has room enough yet to turn*—and, as it is rather manifest that Virginia considers our charge of abolitionism against Harrison a *humbug*, and as the whole South will probably fall into the same opinion, (in which, in my judgment, they would not be very far wrong,) the propriety of taking the opposite ground is well worthy of consideration. *Van's affinities are with the North*; so that if it can be made clearly to appear to be his interest to take this backward leap, his *Southern principles* are not yet more than cobwebs in his way. *We must think of this.* In the mean time, it is the desire of the President and his managing friends here that you not only continue to brand the opposition as *Federalists*, but call them Brɪᴛɪsʜ Wʜɪɢs. This is rendered necessary by the fact that the opposition have just discovered that Van Buren voted against Madison and the War, and supported Clinton and the Peace party. By anticipating the ground and charging the Whigs as under British influence, we shall take off the edge of this assault, and avoid the effect of another reminiscence against the President—I mean his instructions to M'Lane, on the West India Question, which the Whigs impute to him as a truckling to Great Britain. Besides this, you know, Martin has been very assiduous of late in courting the good opinion of Victoria—so, by all means, drive at THE BRITISH WHIGS! Keep your eye upon Amos Kendall, who has consented to act as fugleman. His health is so much shattered by the diseases of the Post-office, that he is compelled to retire; and as his physician prescribes 'the excitement of composition' as his only cure, he is about to devote himself to the Extra Globe, in which sheet he will be able to indulge his imagination in the creation of those chaste and prurient fancies for which he has been remarkable from a child. The pure and simple inventions of that paper are ass's milk to his wasted constitution."

Thus admonished, our Central Committee proceeded in their labors with the most spirited activity; and it was not long before the whole Union was ringing with our charge against the British Whigs.

It was at this juncture that I suggested to the committee the propriety of making this compilation of the Annals of Quodlibet. I explained to them how important it was that the world should be made acquainted with the history and character of that New-Light philosophy which had worked such wonders in our Borough. It was very obvious that even our friends were not fully aware of the height and the depth of this sublime theory, nor of its extreme efficacy in the administration of the government. It had taken the world by surprise, and had grown up, in a few years, into a system which no naturalist had yet defined; and had assumed an importance in the affairs of this country which few persons were able fully to appreciate. Impressed with this conviction, I disclosed to the committee the purpose which, for some time past, I had secretly cherished, of collating from my manuscripts all such particulars in the history of Quodlibet as might serve to elucidate this subject. The committee knew that my materials were ample; and they had more than once been pleased to express their admiration of those poor talents which I had oftentimes exhibited in the effusions of my humble pen. The subject was now brought up to the notice of the committee on the motion of my friend, Mr. Younghusband, in a resolution too laudatory for my modesty to insert in this book. Readily and cheerfully did the committee condescend to assign this task to my endeavors;—confiding the matter and the manner thereof to my sole discretion, with the single injunction that I should abstain from all such incidents of mere personal or private concernment, as might by captious or invidious critics be designated as savoring of romance. Faithfully, as in my judgment, I could, have I obeyed this injunction; and with the frankness and veracity of one who chronicles for posterity rather than the present times, have I set forth all such matters of fact and comments of opinion as shall guide my readers to a true knowledge of the doctrine of the New-Light Quodlibetarian philosophy.

CHAPTER XIX.

DESERVED COMPLIMENT ON MR. VAN BUREN'S EXPLOIT OF THE FLORIDA WAR—THE AFFAIR OF THE TRUE GRITS AND SERGEANT TRAP—TRUE GRITS SUFFER A DEFEAT—FLAN SUCKER'S OPINION UPON THE SUBJECT —HIS ACCOUNT OF AN ACTION AT LAW BETWEEN JOE SNARE AND IKE SWINGLETREE.

Just at this period the True Grits once more began to give themselves airs of importance in Quodlibet. The Tigertail affair had stunned them, as a blow sometimes torpifies a snake; and like that same snake, which after a long period of consequent inactivity wakes up in the possession of new powers of mischief, so woke up the True Grits.

The Florida war, which has been raging on the part of the Indians, and simmering on our part, for nearly five years past, is undoubtedly the greatest of all Mr. Van Buren's exploits, and that which will be longest remembered in the history of this energetic President by posterity. It has developed the genius of our New-Light Democratic administration in stronger colors, and speaks more conclusively in favor of the perseverance and resource of our Great Chief, than any other of the numerous brilliant acts whereby he has illustrated the principles of that unterrified and unflinching Democracy, to whom fortune and General Jackson in partnership, have intrusted the destinies of this Republic. That war was not only the most righteous and unavoidable in its origin, but it has also been the most chivalrous in its character, the most economical in its management, and is likely to be the most productive in its results—if it should ever please Bill Jumper, or Sam Jones, or Micanopy, or their heirs and representatives, to allow it to come to a conclusion—that has ever been waged between two great nations; and will unquestionably cover our Commander-in-chief of the army and navy of the United States with as thick a coat of glory as it has already covered the bravest and keenest-nosed of our bloodhounds with a coat of mud:—and that is, perhaps, about as thick a covering as a hero of the President's mould might be supposed able to stagger under, in that long journey of fame by which he is to march down to after-times.

Among other vigorous measures taken in the prosecution of this stupendous war, was one that produced no small sensation in Quodlibet. A tall, raw-boned, slender, and very straight figure of a man, of a singularly red head and remarkably freckled face—the said figure being decked in a suit of army regimentals highly bedizened with worsted lace and cord, begirt with a huge saber, and wearing a plume three feet long—made its appearance recently in the Borough. This personage rejoiced in the name and title of Sergeant Trap.

He was accompanied by a drummer four feet six inches high, of a remarkably fierce military aspect; and by a fifer six feet four, quite as remarkable for the length of his arms and legs, and the shortness of his sleeves and pantaloons— both inferring, from their general effect upon his exterior, a rustical and imbellicose mode of life which reluctantly accommodated itself to the military requisitions of his station.

The Sergeant and drummer were strangers to our folks; but the fifer was no other than Charley Moggs, long known as the boss loafer of Bickerbray, and who was famed for a *single* accomplishment—the perfection with which he executed, upon an octave flute, that difficult but favorite piece of music which goes by the name of "Sugar in a Gourd;" which accomplishment was the foundation of his present astonishing promotion under Sergeant Trap, who had come to Quodlibet, in pursuance of orders from Mr. Poinsett, to pick up as many spare heroes for the Florida war, as might be found in our environs, willing to dog the Indians in company with our gallant blood-hound allies lately arrived from Cuba.

The Sergeant took a small frame house next door to Sim Travers's Refectory —or rather, as Sim called it, his Drinkery. Here he hung out the stars and stripes, by a pole which was secured in the second story window, and from which the flag vibrated in graceful undulations, almost sweeping the street when the wind lulled, and filling the hearts of Sim Travers's customers with emotions of martial glory.

Now, Sergeant Trap had not the good fortune to be a New Light; but, on the contrary, had the misfortune to be perfectly neutral in politics—and, coupled with that, the additional misfortune to be sometimes in want of money. In the course of some two or three weeks residence in the Borough, he had contracted a sort of intimacy with Peter Ounce, the landlord of The Boatman's Hotel at the upper end, and on the opposite side of the Basin. This intimacy mainly grew out of the circumstance that Ounce's hotel furnished very pleasant quarters to the Sergeant, and had also contributed some five or six recruits to his standard. Peter Ounce, although a Whig, is a kind-hearted, sociable man, and disposed to make friendships with those about him; and the Sergeant having run up a score at the bar, fell into the relation of a debtor to Peter, which it was not always convenient for him, at a moment, to obliterate. Besides this, Sergeant Trap had, once or twice, borrowed small sums from the landlord, and received from him sundry manifestations of good-will, which laid him, in a certain sense, under obligations to Peter. The result of it all was, that the Sergeant took a great liking to his landlord—and, following the suggestions of that feeling, rather encouraged his men, when they had a little money to spend in slaking their thirst, to throw it in the way of Ounce.

This state of things existed for some time before it was brought into public observation. Ounce's liquors were good and cheap, the company about his hotel was jovial, and Peter himself obliging—in consequence of all which Sergeant Trap's men went as often to the Boatman's Hotel as they did to Sim Travers's Drinkery, which was next door to the rendezvous. Sim Travers, who always kept a sharp eye to his business, was the first to notice the visits of Trap's men to his rival's bar, and for some time he bore it with a sulky and uneasy silence. After awhile, sundry inarticulate murmurs escaped him denoting vexation; and at length he openly began to shake his head and talk about *the duty* of soldiers and officers *in the employ* of the Government. "*We* work for the Government," said he, "and the Government ought to work for *us*. If public money *is* to be laid out, them that goes through fire and water has the best claim. These Whigs are ready enough to touch the cash when there's profit to be got; while them that sticks by Government in all their eternal choppings and changings is to be lookers-on. To the Wieters belongs the Spiles; if that ain't a motter, what's the use of having it? Go it full, or give it up—that's what I say."

Sim continued to repeat these sentiments for some time, without seeing things alter for the better. Peter Ounce still continued to divide the profits of the rendezvous with him. At last Sim became violent. "I'll make it a committee matter," said be. Thereupon he went immediately to Eliphalet Fox, and opened to him his whole burden of grievances. "I'll fix it," replied Fox, very much in the tone of a man of business; and Sim went home in excellent spirits.

The next Whole Hog had a paragraph touching this subject. "If," said that paper, "there be one principle which has been more sacredly established than any other by that great revolution through which we have just conducted the nation, in redeeming it from the oppressions of Monopolists and Privileged orders, it is the deep and fundamental truth that, To those who have won the victory belong its fruits. The Democracy have an unalienable and indefeasible right to all emoluments, issues, and profits accruing from the expenditures of the public money. And, moreover, if there be any class of persons who emphatically *belong* to the Government, it is the men who are enlisted for the Florida war. Few of them are destined ever to return again to the character of citizens: their *lives* are undoubtedly the property of the administration, as every man must see who reflects upon the history of that war. And if their *lives* are thus devoted to the cause of the administration, much more, may it be said, are their *little gains* to be employed in the same cause. Notwithstanding this self-evident truth, we know of men now in this Borough, wearing the livery of the Government, who do not scruple to enrich the coffers of the British Whigs with the money lavished upon them by the bounty of the Government, and which has been wrung from the sweat of the poor man's brow. We trust we shall be understood, without being more explicit. If this abuse continue after this hint, we shall act in a more efficient form:—a word to the wise."

Notwithstanding this very significant paragraph, and the fact that the paper containing it was sent to the rendezvous, and even addressed to Sergeant Trap by name, the practice complained of was in no degree corrected. On the contrary, as if from sheer perverseness and contumacy, the evil, if anything, was rather increased. Eliphalet Fox waited a few days to see how his paragraph worked. Sim Travers came to him with a face now much more in anger than in grief. "It doesn't work at all," said Eliphalet, adverting to his paragraph, and anticipating Sim's complaint. "Never mind, my friend," continued he, "this is *my* quarrel. Go home: leave all to me!"

Sim went home, confident that he should have ample redress. "If I don't get it," said he, as he walked toward the Drinkery, ruminating over his wrongs, "blow me if I don't quit the party. I'm not one of them fools to go thorough-stitch, and get nothing for it—blow me!"

"I'll see justice done to Sim Travers," said Eliphalet Fox, with an atrabilious look, when he was left alone, "or die in the attempt—blast me!"

After this blowing and blasting, Sim went about the Borough telling every man of the persecution he was suffering from the Whigs; and Eliphalet Fox went about to get up the old Tigertail Convention and bring the matter before them.

The next evening the convention met, and a Secret Committee was raised with instructions to write a *lettre de cachet* to the President, explaining the flagitious conduct of Sergeant Trap, and demanding his immediate dismissal from the army. This letter was written by Eliphalet Fox, and was signed by him and William Goodlack, besides Sim Travers and Thomas Crop the constable, which two latter made their mark—these four being the Secret Committee. The letter was duly dispatched to Washington to be presented by the Hon. Middleton Flam, who was *required* by the committee to render this service, from a suspicion that at bottom he was not very favorable to the True Grits. "Catch a weasel asleep!" said our worthy representative when this letter reached him. "Gentlemen, I'll do your bidding, by all means." And so, being wide awake, and fully determined to give the True Grits no cause of complaint against him, he went straight with the *lettre de cachet* to the President. In a few days the committee received a letter from Mr. Flam, informing them he had done everything they had demanded: that the President had read their confidential communication, and without hesitation replied, that if Sergeant Trap had been a *civil* officer, he would have dismissed him without further inquiry, in deference to the respectability of the committee;—but that, as Sergeant Trap belonged to the *army*, he found himself reluctantly compelled to proceed in a more formal manner, and that consequently he should direct a Military Court of Inquiry to take cognizance of the case: that this Court would sit in Quodlibet where the prosecutors were requested to be ready to prove the enormities alleged against Sergeant Trap.

"A Court of Inquiry!" exclaimed Fox, with great emotion. "Is the thing to be made public? We are deceived, betrayed:—I know by whom," he added, significantly nodding his head.

"A Court of Inquiry!—proofs, and all riglar—upon oath?" exclaimed Sim Travers.

"I'm blest if I go before any court!" said Tom Crop.

"By blazes, I won't!" said Billy Goodlack. "There's *something* in this here thing—else why don't the President go smack forward on the letter?"

"I'm no prosecutor," said Eliphalet Fox.

"I'm not a persecutor, nother," said Tom Crop. "By blood! I scorn it."

"I'm not going to put my hand on the book, upon it," said Sim Travers. "If a man can't lodge a complaint without being hauled into court, the party's broke: a fig for the money! who cares about it?"

"That's my identical sentiment!" said Billy Goodlack. "By blazes, I'm no prosecutioner!"

The committee was certainly thrown into great consternation. The cause of this is said to have been that in representing the case of Sergeant Trap to the President by letter, upon which they expected an immediate order dismissing the offender from service, they had charged him with a long list of misdemeanors against the welfare of the Great New-Light Democratic Party; which they knew, in the first place, had no sort of foundation in fact, and therefore might be found extremely difficult of proof; and the attempt to investigate which, in the second place, they were aware might bring the True Grits into collision with each other in a manner not very conducive to the harmony of the party. They were, therefore, not a little thrown aback when they were apprised of the President's determination to make the charges a subject of inquiry.

We cannot sufficiently commend Mr. Van Buren's caution in this matter, and the sound New-Light Democratic view he took of the subject. Here was a grave charge preferred against one of his own servants, imputing to him a disposition to deal with Whigs—nay, an *actual* dealing with them, when there was a New Light to be found in the same town capable of furnishing the same commodity. Doubtless, upon this nefarious transaction being fully proved, Mr. Van Buren, like a genuine, unadulterated Quod, as he is, would dismiss the offender from service, or even inflict on him other punishment, if it fell in his way. But in so serious a case he was determined not to be premature in his action: he would not proceed—unless, indeed, the offender had been a civil officer—upon such testimony as the confidential letter of a committee. He takes the only just course—(in this I have reason to believe he was fully seconded, perhaps even prompted, by our sagacious representative, the Hon. Middleton Flam)—and that is a formal, solemn, judicial inquiry into the conduct of Sergeant Trap, to ascertain whether he *really had* purchased liquors to the prejudice of the Great New-Light Quodlibetarian Democratic Party. Truly have we reason, day by day, to rejoice in a President of such magnanimity, such justice, such innate republicanism, and withal such dignity!

The Court of Inquiry met. It was composed of officers of high rank. After a long and patient investigation, and the most accurate ascertainment of the number of gills of rum, whisky, and brandy sold to Trap's recruits by Sim Travers, and by Peter Ounce, and a careful arithmetical computation of the value thereof in money; and, after a laborious examination into Sim Travers's politics, as also into those of Peter Ounce, the trial resulted in the conclusion that Sim Travers was not so good a New Light as he professed to be, (this was founded on evidence that Sim had said "he would leave the party if he couldn't get his share of spiles,") and that Peter Ounce's politics were, in fact, not known to Sergeant Trap at the time he dealt with him: whereupon Trap was acquitted of each and every charge brought against him; although Theodore Fog, the Counsel for the Secret Committee, took upon himself to inform the Sergeant, somewhat authoritatively, that as he was now aware of the dangerous tendency of Ounce's principles, the President would expect him to close all accounts at the said Peter's bar, and to be more circumspect the next time.

It was generally admitted, and indeed was the common talk of the Borough, that in this notable trial Eliphalet Fox dodged, that Billy Goodlack dodged, that Sim Travers dodged, and that Tom Crop actually skulked. And the general effect of the whole was to cut the combs of the True Grits so thoroughly, that it is believed they will never rise again. Flan Sucker made a jest of this, very much to the annoyance of his friends—for Flan had taken a violent fancy to Sergeant Trap, and even at one time, it was supposed, had an idea of enlisting. He used to sit up with the Sergeant of nights and drink a good deal with him through the day, and by this means very naturally became quite a crony. He therefore exulted much more than a True Grit, it was conceived, ought, at the Sergeant's triumphant acquittal. "Sargeant Trap," said he, "Locumsgillied Liphlet Fox;" and as this expression requires an explanation, he gave it, to this effect.

"Joe Snare, the bailiff over here in Tumbledown, fotch a suit before Squire Honeywell, agin Ike Swingletree for twenty-five dollars, on a cart which Joe sold him. Joe drawed up a note of hand for Ike to sign, which Ike did; and Ike never thought no more about it. Joe kept askin' for his money, year after year, year after year, tell at last he got tired, and so fotch the suit. Ike found out at the trial that the Squire was goin' to give judgment agin him; so what does he do but sashrary the case!—whereby the case was tuck up to the Court. Well, when they came on to trial there, Ike had a lawyer who found out that the note of hand was more than three years old, and there hadn't been no promise to pay in the mean time. Thereupon the Court told Joe Snare, if he hadn't nothing to say agin' it, they must give judgment for Ike on the Statute of Lamentations. Is it that, your honor? said Snare—for Joe being bailiff was pretty well up to law, and pled his own cause;—well, may it please your honor, maybe the statue is agin me, but, your honor, I drawed up the note of hand myself, and if you'll just be so kind to look in the corner under the dog's-ear, you'll see two letters at the eend of Ike Swingletree's name tantamount to L. S., which, as I understand, your honor, goes for *Locumsgilly* —whereby it takes twelve years, if I'm not mistaken, to kill the note of hand, bekase that's a bond. The judge looked and looked, and then sot up a laugh; and Ike Swingletree began to turn a little pale. Joe, says the judge, you're right, says he: that alters the case, and you must have the judgment. Joe, says he, you have beaten the lawyer and his client both—you're a clever fellow, and will get your money. So Joe accordingly got the judgment, and came off mightily pleased. And when he was tellin' me about the matter next day, he burst out in a great haw-haw, and couldn't hardly talk for laughing: Ike Swingletree, said he, sashraried *me*, but I reckon I Locumsgillied *him*.

"Well, that's just what Sergeant Trap has done to Liphlet Fox—Locumsgillied him beautiful."

CHAPTER XX.

THESE CHRONICLES DRAW TO A CLOSE—THE NEW LIGHTS NOT
DISPLEASED WITH ELIPHALET FOX'S DISCOMFITURE—PASSAGE OF THE
INDEPENDENT TREASURY BILL, AND REJOICING THEREON IN
QUODLIBET—CHANGES—INTERESTING LETTER FROM THE DIBBLE
FAMILY—MR. FLAM RETURNS TO QUODLIBET—HIS VIEWS OF THE
CANVASS—THE PRESIDENT'S RELIANCE ON THE INTELLIGENCE OF THE
PEOPLE—IGNOMINY AND INSULT OF FEDERALISM—ELECTIONS IN
KENTUCKY, INDIANA, AND NORTH CAROLINA—ALABAMA, MISSOURI,
AND ILLINOIS—PRESIDENTIAL ELECTION—CONSTERNATION OF THE
QUODS—MEETING OF THE CLUB—QUARREL OF THEODORE FOG AND
HON. MIDDLETON FLAM—DEFECTION OF FOG AND SUNDRY TRUE
GRITS—SECOND SPLIT—GREAT UPROAR AND CONFUSION.

My patient and indulgent reader will doubtless agree with me that it is time
these gossiping chronicles were brought to a close. Indeed, I am so near upon
the heels of the day in which I write, and the printer so near upon mine, that
little remains to be said. I shall therefore dispatch what remains of my
memoranda with such speed as shall suit my reader's longing for the end.

Although the New Lights in general bore no ill-will against that division or
faction which has been distinguished in these pages by the name of True
Grits, yet I must say we were not wholly displeased at the result of Serjeant
Trap's trial. On the contrary, many of us chuckled in secret thereat. Eliphalet
Fox we have ever acknowledged to be a useful man and a zealous—and we
have not been backward to award him such meed as he deserved. But it must
be told that in Eliphalet there lurks a scantling of ambition to climb higher on
the ladder than our party is yet willing to afford to one of his degree. And
Eliphalet moreover is suspected—Heaven forfend that I should do him
wrong!—in regard to the Hon. Middleton Flam our representative, and those
who are not altogether well disposed toward him, I mean Theodore Fog's
adherents, (for it is manifest Theodore is looking to a seat in Congress,)
utrosque parietes linere, as the Latin proverb has it, which in the vernacular
signifies to wear two faces—by no means an uncommon, though a very
objectionable sin in political affairs. This may be a groundless suspicion, as I
would fain hope it is; but it is believed by many, and therefore the more
reason was there for some secret rejoicing in Quodlibet at Eliphalet's failure
in the matter of Sim Travers. It unquestionably hath made our editor of the
Whole Hog more modest and seemly in his behavior of late.

The course of the canvass has been growing every day more and more
intensely interesting to our New Lights; and, bating some few aberrations into
which we have fallen, daily gives us greater promise of the consummation of
all our wishes. The passage of the Independent Treasury bill has brought us

fresh occasion of rejoicing and confidence. After a long, and, as Tom Crop says, a bloody struggle, lo! it is at last the law of the land, and all our wishes are crowned. "It is," as Mr. Flam has declared, "the unmingled, unaided, spontaneous result of popular sagacity—springing not from executive dictation, nor the influence of party discipline, but from the intuitive and instinctive wisdom of millions of freemen ground to the dust by the tyrannical pressure of associated wealth. It is the law of the land in spite of the groans of merchants, the wailings of agriculturists, and the murmurs of mechanics. It seals the fortune of our great chief, and proclaims the immortal triumph of the New-Light Democracy."

When the tidings of this joyful event reached us in Quodlibet, our first care was to fire one hundred guns; the next was to illuminate the Borough, and to bring out all our flags and lanterns; after this the New Lights were called together in the Court-House, where addresses were delivered by Agamemnon Flag and Theodore Fog—the latter of whom actually outdid himself in an effort that would have exalted the fame of Patrick Henry; and to close this jubilee, the Central Committee passed a resolution declaring the bill the Second Declaration of Independence. For this brilliant series of events we have to thank that sturdy devotion to State Rights which shone with such conspicuous luster in the annihilation of New Jersey by the New Lights, in the House of Representatives. But for that glorious stroke of policy the bill would again have been crushed by the serpent of opposition. Now that we have gained it, British Federal Whiggery is forever prostrate.

A fortnight after this event brought us the cheering tidings from Louisiana, to which many an anxious eye had been turned. The elections there have resulted in a splendid victory—a victory, indeed, not indicated by the polls, where the majority was *seemingly* increased against us—but manifested in the spirit with which our people everywhere received the tidings. Until this spirit became manifest, it might be said our hopes were even wavering; but forthwith an unwonted confidence in our success has spread abroad. The sagacious Mr. Doubleday, whose face may be called the barometer of our party, and to whom we all look for predictions of the future, now wears a countenance wreathed in smiles, and tells us that, from what he knows of the changeableness of that State, "we may make ourselves altogether certain of the victory in the fall."

In running over the events of the day, nothing is more deserving of our animadversion than the ostentatious display, by the British Federal Tory Whigs, of the *changes* among the people against the New-Light Democracy; —as if here and there the change of some recreant Democrat, who is afraid to follow his leader and chooses to have opinions of his own, could stay the mighty torrent of attachment to the fortunes of our chief. We do not deny these changes; but rather rejoice that men, so little worthy of being called true Quods, should leave our standard to the tried soldiers who have marched behind it in all its vicissitudes, and fought its battles through the whole field of political experiment. By such only can our glorious cause be upheld. But we can recount changes as well as they.

I might select thousands from our newspapers; and I forbear to do so only because I think it unworthy of the good sense of a Quod to parade the names of converts to our party; thus assimilating, as it were, the people to a flock of sheep, and expecting that more will follow because many have gone before.

There is, however, one case which I am sure I shall be excused for bringing before my reader. It is that of the Dibble family of Wisconsin. It was brought to the notice of our Central Committee by Zachary Younghusband, who came into possession of the original manuscript through a brother Postmaster, Mr. Straddle, who resides in the neighborhood of the converted family, and who, in fact, was the amanuensis used upon the occasion. Our committee thought this document of sufficient importance to be copied into the Whole Hog; from whence it is likely to be transferred into every New-Light Democratic paper of the country. It certainly exhibits very conclusive as well as very abundant reasons for change; and may be said to contain the best epitome of the popular objections of the New Lights to the election of General Harrison which has yet appeared in print. An aged and widowed father with five sons —all heretofore steeped to the lips in the slough of British Whiggery—have had the independence to rise, in the majesty of freemen, and boldly assert the highest prerogative of an American citizen—the right of thinking, speaking, and voting in such manner as a patriotic, disinterested New-Light Postmaster, whose opinions are above all suspicion, might direct them. The letter of this never-sufficiently-to-be-admired family will speak for itself. I have only to remark that, in transcribing it, I have taken the liberty to correct, what indeed I must call, some glaring faults in the orthography—which are to be attributed solely to Mr. Straddle, the Postmaster, who reduced the instrument to writing, and who, by-the-by, let me say, should be advised to give more of his attention to the useful art of spelling—but in no other point altering word, syllable, or letter.

It it is somewhat fancifully headed

"GO IT, YE CRIPPLES!

"This is to give notice, that we who have put our sign-manuals to the foot thereof, being till now snorting Whigs, having heard our

Postmaster, Clem Straddle, Esq., say that he knows General Harrison sold five white men as slaves off his plantation, and *is* for abolition, and whipped four naked women on their bare backs, and *is* for imprisonment for debt, and moreover *is* for making a King, and goes for raising the expenses of the Government up to fifteen millions, and *is* a coward and wears petticoats, and *is* kept in a cage, and wants to reduce wages, and for that purpose is a going to have a standing army of two hundred thousand men, which our free and independent spirits won't bear, and wants to give the public money, which comes from the sweat of our brows, and public lands, to Sam Swartout and Price, and a gang of British Whigs, which we consider against the Constitution, and moreover we don't believe he won't answer, and has got no principles excepting them what he used to have, and is against the Independent Treasury which was signed Fourth of July, whereby it is the Declaration of Independence; and the aforesaid Clem Straddle, Esq., which writeth this for us and in our names, being against all office-holders which the British Whigs is a striving after, and tells us to vote for Van Buren, we being an affectionate father and five orphan children without any mother, and never had any since infancy, make known that in the next Presidential election in this Territory, if we had a vote, and if not we shall vote in Missouri, we goes against Tip. and Ty. and all that disgusting mummery of Log Cabins, Hard Cider, Coonskins, Possums, and Gourds, in regard of their lowering morals, and goes for Jackson, Hickory Poles, Whole Hogs, and Van Buren, as witness our hands and seals.

MALACHI +hismark DIBBLE, Parent.

WASHINGTON +hismark DIBBLE

JEFFERSON +hismark DIBBLE

MADISON DIBBLE

FAYETTE DIBBLE

SQUINTUS CURTIUS +hismark DIBBLE

"*Note.*—Washington and Jefferson is voters, Madison and Fayette is at school, and signs for themselves, and Squintus Curtius is rising nine."

This letter, it will be admitted by all unprejudiced persons, bears the most expressive testimony to the natural and unsophisticated character of its authors; and furnishes us gratifying evidence that the great Reform, which it has been the labor of our committee to promote, has begun at the right end, and that the result must be the infallible and universal triumph of New-Light Democracy over the whole Union.

Upon the adjournment of Congress, late in July, the Hon. Middleton Flam returned to Quodlibet, to infuse new energy into our indefatigable committee. Through him we were apprised of many matters of deep interest touching the progress of the Campaign, which was now growing amazingly active. Being in the confidence of the President and Amos Kendall, he could tell us divers things which were not intrusted to the party at large; and let us into the secrets of the little and big wheels which were at work in Washington and other places.

These communications were generally of a character to increase the already sufficient confidence of the party in the re-election of the President, and still more, if possible, endear him to the multitudinous friends who expected, in that event, to receive the long-sought and well-earned rewards due to their personal devotion to his cause. Mr. Flam had surveyed the whole field of contest, and had arrived at an accuracy of information in regard to the vote of each State—and, indeed, of almost every county in the Union—that, to the unstudied in such matters, would appear to be miraculous—very little short of the gift of prophecy. It is astonishing to see what proficiency an old and practiced politician arrives at in predicting, months beforehand, the precise majorities of the Democratic party over all other parties, in every election, and especially in settling the result of a Presidential election. Our sagacious member on this occasion assured us, greatly to our exhilaration, that we should see, in the Western and Southern State elections which were about to take place, a most triumphant vindication of the administration, as well as a most conclusive evidence of the hold which the President has gained upon the affections of the people. "Indiana," he said, "is undoubtedly with us by an overwhelming majority; Kentucky is redeemed, regenerated, and disenthralled, beyond a shadow of doubt—(a favorite oratorical expression of his;) and North Carolina is prepared to hurl the thunderbolts of her contemptuous scorn against British Whiggery, with the red right hand of an offended Jove. Depend upon what I tell you, gentlemen. I have carefully surveyed the field. I am not accustomed to speak without knowledge. I am never mistaken."

Assured and invigorated by these encouraging words, we accordingly wait with cheerful trust in the coming event.

Some nervous New Lights affect to see signs of alarm in the unwonted disquietude of the President. Rumors reach us that he does not sleep well; that he writes many letters, slightly variant in sentiment, to opposite sections of the Union; that he manifests symptoms of an over-excited zeal to demonstrate the exceedingly prosperous condition of the party. Besides this, the Vice-President, it is said, thinks it his duty "to take the stump," which is considered rather an ominous departure from "the usages of the Democratic party," and, in fact, is looked upon as a proof that our leaders are growing a little faint-hearted. But what can be more consistent with the principles and professions of the New-Light creed? Have we not exploded Mr. Jefferson's old and unprofitable notion, that the office-holders ought not to interfere with the freedom of the elective franchise? Is it not a fundamental point in our philosophy that the offices are "the spoils," and that the men who hold them owe it to themselves and their posterity to fight for them in every way known to Democratic warfare?—How appropriate then is it that our highest and greatest officers, having the largest stake, should be in the very front of the battle! Is it not especially incumbent on the President, being the illustrious head of the unterrified new Democracy, to show a laudable anxiety for the issues of the campaign, to write letters suited to every emergency, to rectify constitutional mistakes, and to mystify every unpleasant fact that might have a tendency to divide the party or discourage its hopes? If he did not diligently devote himself to such work he would not be worthy of that high place we have assigned him in the Quodlibetarian school.

Mr. Flam, moreover, assures us that the President has a profound faith in "the intelligence and firmness of the people," and is unwearied in his endeavors to make that clear to the most careless or indifferent observer. Mr. Flam himself urges it upon the Club as highly important; that we should give great prominence to this idea of an absolute belief in the intelligence of the people. He reminds us, that it is a cardinal maxim in the tactics of the New Lights, when a politician or a party is suspected of any unwholsome opinion, to repel the effect of this suspicion by frequent affirmation and repetition of words and sentiments which in the popular judgment shall be held to contradict it.

Another card in the game our member recommends on the same august authority: that is, to dwell persistently upon the *Federalism* of our opponents, and to speak of it, on all occasions, as a term of "ignominy and insult," by which, he says, many virtuous and innocent-minded Democrats may be beguiled into the belief that none of our chief and most authoritative leaders ever belonged to that venerable party which once gloried in the name of Federalists.

These and many other valuable suggestions were communicated by our

Honorable Representative to the Club, as matters of moment in the conduct of our affairs.

It is wonderful to contemplate the influence of these master-minds upon our Quodlibetarian friends. The President scarcely drops a sentiment from his pen before it becomes as it were expanded into the common air of Democracy. The Globe usually leads off: the Whole Hog follows; and upon their heels the Scrutinizer, with all the rank and file of typographs, brings up a glorious chorus of repetition which leaves no hill or valley, mountain or plain in the whole land uninstructed in the Presidential utterances. Thus is it, even now, with this tribute to the *intelligence* and *firmness* of the people, and this stigma of *ignominy* and *insult* upon the old Federalists.

The Hon. Middleton Flam, Theodore Fog, Agamemnon Flag, and Zachary Younghusband, (for Zachary has turned orator of late,) and, without vaunting, I myself may say that the importance of the crisis has even, on same recent occasions, placed me in the same category—we all give breath to the same sentiment in speeches by day and by night, and "the same keynote," to quote a studied and prepared figure of speech from an admirable oration delivered last week by Agamemnon Flag in front of the Iron Railing—"The same key note of the *Intelligence of the People* rings in the discourses of five thousand Orators, and jangles in twenty thousand resolutions of New-Light Democratic Clubs from the St. Croix to the Sabine; and through all the windings of its devious way the *Ignominy and the Insult of Federalism* murmur on the ear in inseparable treble accompaniment."